W9-ARI-150

DISCARD

Date: 12/28/17

LP FIC SHALVIS
Shalvis, Jill,
Chasing Christmas Eve

CHASING CHRISTMAS EVE

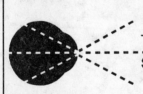

This Large Print Book carries the
Seal of Approval of N.A.V.H.

A HEARTBREAKER BAY NOVEL

CHASING CHRISTMAS EVE

JILL SHALVIS

THORNDIKE PRESS
A part of Gale, a Cengage Company

Farmington Hills, Mich • San Francisco • New York • Waterville, Maine
Meriden, Conn • Mason, Ohio • Chicago

LIBRARY OF CONGRESS CIP DATA ON FILE.
CATALOGUING IN PUBLICATION FOR THIS BOOK
IS AVAILABLE FROM THE LIBRARY OF CONGRESS

ISBN-13: 978-1-4328-4106-5 (hardcover)
ISBN-10: 1-4328-4106-8 (hardcover)

Published in 2017 by arrangement with Avon, an imprint of HarperCollins Publishers

Printed in the United States of America
1 2 3 4 5 6 7 21 20 19 18 17

CHASING CHRISTMAS EVE

PROLOGUE:
#OhPluckIt

Colbie Albright stood in the crowded La-Guardia Airport staring up at the flight departure board. Her chest was tight and her throat felt like it was closing in.

Classic anxiety, she told herself. *Just breathe right through it.*

Not that her body listened to her brain. Her body rarely listened to good sense.

In any case, it was December 1 and people were rushing all around her like chickens without their heads, while she stood still trying to figure out her choice of destination. Her only requirements were warm and tropical. An exotic beach would fit the bill perfectly.

Aruba.

Jamaica.

Oooh, I wanna take you . . .

Great, and now the Beach Boys song was stuck in her head. Doing her best to shake it off, she eyed the board again. So many choices for a twenty-eight-year-old runaway with a packed bag and no regrets.

From inside her purse her phone vibrated and she grimaced. Okay, so there were regrets. Buckets of them that made her suitcase feel like a thousand pounds and sucked the air from her lungs, but she refused to let herself turn tail and go back.

She was doing this.

But even as she thought it, the board changed and a bunch of the flights — all the southbound ones — blinked off and came back on . . . showing as delayed or cancelled.

"A surprise late season hurricane," someone said in disgust next to her. "Of course."

Okay, so she wasn't going south. There was a flight to Toronto in twenty minutes but Toronto was the opposite of warm and tropical, and plus it wouldn't give her enough time to grab some breakfast. Apparently running away really ramped up a girl's appetite . . .

That's when her gaze locked on a flight leaving for San Francisco in an hour. Huh. California, the land of celebrities, avocados, surfer dudes. She'd never really had a chance to enjoy any of those things. In fact, LaGuardia was the furthest she'd been from home in three years. But hey, there was a first time for everything, right?

Right.

She nodded, psyching herself up for this. After years of taking care of her family and working herself half to death, she deserved this. She needed this.

So . . . San Francisco or bust.

It would work, she assured herself. Getting away would allow her to find her muse again, her love for the writing. And so, convinced, she strode to the ticket counter.

Fifteen minutes later, she hit the very long, very slow-moving security line. Surrounded by people complaining about the wait, she was in the process of removing her laptop, her sweater, her shoes, her watch, and her bracelet and was patting herself down to make sure she'd gotten everything out of her pockets when a TSA agent pulled her aside.

"Oh," she said, "I'm not carrying any liquids over three ounces."

The guy shrugged. "Random female," he said. "That your bag?"

"Yes." This was what she got for buying a last-minute one-way ticket and she bit her lower lip as the agent started to go through her things. She favored layers, especially tees and sweaters with loose skirts or yoga pants — even though she'd never been to a yoga

9

class in her life. He pawed through every-thing, pausing at the sight of her bunny slip-pers — which, hey, totally completed her favorite writing uniform.

"My three-year-old kid has these," he said and then kept going, alternately looking up at the X-ray monitor and down at her bag, clearly seeking something specific. He moved aside a lightweight jersey dress and she grimaced as some lacy, silky things were exposed. Maybe her clothes were nothing special but she did have a thing about what she wore beneath them, her one concession to feeling sexy in this crazy life she'd built where she didn't have time to actually *be* sexy . . .

Luckily for his health, the agent's stoic expression never changed. No doubt he'd seen it all and couldn't care less as he dug past her favorite peach lace bra-and-panty set, a box of tampons, and . . .

"Ah," he said, holding up an apple.

"Are apples a problem?" Colbie asked.

"They sometimes look weird on the screen."

"No weirdness here," she said. "Just a morning snack. It's not even poisonous." She added a harmless smile.

He didn't return it, because he was star-ing at some papers she'd paper-clipped and shoved in her bag to read on the plane. "How to murder people by poison without detection," he read aloud.

The woman behind Colbie gasped in horror.

"Okay," Colbie said, pointing to them. "That's not what it looks like."

The woman behind her, cradling a leopard-print cat carrier, had turned and was frantically whispering to the people behind her.

"Really," Colbie said. "It's a funny story, actually."

But the TSA guy was flipping through her notes, not even remotely interested in her funny story. He didn't need to read aloud what he was looking at, because she knew exactly what was there — other Google searches, such as how to get away with murder using a variety of different everyday products that weren't considered weapons. "It's research," she said to the room.

"Yeah, that's probably what I'd say too," a guy said from somewhere behind her.

Colbie didn't look back; she just kept her gaze on the TSA agent, trying to look nonthreatening as she said something she rarely if ever said aloud. "I'm a writer."

"Uh-huh." He pulled out his radio now with an ominous "Female agent, please."

"Oh, pluck it!" she snapped.

The agent narrowed his gaze. "What's that supposed to mean?"

"Nothing bad," she said. "That's the point. See, we've got this swear jar at home, which means I've gone broke swearing, so I say other stuff instead of bad words. Stuff that sounds like bad words but isn't. I don't lose any money that way, and —" She broke off because he didn't appear impressed. "Look, never mind that," she said. "Just believe me, I'm not a problem. You saw the bunny slippers, right?"

"Ma'am," he said, pulling her bag aside. "I'm going to need you to come with me."

"No, really! If you look in my purse, you'll see it's filled with scraps of paper, napkins, whatever, all with handwritten notes on them. I write notes for my books all the time. Plot points. Characterization stuff. Just little things, really. For instance . . ." She looked around and gestured to the woman behind her. " 'Crazy cat lady with a leopard-print cat carrier —' "

"Hey," the crazy cat lady with the leopard-print cat carrier said.

Colbie ignored her. "— or 'friendly, sweet, kind TSA agent with a heart of gold . . .' " she said, and added a flirty, hopefully innocent-looking smile. "I use the notes in my books. It adds color and heart to the story and all that."

The agent's eyes were still suspicious, but at least he opened her purse to check her story. And just as she'd said, it was filled with what probably looked like trash but were in fact little treasures to be revisited and added to her manuscript.

"What do you write?" he asked, unraveling a small square bar napkin and staring at the words she'd scribbled on it: *Icicle — the perfect weapon. It melts and vanishes!*

The agent lifted his gaze and leveled it on her.

"Cheese and rice!" she exclaimed and drew a deep, calming breath. It didn't help. "Okay, listen," she said. "It's not what it looks like. I write young adult action-adventure. Postapocalyptic world." She was hoping to not have to go further than that, but the expression on his face told her she was on borrowed time. "The characters are teenagers with powers they acquired in the radioactive war," she added.

"And these teenagers, they . . . kill people?"

"No," she said. "But the bad guys do. And it's *fiction.* You know, made-up stuff." She pointed to her brain and shook her head, like, *See? Harmless.* "And so really, all this is for naught. It's not like I've got a bomb in my bag or anything."

In hindsight, she probably shouldn't have mentioned the word *bomb*. She missed her flight and almost the next one, instead becoming intimate, very intimate, with a pair of female TSA agents.

She also missed breakfast.

And lunch.

And the nap she'd been counting on since she hadn't slept more than a few hours in so long she couldn't remember what a good night's sleep felt like.

Not exactly an auspicious beginning to her vacation from life, but hopefully all her trouble was behind her now and the rest of the trip would be perfect.

A girl could dream anyway . . .

Eight hours later, she pressed her face to the window of her plane as it banked and came in for a landing at SFO International. They'd been diverted twice for too much air traffic, which turned out to be a blessing because they came in from the north, giving her a view of the Golden Gate Bridge glowing red in the late afternoon sun. The bay was a gorgeous sparkling blue, all of it looking like a postcard, and something in her tight chest loosened. It seemed like the entire world was laid out in front of her and she brought a hand up to the window as if she could actually touch the sight.

This, she told herself. This was *exactly* what the doctor had ordered — if she'd actually gone to a doctor for her anxiety and crippling writer's block. Here she would find herself, so that by the time she went back home in three weeks for Christmas Eve, she'd be happy again.

She was sure of it.

Chapter 1
#SonOfABeanbagChair

"Spencer Baldwin?" an unfamiliar female voice asked.

Shit. Anyone who used his full name was most definitely *not* someone he wanted to speak with. After the past few months, he knew better than to answer his phone without looking at the screen, but with both hands busy directing a drone around the room, he'd answered on voice command without thinking about it.

"Wrong number," he said, the drone hovering with perfect precision — and engineering — above his head. Then, to prevent a repeat call while he was working, he took one hand off the controls and chucked his phone out the high, narrow window of the basement.

Which felt great.

Directing the drone to continue hovering, he moved to the far wall of the huge basement below the Pacific Pier Building and

17

climbed the three-foot ladder that was against the window for just this sort of situation.

Yep. His cell phone had landed directly in the fountain in the center of the courtyard. "Three points," he murmured just as the elevator doors opened and Elle entered.

"Are you kidding me?" she asked in a tone that only she could get away with and not die. "You killed another one? Why don't you just stop answering to the damn reporters — wouldn't that be easier?"

He turned his attention back to his drone, impressed with the changes he'd made in the flight software. "Am I paying you to bitch at me?" he asked mildly.

"As a matter of fact, yes," she said. "You're actually paying me a hell of a lot of money to bitch at you. Why don't I just change your phone number again?"

"He can't," Joe said from the other side of the room. He wore only a pair of knit boxers and stood in front of one of the three commercial-grade washer-dryers, waiting for his clothes. "Me and the guys like it when he gets all the marriage proposals."

"You mean you like the nudie pics that come *with* the proposals," Elle said.

"They send him presents sometimes too," Joe said. "Junk food and panties. That's

18

always fun."

Elle rolled her eyes. "Why are you in just your underwear?"

Joe was an IT wizard who worked at Hunt Investigations two floors up. He was second in charge there, a master finder and fixer of . . . well, just about anything, and fairly badass while he was at it. And although Elle terrified almost everyone on the planet, Joe just grinned at her. "Had a little tussle earlier on the job," he said. "Spence let me in down here to use the machines."

Elle was not impressed. "If by *tussle* you mean a takedown went bad and you got blood all over yourself again, you best not be using those machines."

"Hey, at least it's not my blood. And I'm fine, thanks for asking."

Elle went hands on hips. She managed this building for the owner, who happened to be Spence — and she often mistook her job for actual world domination, trying to run his personal life as well.

But Spence had nixed his personal life a long time ago. It was the Baldwin curse. He could be successful in his business life or his personal life — pick one — but not both. Since he objected on a very base level to going back to abject poverty, he'd long ago decided business was a safer bet than love.

Although, to be honest, he'd made a few forays into attempting both and had failed spectacularly.

"Oh, and did you hear that Spence here is rumored to be one of the top ten nominees for San Francisco's most eligible bachelor?" Joe asked Elle, giving a snort as if this was hysterical.

Spence leaned forward and banged his head against the wall a few times.

"Don't bother," Elle said. "Your head's harder than the concrete. And yes," she told Joe. "I know. I figure that's part of the reason he just threw his phone out the window?"

"I could just scare everyone off your ass for you," Joe said to Spence.

He was kidding. Probably. And actually, Spence was more than a little tempted. This mess was his own fault, for trusting someone he shouldn't have. As a result, the press had been having a field day with his success in a very large way, threatening his privacy and also his sanity.

Just thinking about the "most eligible bachelor" thing had him groaning.

"Listen," Elle said more kindly now. "Go take a break, okay? Then you can come back and shut out the world and work."

It was a well-known fact that Spence's

ability to hyper-focus and ignore everything around him was both a strength and a giant flaw. Great asset for an engineer/inventor, not so great for anything else, like, say, relationships. But truthfully, he was hungry, so a break sounded good. He headed toward the elevator.

"Uh," Elle said, gesturing to his clothes. "You might want to . . ."

"What?" he asked, looking down at himself. So he hadn't shaved in a few days — so what? And okay, maybe he lived out of his dryer, grabbing clean but wrinkled clothes from there in the mornings when he got dressed. Whatever. There were worse things. "Joe's in his *underwear.*"

"Hey, at least I was wearing some today," Joe said.

Elle took in the guy's nearly naked form, clearly appreciating the view in spite of her being very much taken in the relationship department by Joe's boss Archer Hunt. She finally shook it off and turned back to Spence. "You know damn well when you walk across the courtyard talking to yourself, hair standing up thanks to your fingers, all stubbly because you forgot to shave, and those black-rimmed glasses slipping down your annoyingly perfect nose, women come out of the woodwork."

"They do?" Joe asked.

"It's the hot geek look," Elle said.

"Huh." Joe rubbed his jaw, where he too had stubble. "Maybe I should try that sometime."

"No," Elle said. "You can't pull off hot geek. Your looks say sexy badass, not geek, which apparently is like a siren call to crazy women everywhere."

Joe looked pleased. "I'm okay with that."

Elle ignored this and looked at Spence. "After your last romantic fiasco, you vowed to take a break, remember? So all I'm saying is that you might want to change up your look."

"How?"

"I don't know," she said. "Slouch. Get a beer gut. Fart. Whatever it is that guys do to organically turn us off."

"Wait," Joe said. "You gave up sex after Clarissa dumped you, what, two years ago now? Like, *willingly*?"

"Something you should try sometime," Elle said to him.

"Woman, bite your tongue."

"No, really," she said. "How do you even keep all their names straight?"

"Easy," Joe said with a smile. "If I forget their name, I just take them to Starbucks in the morning and wait until the barista asks

22

their name for their cup."

Elle rolled her eyes. "Seriously?"

"Hey, you know I run on caffeine, sarcasm, and inappropriate thoughts at all times."

"I didn't give up sex," Spence said. Okay, yes, his latest project required his 24–7 attention and he hadn't had time to connect with anyone. But quick hookups weren't really his thing anyway. What was his thing at the moment was creating a system for getting meds to people via drones, in far-flung areas where they were nearly nonexistent. Meds and also medical care through camera-equipped drones, allowing doctors to remotely diagnose and monitor patients.

He'd had problems. Accommodating for the atmosphere and varying weather patterns, for one. The security, for another — making sure pirates couldn't intercept and steal the meds and equipment was a high-stakes priority. And then there was the ratio of the changing weight of the cargo to getting enough battery charge to make the long flights, not to mention limited battery life and the struggle to stay connected no matter the conditions. But he was getting close, very close. All he needed was time, uninterrupted time, a rare commodity. He moved toward the door. "I'm going after my phone."

"The one you just killed dead?" Elle asked.

"I'll bring it back to life."

"You're a genius, Spence, not a miracle maker."

When he kept going, he heard Elle mutter "great" to Joe. "Now I've issued some sort of challenge to his manhood and he has to prove me wrong."

The truth was, Spence could rebuild his phone in his damn sleep. What he wished he could do in his sleep was get this project up and running. Maybe a part of his problem was that it happened to be for Clarissa's One-World charity and he'd promised her.

And Spence no longer broke promises.

He took the stairs because he hated the elevator, and when he stepped out into the courtyard, he stilled for a beat. He'd grown up hard and fast and without a home. This building had changed all that for him, and normally the sight of the fountain, the cobblestones, the building itself with its amazing old corbel brick architecture, all worked together to lighten his day.

But when he hadn't been looking, Christmas had taken over the place. There were garlands of evergreen entwined with twinkling white lights in every doorway and window frame. On top of that, all the potted trees that lined the walkways had been done up like Christmas trees.

This being winter in San Francisco, specifically the district of Cow Hollow, the foggy afternoon air burned his lungs like ice. He grabbed his phone from the coin-filled fountain, dried it off on his pants, and shoved it into one of his pockets to restore later.

"Spence!" Willa called out from the pet shop that opened into the courtyard. She ran a pet day care out of her shop and sometimes when Spence needed to think, he often did so while walking her clients for her.

She gestured to the large dog snoozing in the sunspot with a cat on either side of him. "Got time to help me out?" she asked.

"Sure." The dog was a regular client named Daisy Duke, and she came out of a dead sleep at Spence's voice, leaping over the cats in sheer joy as she headed right for him. When she got to him, she jumped up and down in place, attempting to lick his face. Spence calmed her down somewhat, hooked her up to the leash, and hit the courtyard with her, heading toward the wrought-iron gates so he could walk her to doggy Disneyland — the park.

But Daisy Duke wasn't a walker. She was a runner. More accurately, she was a 125-pound bunny, bounding with enthusiastic energy, tugging at the leash.

"Hold your horses, Daze," he said. "Save it for the park." He muscled her to his side, his mind miles away on his drone problems. Lost in thought, he wasn't exactly on his game when a black cat appeared out of nowhere.

With an excited bark, Daisy Duke broke free to charge after it, heading back toward the fountain and the woman now standing there, suitcase at her side, arm primed to throw a coin into the water.

The cat managed to dodge the woman, but Daisy Duke wasn't nearly as dexterous. Barreling forward at warp speed, she clearly saw the problem at the last minute because she let out a bark of surprise. She was probably mostly Irish setter, but Spence was pretty sure she was also part Wookiee. She was huge and uncoordinated, and a few crayons short of a full box. She did drop her head and try to stop, but her forward momentum was too much. Her back end slid out from beneath her and she flipped onto her back, plowing headlong into the woman and toppling her over.

Right into the water.

Jesus. "Stay," Spence said to Daisy and lurched forward as the woman pushed up to her hands and knees in the water, coughing and sputtering. *"Are you okay?"*

Gesturing that she didn't need his assistance, she swiped a hand down her face, muttering what sounded like "I should've gone to Toronto."

She was completely drenched thanks to him, and yet she wasn't yelling. She got serious points for that, he thought. And because she was wearing one of those flowy dresses that gave a man thoughts about what might or might not be under said dress, along with a denim jacket and boots — all of which were now clinging to her and fighting her efforts — he stepped into the fountain to help her.

"The water's . . . warm," she said in surprise. "It's freezing out. How is the water warm?"

He looked down at the water. Green. He could feel coins beneath the soles of his shoes. "That can't be good."

She choked and he did a mental grimace. He deserved the tears. Hell, he deserved fury. But when she lifted her face, he realized she was *laughing*?

She'd found humor in this shitty situation.

He felt something shift in his chest at that, a zing of attraction maybe, which he hadn't seen coming. In fact, he actually wasn't seeing too much at all, since he was now nearly as wet as she, including his glasses. He took them off to wipe the lenses on his equally wet shirt and eye contact was made.

She had big green eyes. Big, green, smiling eyes. "I'm a mess," she said.

That wasn't what he was thinking. Her clothes were plastered to her body. Her very nice, curvy body. He forced his gaze back to her face, then stepped out of the fountain and turned back for her, offering a hand.

She took it but still fumbled because her dress had shrink-wrapped itself to her legs, making moving all but impossible. They struggled a moment, hands grappling for purchase on each other until finally he just wrapped an arm around her waist and lifted her out, then set her down on the cobblestoned ground.

"Wuff!" Daisy had flopped around on her back for a few seconds, trying to right herself. Eventually she'd given up and stayed down, tail wagging like crazy, her tongue hanging out the side of her mouth.

That is, until she eyed something in one of the big potted trees lining the courtyard, now decorated to within an inch of their lives with lights and ornaments.

The black cat.

"Stay," Spence warned the dog and turned back to the woman.

"Thanks," she said, her voice matching her husky laugh. "Appreciate the help . . ." She paused, clearly waiting for him to fill in his name.

"Spence," he said, purposely skipping his last name. Anonymity was hard to come by lately, but he'd made a habit of keeping up the effort.

"Well," she said. "Thanks for the help, Spence." And then she . . . turned to walk away.

"Wait —" He'd gotten her soaked and he felt terrible about that. He wanted to make sure she was okay, that he got her dry and warm. "You didn't tell me your name."

She looked back, seeming oddly reluctant. "Colbie," she said. "My name is Colbie."

"Colbie, I can't let you just walk away. You've got to be freezing cold. At the very least I owe you dry clothes and a warm drink."

"No, really. It's okay." She started to wring out her long, dark hair and paused. "You might want to stand back. My hair needs its own zip code when it's wet."

This made him smile.

"Oh, I'm not kidding," she said.

Out of all the women Spence had known in his life, he couldn't think of a single one who'd be taking this so well, and shit, he realized she was absently rubbing her elbow. Gently, he pushed up the sleeve of her denim jacket and found an abrasion along with an already blooming bruise.

"It's nothing," she said.

Maybe, but her skin was broken and he had no idea what was in that water. "We need to clean that cut and ice your elbow. And I want to pay for your clothes to be cleaned or replaced —"

"Wuff!"

He shot the impatient Daisy a long look that promised no cookies today just as Elle came out of the elevator into the courtyard, striding toward them with a concerned look on her face. "Hi," she said to Colbie. "I'm Elle Wheaten, the building manager. What happened? Are you okay?"

"She took a header into the water," Spence said. "Daisy's fault."

They all looked at Daisy, who was sitting there smiling wide, not a concern in this world.

"I'm taking Colbie upstairs," he said. "To clean out her cut and get her some dry clothes."

Elle turned to him in shock.

Spence understood the surprise. He usually avoided dealing with people, especially people he didn't know. And then there was the fact that his penthouse apartment was an inner sanctum that he didn't let just anyone into. "The gym," he clarified, which was on the top floor next to his apartment. It had its own entrance, separate from his living quarters and office.

"I'll take her," Elle offered, doing as she always did, which was keeping herself between Spence and the rest of the world.

"Really," Colbie said, her voice firm if not a little shaky. "Not necessary. I'm fine."

Spence didn't claim to know all that much about women, but even he knew that *fine* didn't mean fine. The scale went great, good, okay, not okay, I hate you, fine. And as a bonus, she was beginning to tremble from the cold as she gripped her suitcase and tried to walk off — not that her dress was having it.

Colbie stopped fighting it, sighed, and tilted her head back. "Really? Are we serious with today?"

Both Spence and Elle glanced up at the sky. Nothing but clouds. He looked over at Elle, who was brows up, giving him a slow shake of her head. And while it was true that Elle was one of his best friends and he trusted her with his life, he didn't agree with her silent opinion to just let the woman go.

He couldn't. There was just something about the very wet, cute-yet-sexy Colbie No-Last-Name that appealed to him in a way that nothing else had in a long time. So when she tripped over her dress yet again and swore with a low, muttered *"Son of a beach!"* he grabbed for her, keeping her upright.

"Please," he said as her clothes began to soak his. "*Please* let me help you."

At his other side, Elle's mouth fell open. She wasn't used to hearing the word *please* from him. Ignoring her, he kept his gaze on Colbie.

Wary, she rolled her eyes, but gave a slight nod. She'd let him help her out but she wasn't happy about it.

Fair enough.

Chapter 2
#H-E-Double-Hockey-Sticks

Colbie kept a grip of Spence's forearms and it wasn't because she hadn't touched a man in so long she'd forgotten how much she'd missed the tactile feel of hard, sinewy muscle beneath her fingers. Nope, she kept a grip on him because her damn dress was holding her prisoner, making it nearly impossible to move with an ounce of grace.

As if she had any ounces of grace even on good days, of which this wasn't one. In fact, it was a rough day. She'd even venture to say it'd been a rough *year,* but that wasn't strictly true. The fact that she could suddenly pay her bills without using credit cards and racking up more on her mounting debt had truly changed her life in that she no longer was constantly stressed about money. But as hard as it was for her to believe, money hadn't solved all her problems.

Later. She'd obsess later. For now she

stared up at the man who was tall, leanly muscled, and sturdy as a tree, or so it seemed, given that he was holding the both of them upright.

His hair was every shade of brown under the sun, on the wrong side of needing a cut, and seemed to have a mind of its own. His eyes behind the glasses were a warm whiskey brown, eyes that were somehow amused and kind and enigmatic all at the same time. Fascinating, she thought, and fought the urge to find a pen from in her purse and make a note. But if she could have done so without looking silly, she'd totally have done it and written *tall, dark, and yummy stranger with an overly exuberant dog the size of a VW Bug.*

Said dog was panting with happiness at Spence, who shook his head at her as he picked up her leash. "Next time, it's the glue factory for you."

The dog's expression went sheepish and contrite, and Colbie felt her amusement fade. She knew from raising siblings with their far too many pets to count that the bad behavior never came from the animals but their owners. She tried very hard not to let her admittedly crazy personal life dictate her feelings but she had a thing, a big thing, against people who didn't take responsibility for their actions. Like her father. Nothing had ever been his fault either. He'd always been the victim.

"Don't you worry," she told Daisy. "It wasn't your fault." Then she hiked her wet dress up to her thighs and again tried to walk away.

"I'd really feel better if you let us help you," the woman named Elle said to her back.

She was probably worried that Colbie was a lawsuit walking. Elle herself was dressed to rule the world in a badass, gorgeous black and white suit dress with heels to die for. She'd said she was the building's manager, and given the easy affection between her and Spence, and the shorthand way they had of communicating, there was at least some sort of relationship between them. Maybe they were a couple and Elle was feeling threatened.

Except . . . no one looking at Colbie now or even before she'd gone for a swim would consider her a threat standing next to Elle.

Maybe . . . maybe Spence was a serial killer and Elle was worried that she'd have yet another body to dispose of. Okay, yeah, so now she was letting her inner writer take over. But at least she still had an inner writer somewhere deep, deep, *deep* down . . .

Still, serial killer or no, she needed to let someone from home know where she was, and that's when it hit her. Her phone. With sudden panic, she fished through the pockets of her drenched denim jacket and . . . yep . . . pulled out her equally drenched cell phone, still turned off from her flight. She went to turn it on but Spence put his hand over hers. "Wait. Let me dry it out for you first or you'll fry it."

Thinking of all the information in it, information that linked her to her pen name and a huge career she still hadn't gotten comfortable with — so much that she'd literally run away from it — she hugged the phone to her chest. "I've got it."

Spence and Elle glanced at each other again with unspoken questions that Colbie didn't intend to answer. She thought of the e-mails she'd left, none telling anyone exactly where she was, just that she needed to be alone and unplugged for a few weeks.

Getting out of New York had been huge for her, and nothing short of miraculous. For five straight years she'd worked twelve to fourteen hours a day without a single break — longer if on deadline — trying to keep everyone in her life happy and taken care of. She'd begun to dream about her prepublished days when she'd been a writer by night, an eager waitress by day, soaking up everything around her like a sponge, shamelessly eavesdropping on customers, studying people, making up stories about them in her head.

She'd lost that joy and in doing so lost her ability to write at all. If she wanted to save her burgeoning career, she needed this break, needed the time away to refill her well or she'd be back to waitressing. There was nothing wrong with that but she was hoping instead to find her love of writing.

Then she'd go home in time for Christmas, at which point she'd plaster a smile on her face and get on with the insanity of her life.

"Here. You're cold." Spence handed Daisy's leash to Elle and shrugged out of his own jacket and wrapped it around Colbie's shoulders, careful not to actually touch her as his fingers drew it closed in front of her. It was blessedly warm from his body heat and she had to fight not to inhale his scent, which was some glorious guy smell.

Now that the shock of the trip and her unexpected dip into the fountain was wearing off, she realized Spence was right — she was seriously cold. Trembling with it, including chattering teeth.

She'd been in the city for all of an hour. She hadn't even found a place to stay yet. She couldn't imagine how many texts and voice mails were waiting for her from her mom, her brothers, her two staff members, Janeen and Tracy, and her agent, Jackson — not that she could get to them anyway with her phone possibly destroyed.

Which, actually, had its upside . . .

"I've got hot tea," Elle said.

The thought of hot tea appealed to Colbie on every single level and she bit her lower lip in indecision.

"She's got a million different kinds too," Spence said, watching her with a hint of humor, like he knew she was arguing with herself. "She specializes in flowery and fruity shit."

Elle sighed.

Colbie laughed but . . . "I don't know you," she blurted out. Embarrassed, she grimaced. "I'm sorry. It's just that I came here to be alone."

Elle nodded. "I get that. And so does Spence, more than anyone I know. He'd be a complete shut-in if we let him. We routinely have to drag him around with us and force him to be social."

Spence looked pained. "I'm not that bad."

"Wanna bet?"

He shook his head but didn't take his gaze from Colbie. "I want you to know that you're safe here in this building. I promise you that."

He had incredible eyes and that combined with a killer smile, and she was sucked right in. Her problem was simple. The promises of people she loved had never meant jackshit, so she certainly couldn't accept a promise from a stranger. And yet, her gaze locked with Spence's, she found that she somehow wanted to.

"This way — follow me," Elle said and started walking, Daisy trotting along after her.

Colbie stared at them. "Do people always just do what she says?"

"Always," Spence said. "Resistance is futile. Come on, I've got ya." He took her stuff and led her past the wrought-iron gate that would've taken her back to the street.

The irony was that she'd come into the courtyard on her way to the hotel she'd Googled only because of the fountain. The one with the crazy love legend that had appealed to the writer deep down inside her.

Ahead of them, Elle and Daisy took the stairs, which was impressive because Elle was wearing some seriously kickass heels.

Thankfully, Spence bypassed the stairwell

and hit the button for the elevator.

"Your girlfriend —" she started.

"Not my girlfriend."

"Okay, then," she said, not sure why that sent a thrill through her. "Your dog is taking the stairs."

"Because she's not in danger of hypothermia. And she's not mine either. A friend owns South Bark Pet Shop on the farside of the courtyard. To clear my head, I sometimes help her out and walk her day care clients."

So Daisy wasn't even his, a fact that oddly relieved Colbie. He hadn't been shirking responsibility of his own pet.

Which meant she'd jumped to conclusions about him and she didn't like what that said about herself. "So . . . you're a professional dog walker?"

He laughed as the elevator doors opened. "No."

They stepped on and he pulled out a special keycard, sliding it across the card reader as she looked at him. "Dog walking is a perfectly respectable profession," she said.

"Of course it is. But that's not what I do."

She waited, but he didn't say what he *did* do — and that's when she caught sight of herself in the mirrored walls of the elevator and did her best not to gasp in horror. Her hair was so much worse than she'd imagined, and she'd imagined it pretty bad. The waves had exploded around her face and shoulders like she'd stuck her finger into an electrical socket. Letting out a shaky breath, she turned her back to the wall so she couldn't see herself. Better.

"So where you visiting from?" Spence asked, his hair also tousled but looking ridiculously effortlessly sexy.

Where was she from? "Another planet entirely," she said.

He did that brow arch again, which somehow with his glasses and those piercing light brown eyes was hot as hell and loosened her tongue. "I mean a life that *seems* like another planet from here," she clarified.

He studied her a moment, leaning back against the elevator wall like he didn't want to crowd her. "And you . . . ran away."

"Sort of."

"Are you in trouble, Colbie?"

The way he said her name did something to her low in her belly. "No." Yes. Most definitely, yes. Her deadline was barreling down on her and instead of working on her book, she was three thousand–plus miles from home. "There were . . . things I couldn't control in my life, so I decided instead to control the way I responded to it all. It's my superpower."

He smiled, and oh boy did he have a nice smile, so she returned it. "New York," she said. "I'm from New York."

"That's a long way to run."

Hopefully long enough. As the oldest sister to twins Kent and Kurt, the two brothers she'd mostly raised herself, both of whom had so far refused to grow up, she'd have liked to go even farther. And then there was Jackson, the agent who'd single-handedly put her on the map in her career. Until not too long ago, he'd been one of the most important people in her life. So important that she'd fallen for him hard, and she'd believed he was doing the same.

Oh how woefully, pathetically wrong she'd been. Remembering her humiliation over what had happened, she felt her face burn.

So yeah, she'd desperately needed to get away, and far away. After a lifetime of taking care of everyone around her, she just needed to be left alone for a little bit, needed that quite badly. Just her and her laptop and her thankfully vivid imagination.

Except it wasn't so vivid lately, was it. Not since she'd become an entire huge franchise that she alone maintained. The pressure was killing her. Her brothers and their incessant

neediness were killing her. Jackson was killing her.

Everything was killing her and she'd lost
it. Lost herself.

"I'm going to ask you again," he said very
gently. "Are you in some kind of trouble?
Do you need help?"

"No," she said and repeated it when he
didn't look like he believed her. "No," she
said more firmly. "I'm really not in trouble.
I'm . . ." She sighed. "Well, what the H-E-
double-hockey-sticks. I'm a fiction writer,"
she admitted.

His mouth twitched. "H-E-double-
hockey-sticks?"

She shook her head. "Don't ask. It involves
a swear jar and me going broke."

He laughed. "Creative swearing. I like it.
So you're a writer. Who ran away from New
York."

"I hit a wall. I need some inspiration. I
was thinking a tropical beach, but then a
surprise hurricane thwarted me, so here I
am. And so far it's been the right call. On
the cab ride here, I saw a gorgeous bridge, a
sparkling bay, and streets lined with elegant
Victorian houses."

"And then a horse of a dog and a fountain
up close and personal," he said with a smile.
"With all that inspiration, I bet your first

book flies right out of you."

She opened her mouth to correct the notion that this would be her first book. In fact, she'd written three, the first of which had a movie coming out on Christmas Day. In her mind, she'd finished off the series, but her publisher wanted to add a fourth book and they wanted it by the first of the year.

One month from now.

As a result, she felt like there was an elephant sitting on her chest. "That'd be great," she said.

"So what do you do to support yourself while writing?"

"Waitress," she said, citing what she'd done all through college and up until the day she'd gotten her first big deal. See? She wasn't a complete liar. She was merely an *omitter,* and that was totally allowed with perfect strangers, no matter how hot they were.

Look at her learning something from Jackson after all . . .

"Do you live or work in this building?" she asked.

"Yes."

She smiled at his vague answer. She wasn't the only secret keeper.

"So why Cow Hollow?" Spence asked. He

44

was still leaning against the far wall, giving her as much space as he could. Not that it mattered. He was tall, broad shouldered, and long legged. He alone nearly filled up the elevator.

"I've never been to San Francisco before," she said. "And when the cabbie at the airport asked me where to, I told him to surprise me."

This got a bark of laughter from Spence.

"True story," she said, smiling in spite of herself because he had a nice laugh too. Contagious really, even if she could tell he didn't do it very often. "With a name like Cow Hollow, how could I resist checking this area out? Plus he told me more about the myth of the fountain in the courtyard, that if you wish for true love with a true heart, you'll find it."

"Is that what you were wishing for when Daisy Duke knocked you into the water?" he asked. "True love?"

Actually, the opposite. She wanted to never be hurt by love again, but that was way too personal to admit. "I was wishing for peace and quiet for as many days as I could get. I figured any fountain with such a good reputation wouldn't mind granting such an innocuous wish, right?"

He smiled, and like the other times,

something fluttered deep in her belly. Something most definitely not peaceful or quiet. She might be cold and drenched and completely exhausted, but she wasn't sorry. About any of it. The truth was, something about this building energized her, gave her a sense of an adventure that had been missing from her life. And *that* gave her a piece of what she just realized she'd been missing — *hope.*

CHAPTER 3
#MOTHERFORKER

The elevator doors opened onto the fifth floor, Spence's private floor. He guided Colbie off the elevator into a lobby with four doors. One led to the stairwell — which Elle came out of with Daisy Duke in tow, perfectly behaved now, of course.

Two more doors led to Spence's private penthouse apartment and office. The last one opened directly into his gym. They went through that door, and while Elle flicked on lights and hit the alarm pad to enter his code, Spence heard Colbie gasp. He turned back quickly to find her staring in awe out the windows at the sun setting over the bay.

"Wow," she breathed, still shaking but taking the time to eye the 180-degree vista of the city as she hugged herself in his jacket. He knew that from where she stood, she could see the rest of Cow Hollow, and past that, Fort Mason Park, the Marina Green, and the bay.

And he thought it was pretty wow too. He loved this view. It was one of the many reasons he'd bought the building in the first place.

"I wouldn't be able to work out to this view," she said.

"Never gets old for me either." Spence pulled out his phone to crank up the heat from his app before remembering he hadn't dried the phone out yet. He had to actually use the control panel on the wall before going to her at the window. When he was stuck in his own head and unable to get anywhere with his work, he liked to stare out at the city that was more home to him than anywhere else had ever been.

"I love it," she breathed. "I feel like from right here I can see all the way to the ends of the Earth."

He knew what she meant. Out beyond the bay stretched the Pacific Ocean in all its deep-blue majesticness, clear to the gently curved horizon.

"I could so write to this view," she went on in a hushed, amazed voice and turned to Elle, who was working out her thumbs — on her phone. "This is such a great building. I saw the pub downstairs. And the coffee shop and that cute reclaimed-wood furniture place. What else is there?"

"More shops and businesses," Elle said, her thumbs still going, Daisy Duke at her side falling asleep standing up. "An eclectic mix on the first and second floors. Residential apartments on three and four."

"I don't suppose you have any apartments available for a short-term rental?" Colbie asked hopefully. "I'm only going to be here until Christmas Eve but would happily pay for the whole month to stay here."

"Sorry," Elle said. "But no."

Spence met Elle's gaze. She was the mother figure he didn't need, the bossy-as-hell sister he'd never asked for, and his favorite and most important employee, but she was also a colossal pain in his ass. "What Elle means," he said, "is that she doesn't know of anything offhand but I'm sure she could check it out for you."

"Hmm," Elle said and nudged a trembling Colbie toward the shower area. "The restroom's through that door. Fresh towels under the sink. Go get warmed up."

Colbie, apparently too cold to further argue, nodded. She shut the door behind herself and they heard the lock click into place.

Cute, sexy, *and* smart.

"Are you kidding me?" Elle asked him, keeping her voice low.

"What?"

"Don't 'what' me. You know what. You're in the middle of saving the world right now for Clarissa, remember? So please tell me what the hell you think you're doing."

They heard the shower come on from inside the bathroom. "Look," he said, trying to not picture Colbie stripping out of her clothes. "I got her into this mess. This is the least I can do."

"No," she said. "The least you could do is give her a hundred bucks for her trouble and send her on her way."

"Cold, Elle, even for you."

"Did you even get a last name on her? Or what she does for a living? Did you vet her in any way?"

"For what?" he asked. "*I'm* the one who ruined her day, not the other way around."

"And how about the way she reacted to you even thinking about touching her phone? Did you notice that little red flag?"

"Of course. And I wouldn't have let a stranger touch my phone either," he said. "Hell, I barely let you touch it."

"You know what I'm getting at," she said. "Maybe she has something to hide, Spence."

Or maybe she was in trouble. She'd denied that but he couldn't help but think of her sweet eyes and the haunted depths he'd seen in them. "She needs a place to stay. Give her the empty furnished apartment I'm holding on the third floor."

"We don't do short-term rentals here. By your own decree."

"We do today."

There was a beat of silence. Since Elle was never silent, it had to be shock.

"You hold that open for a reason," she finally said.

"Yeah, and so far Eddie's refused to come in off the streets, hasn't he." Yet another problem he hadn't been able to solve, which tightened the ever-present knot in his chest. "Make the rent cheap because she's a struggling writer — she probably doesn't have much money."

Elle's mouth fell open. "She's a *writer*? Are you kidding me?"

"Not a reporter," he said. "A fiction writer."

Elle just continued to stare at him. "Are you even listening to yourself?"

"Look, I got her knocked into the fountain and it's butt-ass cold out there, and she rolled with it." He remembered Colbie's throaty laugh and it made him smile even now. "She's been a really good sport about it."

"Maybe she had a good reason," Elle said.

"Maybe she was trying to get close to you. Hell, maybe she *is* a reporter and the whole thing's a setup."

"Come on," he said. "She couldn't have known Daisy Duke would send her sprawling into the fountain. This happened on my property — I'm making it right, end of story."

"Fine." Elle pulled out her phone, which had gone off four thousand times in the past four minutes. "But I'd like to remind your stubborn ass that you've not been yourself since this whole media thing. You need to be more cautious about connecting with a stranger who appeared basically out of nowhere."

"She's not running a con on me."

"I'm not saying she is, but we both know you've been screwed over, *twice* if we're counting, and you haven't come to terms with the betrayal yet. So just be careful, okay? That's all I'm saying." She pointed at him. "And remember, you're the smartest person in this building and probably the smartest person I'll ever meet. Use your powers for good."

He had to laugh. *"Ditto."*

She blew out a sigh, gave him a quick hug, and then she and Daisy Duke were gone.

Spence let his smile slip as he walked

across the room to check the thermostat again. He'd heard what Elle had to say, and he got it. He *was* still stinging, and he wasn't himself. Added to that was the project for Clarissa. The *unfinished* project. It was critical work, more important than anything he'd ever done, and it was kicking his ass. He was on a deadline and could feel it breathing down his neck every single day that passed. He could afford no break in his concentration and efforts.

A problem now that 99 percent of his brain had short-circuited over the thought of Colbie naked in his shower . . .

He heard the water go off and he pictured her wrapping herself in his towel. Dripping wet . . . Shoving his hands in his pockets, he moved to the window and looked out at the view that had so impressed her. Once upon a time he couldn't have imagined living in a place like this, much less owning it. But he'd conquered the shitty hand that life had dealt him.

And he'd do it again if he had to.

The bathroom door opened, and even better than his fantasy, Colbie emerged from a cloud of steam, her willowy body wrapped in one of his towels, her exposed skin gleaming and dewy damp. Her hair had been piled on top of her head, but wavy strands had escaped, clinging to her neck and shoulders.

He couldn't tear his gaze off of her. There was just something so uncalculated about her, so . . . natural and easy. She was like a beacon to him, which was both crazy and more than a little terrifying.

Clearly not seeing him against the wall, she moved with an effortless grace to the suitcase she'd left at the door. Bending low enough to give him a near heart attack, she rifled through her things, mumbling to herself that she should've researched more about how to be a normal person instead of how to kill someone with an everyday object.

"Do you kill a lot of people, then?" Spence asked.

"Motherforker!" she said with a startled squeak of surprise, whirling to face him, almost losing her grip on the towel.

Five days a week, Spence worked out hard in this gym. Mostly to outrun his demons, but the upside was he could run miles without losing his breath. But he lost his breath now.

And that wasn't his body's only reaction.

CHAPTER 4
#SHIITAKEMUSHROOMS

At the unexpected sight of Spence, Colbie startled hard. How was it that he was the one who needed glasses and yet she'd not seen him standing against the window? "No, I don't kill a lot of people," she said cautiously because she was wearing only a towel in front of a strange man. "But I'm happy to make an exception."

He laughed, a rough rumble that was more than a little contagious but she controlled herself because, hello, she was once again dripping wet before the man who seemed to make her knees forget to hold her up.

"I didn't mean to scare you," he said and pushed off the wall to come close.

She froze, but he held up his hands like, *I come in peace,* and crouched at her feet to scoop up the clothes she hadn't realized she'd dropped.

Leggings, a long forgiving tee, and the

peach silk bra-and-panty set that hadn't gotten so much as a blink from the TSA guy.

But it got one out of Spence. He also swallowed hard as she snatched them back from him.

"Hold on," he said and caught her arm, pulling it toward him to look at her bleeding elbow.

"Sit," he said and gently pushed her down to a weight bench. He vanished into the bathroom and came back out with a first aid kit.

It took him less than two minutes to clean and bandage the scrape. Then, easily balanced at her side on the balls of his feet, he did the same for both her knees, which she hadn't noticed were also scraped up.

"You must've hit the brick coping as you fell in the fountain," he said and let his thumb slide over the skin just above one bandaged knee.

She shivered, and not from the cold either. "Not going to kiss it better?" she heard herself ask before biting her tongue for running away with her good sense.

She'd raised her younger twin brothers. Scrappy, roughhouse wild animals, the both of them, so there'd been plenty of injuries she'd kissed over the years.

But no one had ever kissed hers. Not

surprising, since most of her injuries tended to be on the inside, where they didn't show. Still, she was horrified she'd said anything at all. "I didn't mean —" She broke off, frozen like a deer in the headlights as Spence slowly lowered his head, brushing his lips over the Band-Aid on her elbow, then her knees.

When he lifted his head, he pushed his glasses higher on his nose, those whiskey eyes warm and amused behind his lenses. "Better?"

Shockingly better. Since she didn't quite trust her voice at the moment, she gave a jerky nod and took her clothes back into the bathroom. She shut the door and then leaned against it, letting out a slow, deliberate breath. Holy cow, she was out of her league. He was somehow both cute *and* hot, and those glasses . . .

He hadn't touched her other than the first aid and then those sweet kisses on her scrapes — which *she'd* asked for — and yet she felt more trembly than she had when she'd been freezing.

Clearly she'd gone too long without a social orgasm.

She dressed quickly and glanced at herself in the bathroom. In spite of herself, she looked . . . well, flushed. And her eyes were sparkling. And something else — she was smiling. What was wrong with her? She'd had a very long day but still she felt . . . invigorated.

From the other side of the door came a single knock. An alpha man sort of knock, one that suggested curiosity and a slight impatience. "Almost ready?"

"For what?" she asked, still staring at herself in the mirror.

"First aid, take two."

Oh boy. She stepped out of the bathroom. "Listen, I think maybe I gave you the wrong idea —" She broke off because Spence was at the door to the gym now, holding it open for her.

"Leave your stuff except for your phone," he said. "We'll come back for it."

You wanted adventure, she reminded herself. And if they were leaving here, it meant he didn't have nefarious intentions. At least not at the moment.

She wasn't sure if she was relieved or disappointed.

As if maybe he could read her mind, his lips quirked in a barely there smile as he led her back down to the ground floor. Night had fallen as they walked through thick fog across the beautifully lit cobblestoned courtyard. Past a coffee shop, pet shop, tattoo parlor, furniture shop, and straight into a pub named O'Riley's.

The place was cute. The tables were made from whiskey barrels and the bar itself had been crafted out of what looked like repurposed longhouse-style doors. The hanging brass lantern lights and stained glass fixtures, along with the horse-chewed old-fence baseboards, finished the look that said antique charm and cozy, friendly warmth.

She immediately felt right at home. Music drifted from invisible speakers, casting a jovial mood, but not so loud as to make conversation difficult. Spence had her by the hand and tugged her through a surprisingly large crowd straight to the bar, where at the far right were two open barstools.

Spence nodded to the guy behind the bar as they took a seat.

"Good timing," the guy said. "Archer's in the back being Archer. I need you to go kick his ass in pool to put him in his place."

Clearly there was a familiarity between these two, an ease and connection that spoke of either brothers or a longtime friendship.

"Later," Spence told him. "I need my usual, with two sides: a bag of ice and another of uncooked rice."

The guy, good-looking and wearing a

59

T-shirt that read *I Am O'Riley,* smirked. "You threw your phone out the window again, didn't you?"

Spence ignored this, gesturing to Colbie. "Colbie, this is Finn O'Riley."

Finn smiled. "Nice to meet you."

"She's in the city for the first time," Spence said. "And thanks to me, Daisy Duke dumped her in the fountain. We need food to refuel, ice for her elbow, and rice for her phone to hopefully redeem us in her eyes."

"Tall order," Finn said and pulled out his vibrating phone to read a text. "Huh," he said and gave Spence a funny look. "So, uh, there's a 9–1–1."

Spence shook his head. "Let me guess. Elle."

Finn nodded. "Wants me to rescue you."

Colbie tried not to take umbrage at that and failed, but Spence just laughed.

"Tell her she needs to get a grip," he said.

"Do I look crazy?" Finn asked and slid his phone into his pocket. "Besides, we both know she's paranoid for you for good reason after all that media crap."

Spence lifted a shoulder but didn't comment.

"Food, ice, and rice, coming up," Finn said and vanished into the back.

Colbie looked at Spence. "Are you sure you're not in a relationship with Elle?"

"No, I'm in a relationship with bad judgment." He pointed to the other side of the room. "See that guy through the back doors playing pool like he was born to it?"

Colbie turned and looked. The man leaning over the pool table lining up his shot was . . . holy moly hot.

"That's Archer Hunt," Spence said. "Elle's his. But more importantly, he's 100 percent all hers. They're both crazy, but they make it work." He lifted her arm and again eyed her elbow. "Still swelling." He gently probed at it.

"It's not broken," she said.

"How do you know?"

It was more of a hope than actual knowledge, so she pulled away just as Finn came back. He tossed two baggies at Spence, who caught them in midair and offered her the one holding the raw rice. "Put your phone in here," he said. "Ziplock it. The rice will draw the moisture out of your phone and, with any luck, it'll still work a few hours from now."

Colbie had heard of the trick but she still hesitated.

Spence met her gaze, his eyes warm but curious. "Problem?"

61

"Would you think I was an awful person if I secretly hope my phone's broken forever?"

He gave a wry laugh that told her more than words could how very much he sympathized with her. "You're talking to the guy who earlier today threw his phone out the window," he said.

"So . . . we both fantasize about going phoneless?"

His smile said he fantasized about other things as well, and her body did that inner quiver thing again. She slipped her phone inside the baggie and then dropped it all back into her purse.

"Next," Spence said and pressed the ice bag to her elbow.

Finn came back with a huge platter of chicken wings and deep-fried zucchini. Colbie eyed the platter and then Spence's extremely fit body with disbelief.

He shrugged. "That's what the gym's for."

Colbie couldn't even *look* at a French fry without gaining weight, but her stomach growled, reminding her she hadn't eaten since the sad pack of three whole peanuts on the plane.

They dove into the food and she asked one of the questions that were killing her. "Tell me about this amazing building."

"It is pretty amazing, isn't it?" He smiled.

"The fountain actually came first. The building was built around it back in the mid-1800s, when Cow Hollow was still actually filled with cows."

"Wow. Really?" Hard to imagine San Francisco as anything but the incredibly hilly, unique, busy but somehow also laid-back, quirky city it seemed to be.

"This building was a compound for one of the biggest ranching families in the state at the time," Spence said.

"When did the infamous legend come into play?" she asked. "The one where if you wish for true love, you'll find it."

He looked both pained and amused. "Shortly after. Some idiot made a wish and got lucky. Most of the businesses in the building perpetuate the legend because it makes good press and brings in foot traffic."

"But you don't believe," she said.

Finn was back, refilling their drinks, and spoke for Spence. "It's more like he can't help but believe and he's terrified." He grinned when Spence shot him a dry look.

"Explain," Colbie said.

Finn was happy to. "Not one but *three* of us owe our love lives to that fountain. So Spence's been giving it a wide berth."

"Because . . ." she eyeballed Spence ". . .

he doesn't want to be happy?"

Finn snorted and moved on.

"He thinks he's funny," was all Spence would say on that. He studied her over their tray of food. "So what's your three-week plan while you're here besides writing?"

"Rest," she said. "Eat. Be a tourist. I made a list of things I want to do."

"Let's see it."

She hesitated, wishing she hadn't said anything, because there were some really embarrassing things on that list . . .

"I won't laugh," he said.

She grimaced. "Yeah, I'd need that in writing first."

He produced a pen from his pocket and grabbed her cocktail napkin. "I, Spencer Baldwin, hereby solemnly promise not to laugh at your to-do list," he said as he wrote and signed the napkin. He pushed it toward her. "There. A binding contract."

She opened her purse to locate the list and had to paw through a bunch of her various notes to do so.

"How do you ever find anything?" Spence asked, not with any censure at all but with actual genuine fascination.

She shrugged. "My purse gets sad when it's all neat and organized." She finally got a hand on her list. The first eight items were places she wanted to see in San Francisco. Number nine was learn how to drive, something she'd not been able to do in New York. Nothing all that embarrassing. But number ten. Number ten took the cake. She grabbed his pen to scratch it off before giving him the list, but he put his hand over hers.

"I promised not to laugh, remember? And I don't break promises, Colbie."

"Ever?"

There was a rather fierce light in his eyes. "Not anymore."

That was interesting enough that she let him pull the list from her fingers. She knew the exact moment he got to number ten because he had to fight a smile when he lifted his gaze to hers.

"Ten's my favorite," he said and read it aloud — like she didn't know what she'd written. "A wild, passionate, up-against-the-wall, forget-my-name love affair that makes me weak in the knees when I think about it — but only a very *short* wild, passionate, up-against-the-wall, forget-my-name love affair because . . ." he paused, probably to control himself, before continuing ". . . I don't have the time or stamina to maintain that level of sexual activity, much less a relationship."

She moaned and closed her eyes.

"Pretty detailed," he said, running a hand over his deliciously scruffy jaw to hide the smile she knew he was fighting.

"I told you!" She snatched back the list. *"Shit."*

"Thought you didn't swear."

"I don't," she said, "but that's a body function, so it doesn't really count as a swear word." She sighed.

Not Spence. He out-and-out laughed, tipping his head back to do it, and it was such a nice sight that she had to crack up too. "You promised not to laugh," she reminded him.

"I'm not laughing at your list, so it doesn't count. My grandma used to swear by saying 'Shiitake mushrooms!' That was her favorite."

When he spoke with good humor, or actually whenever he spoke in general, his voice sounded like sex personified and it had her wriggling in her seat, no longer embarrassed but something entirely new now.

She blamed the combo of that sexy stubble with the glasses.

"I like your list," he said. "But you could do even better."

She felt some of her bones liquefy. "I'm going to assume you're talking about items one through eight."

He just smiled.

Okay, so she was going to *pretend* he was talking about one through eight. "I got some of those things from Googling what's a must-see in SF," she said. "If you can't trust Google, who can you trust?"

"Google isn't always the best avenue of research."

"No?" she asked, feeling a little defensive at that because number ten was still ringing in her head. And also because, well, her pride was injured. Research was her thing. Living in front of her computer had been how she'd built the crazy world that existed in Storm Fever, the series penned by her alter ego, CE Crown. "I suppose you're going to tell me what *is* the best avenue of research," she said.

"You gotta stretch yourself. You could question the people who actually live here, experiencing the city through them."

"But I don't know people who live here," she pointed out.

"Don't you?" He dunked a piece of fried zucchini into ranch sauce until it was more ranch than zucchini and then popped it into his mouth. When he'd chewed and swallowed, he flashed her a smile. "You know me, right? And I'm an open book."

That made her laugh. Spence Baldwin was

good-looking, smart, and funny, and he had good taste in friends and food, but he wasn't an open book, not by any stretch of the imagination — and her imagination was good, very good. He had secrets in his eyes, secrets that haunted him.

And so do you . . .

"I can tell you all sorts of things about this city," he said.

"Such as?"

"Such as it's seven by seven miles perched on a peninsula of forty-three hills."

"Wow," she said. "You're right. I didn't know that."

"I had a crush on Mrs. Stein, my fourth-grade teacher. I used to memorize all the geography facts to please her."

She laughed.

"All better?" he asked.

She looked down and saw the mountain of bare chicken bones on her plate and had to laugh. "I was starving."

Spence nudged the zucchini her way and she bit her lip, torn. On the one hand, she was full. On the other, the zucchini looked amazing. She blew out a sigh and ate one. "Oh. My. God."

"Right?"

"Shh." She took another while he laughed. And then another. When she finally leaned back, Spence was smiling at her.

"What?" she asked.

"Cute."

She resisted squirming in her chair because she hadn't straightened her hair or reapplied makeup, and she knew what she looked like.

Harried.

Tired.

Overworked.

Stressed.

And definitely *not* cute. "Thanks for feeding me. And for the ice and rice." She slipped off the stool. "But I've gotta go."

"Where to?"

To get her life together . . . "I still need to find a place to stay."

"How about right here?"

Chapter 5
#SonOfANutcracker

Colbie had just taken a sip of water when Spence said those words.

"How about right here . . ."

As a result, her sip of water got sucked into the wrong pipe and she choked and very nearly snorted water out her nose. This would've been no surprise at all to anyone who knew her, but she was really trying to be mysterious here.

And sexy, a voice inside her head said. *Admit it — you want him to think you're mysterious and sexy.*

He handed her a napkin.

"I'm sorry," she said, cleaning herself up. "But I can't stay with you. I'm not . . ." She shook her head. "I'm not interested in any sort of relationship. I'm only going to be here until Christmas Eve, so I really have no business starting something. I mean, not that you're not . . . well, *really* nice to look at, but —"

"There's a studio apartment on the third floor," he said, looking amused. "Furnished. Available. Elle's getting a key to show it to you."

"Oh." She felt her face flame. Wow, she was such an idiot. A socially inept idiot, which was yet another reason on her long list of reasons for running away for the month. She had no skills for navigating these kinds of waters, none. She needed a GPS for her life. Was there an app for that? Someone needed to invent that and pronto.

He was smiling outright now. "You done with your panic attack?"

She blew out a breath. "Yes." She shook her head at the both of them. "And while it's very kind of you to ask Elle to get me a place, I don't want to impose."

"No imposition," he said. "The apartment's empty."

She bit her lower lip and studied him.

He smiled. "It's sad when it's empty."

She burst out laughing and it felt so foreign that she laughed some more. Maybe, she thought, maybe today, even with the rough beginning, was supposed to happen. Maybe being here, *right* here, was exactly what she needed to get back on track. "Why would you help a perfect stranger?"

"We're not strangers," he said. "We went

71

swimming in the fountain together."

"But I don't even know what you do for a living," she said just as Finn came back to top off their drinks again.

Finn slid a look at Spence like he was really curious about how Spence would respond to this.

Spence didn't respond.

Colbie tried Finn. "Want to tell me why your friend is so mysterious about his job?"

"No can do," Finn said, but he said it very nicely.

She eyed Spence again. "How about if we play Twenty Questions."

"Sure," he said agreeably.

"If I get close, are you going to admit it?"

He just smiled.

"Never mind," she said. "It won't matter, because I'm good enough to be able to tell if you're lying."

Finn snorted. "I like you. I like you a lot, so I feel like I've got to tell you this . . ." He leaned in as if imparting a state secret. "There's a bimonthly poker game that goes on in the basement. It's highly competitive. And Mr. Poker-Face here almost never loses. Our boy's got some serious game."

"Elle used to win every time," Spence said casually. "But that was before they let me join in. Now the two of us aren't allowed to play on the same night."

"Because they're both asshole losers," Finn said.

"Hey," Spence said. "Don't sugarcoat it or anything."

"I don't sugarcoat. I'm not Willy Wonka." And then he moved off to serve other customers.

Colbie looked at Spence, who seemed like the very picture of laid-back and easygoing and not even close to anything like fiercely intense or competitive. "So you play poker," she said, "which means you're a thrill chaser. What else? Do you play any dangerous sports?"

"Yeah. Sometimes I disagree with Elle."

Colbie laughed. "You don't like to lose?"

"I don't know," he said modestly. "Because I never do."

Oh boy. "Are you a lawyer?"

It was his turn to laugh. "No."

She looked at his hands, taking them in hers, turning them over, running a finger along his work-roughened palms. "Are you a builder?"

He stared at her for a long beat. "No. But you're getting warmer."

She blew out a breath and studied his clothes. Sexy-guy jeans. An expensive-looking, perfectly fitted black button-down

73

in a material that made her fingers ache to touch. It was opened over a T-shirt that had a series of math equations on it. Or maybe physics. "College professor?"

"No."

He had Oakley aviator sunglasses on top of his head and his regular glasses on his face, making her smile. His hair was wind-blown and still in need of a cut, but clearly his last one had been excellent. "You *do* work though," she said. "Right?"

Again something flickered in his gaze. "One hundred percent."

"All the time, actually," Finn offered on another pass-by.

"Porn star?" she asked.

Spence grinned. "Ah, man. You recognized me."

She had to laugh. "You're a hard man to read."

"Tell us something we don't know," Elle said, slipping onto the stool next to Spence. She handed him a key. "The spare to the third-floor apartment."

Colbie found it odd that Elle gave the key to Spence. What did he have to do with the rentals if she was the building's general manager?

"Let's go see the apartment," Spence said, standing, dropping some cash onto the bar.

"Oh," Colbie said, opening her purse, shoving aside some notes to look for her wallet. "Let me —"

Spence put a big warm hand over hers. "I've got it."

"I appreciate it," she said. "But I have this thing." She met his gaze. "I don't let men pay for my food, because then . . ." She broke off and shook her head. Because then they thought she owed them. Maybe that had been just Jackson, but the memory of how badly she'd misread that situation was sobering and she intended to stand by her resolve.

"Because then . . . ?" Spence pressed.

"I just don't like to owe anyone."

"Okay, how about this," he said. "Since you're going to be around for a few weeks, you can get the next round of chicken wings and zucchini chips. Can you handle that?"

She considered it. Surely she could find him during her three-week stay and make sure she repaid the favor by feeding him at least once. "I suppose so, yes."

He smiled at her.

Elle, looking annoyed, led the way, her heels clicking, clicking, clicking as they walked back through the courtyard, which was so cute and charming that Colbie couldn't wait to grab her laptop and sit on one of the wrought-iron benches and write, a thought that had her heart pumping.

She wanted to write! That was a good sign.

"It's a studio," Elle warned her on the third floor, just outside the front door. "So it's small."

"Small is fine," Colbie said. "Thank you so much."

Before Elle could unlock the door, an old woman poked her head out of the apartment across the way. "What's going on out here?" she wanted to know.

Elle waved at her. "Hi, Mrs. Winslow. We're just showing the apartment to a possible new tenant, that's all."

Mrs. Winslow cupped a hand to her ear. "What's that?"

Elle raised her voice. "You might be getting a new neighbor!"

" 'Bout time. Is he a young hottie?"

"Well . . ." Elle looked like maybe she was trying to hold back a smile.

"It's okay if he isn't young. A silver-fox hottie would probably be just as good. I guess age don't matter too much, as long as he's still got what it takes." She looked Spence up and down. "Is it you, Spencie? Because I could totally handle you."

To his credit, Spence just smiled. "You think so?"

"I know so," Mrs. Winslow said smugly and then ruined it by hiccuping and giving them all a whiff of whiskey.

Spence looked pained. "Do you remember what we said about alcohol?"

"Yes." She beamed. "That the Jack mixes with everything but good decisions. Don't worry though — I never mix the two."

Elle snorted and opened the door. "Take care, Mrs. Winslow."

When they were inside with the door shut, Elle shook her head at Spence. "You shouldn't encourage her."

"She's still mourning."

"I know. And I also know that you're bringing her food and taking care of her. It'd be incredibly sweet if I didn't also know you were the one who got her 'the Jack.' "

"It was what her husband used to drink," he said. "She's having a hard time. So I bring her stuff."

Okay, so the guy saved people from the fountains and old ladies from grief. He seemed too good to be true, which — in Colbie's experience — meant he wasn't to be trusted. She needed to remember that when he looked at her with those startlingly clear eyes.

Shaking that off, she took in the place. It *was* small but also . . . cozy. The furniture was sparse but nice. Really nice. The bed looked brand-new, and sitting on top of the mattress was an unopened set of good-quality sheets and a pair of down pillows. A bar-top counter divided the kitchen from the living area, and there was a dumbwaiter that fascinated her and . . .

A black cat.

"That's the cat who spooked Daisy Duke into charging Colbie," Spence said. "It must've come up on the fire escape." He headed to the opened kitchen window to check it out. "Do you know who it belongs to, Elle?"

"No. I've never seen it before."

"I'll get it and take it outside —" Spence broke off when he turned back around and found Colbie holding the cat.

"It's a she," she said, hugging the poor thing. "And she's so thin and gangly that I think she's just a teenager."

Elle shook her head. "Don't worry. She's not your responsibility —"

"Oh, she's totally welcome to share the place with me," Colbie said and, still holding the cat, walked across the floor.

Her floor.

She looked out the window and took in the view. God, the view. She couldn't wait to get out there, to listen to tidbits of conversation as people walked by, letting it all stoke the flames of her imagination as she wrote.

It was such an ache that she nuzzled the cat to hide the fact that her eyes were burning with relief.

She really had done the right thing by coming here.

"So what do you think?" Elle asked.

"Are you kidding? I love it. I'll take it." Colbie took a peek in the bathroom. Catching a glimpse of herself and the black cat in the mirror, she smiled.

The cat stared at her, not unfriendly but not exactly ready to be besties either. "It's okay," Colbie told her. "I'll grow on you." She moved to leave the bathroom but stopped when she heard Elle talking.

"She didn't even ask how much."

"So?" Spence asked.

"So, you don't think that's . . . weird?"

Colbie — and the cat — walked into the room and looked at Elle. "How much?"

Elle had the good grace to grimace. "Okay, maybe I'm a little overprotective."

"I get it," Colbie said. "I'm the same. So really . . . how much? And do you want me to fill out an application?"

"Yes." Elle pulled an app from her purse and named the price.

Colbie nodded. "I'll fill this out and bring it to you with the cash for the month's rent right away."

"It's getting late. In the morning will be fine," Elle said. "And you don't need to pay in cash. You can pay through an app or with a check."

Colbie wasn't ready for her world to track her. She'd brought cash. "Is cash a problem?"

Elle slid Spence a look, sighed, and shook her head. "No problem."

CHAPTER 6
#SonOfACheez-It

Later Colbie got in her bed. The black cat had come and gone a few times. Worried about her, Colbie had left the window open just wide enough for her to seek shelter if she needed. Then she lay in bed in the dark thinking about her crazy day. Crazy but good, she decided. Shockingly good.

But that was because she hadn't yet looked at her phone. Remembering, she got out of bed and fished the bag of rice from her purse. She pulled out the phone and turned it on.

Notifications began to fill her screen. She chose to start with a group text with her assistant, Tracy, and publicist, Janeen.

Tracy:
Hey, Editorial wants to know your projected delivery date for the manuscript.

Janeen:

Whoa, hold up there, missy. First I want to know Colbie's projected delivery date for the articles and blogs she's supposed to write for promo.

Tracy:

Don't make me sorry I put you on this convo, Janeen. Colbs — I didn't tell Editorial that you ran away from home to find yourself, because I didn't want to set off a panic avalanche. Why should everyone panic when I'm doing enough for all of us?

Tracy:

P.S. At least tell me you're on a warm beach somewhere with a really hot cabana dude pouring you wine?

Janeen:

Oh, *you're* panicking, are you, Trace? How about me? Colbie hasn't done a damn thing on her list! Listen, Colbs, I get it. You needed to get away. *Fine.* But at least go thru your damn e-mail and send me back the articles and posts I need pronto. P.S. Miss you, but I'd miss you more if you'd GO THROUGH YOUR E-MAILS.

Colbie answered with I'll send everything soon, making sure not to define *soon*. Then she silenced her phone and slept like a baby, at least until around two a.m. when something shook her bed.

She sat straight up with a gasp and came nose-to-nose with the black cat.

"Meow."

"You need a curfew," Colbie said.

The cat, noncommittal, turned in a circle three times and then plopped on Colbie's feet and closed her eyes.

Fine with her — her feet had been cold anyway. She fell back to sleep, waking only when daylight was streaming in through the window.

"Wow," she said to the cat in genuine shock. "A whole night's sleep, with the exception of your arrival. It's a miracle."

The cat looked pleased, like it'd been all her doing.

Colbie picked up her phone. She had texts from her brothers, which she ignored for now. Same with Jackson's. "Whoa," she said, surprised to see a text from her mom. Colbie had bought her an iPhone Plus so she could text with ease rather than always calling. So far her mom had refrained.

Until now, apparently.

Mom:
Love you that's it send Siri send it Siri are you on crack send the message to Colbie

Colbie laughed and sent a return *I love you* text just as a certain black cat's face came right up against hers, gold eyes very serious.

"Meow."

"Let me take a wild guess. You're hungry?"

The cat's eyes said *duh.*

Colbie got up and showed the cat her bowls filled with water and the cat food she'd purchased last night at the store when she'd been stocking up for herself. "Do you feel like Cinderella?" she asked the cat. "Because I do."

"Meow."

Colbie smiled. "Maybe I'll call you Cinder for short."

With a low, approving chirp, Cinder dove into her food, apparently feeling as completely at home as Colbie did.

Colbie showered and dressed and took a deep breath before reading the twins' texts.

Kent had locked his car keys in the car. While it was running. In a blizzard.

Shock.

Kurt had been fired from his sandwich

shop job for hitting on the boss's daughter.

"Son of a Cheez-It." Instead of responding, or giving in to the stroke she could feel coming on, Colbie set her phone aside and filled out the rental app Elle had given her. "Should I list you as my roommate?" she asked the cat.

Cinder rolled onto her back on the hardwood floor in the sole sunspot and closed her eyes in bliss.

"I'll take that as a yes. You don't listen to rap at earsplitting levels in the middle of the night or ask for money, right?"

"Meow."

"Good enough."

Five minutes later, Colbie brought the application and her rent money to Elle's office on the second floor. Elle wasn't alone in the office. She had two others with her, and they were all eating muffins from the downstairs coffee shop.

"Willa owns the pet shop," Elle said by way of introduction, pointing to her friend on the right. "And Kylie here works at Reclaimed Woods, the furniture shop."

Kylie offered Colbie a muffin while asking the room a question for the ages. "How am I supposed to stay in shape when the best part about life is food?"

"You could exercise," Elle said.

"I do," Kylie said. "My cardio of choice is online shopping."

"Very mature."

Kylie laughed. "I am mature. But not, like, *mature* mature. I mean, I pay my bills on time but I still have to say stuff like 'righty tighty, lefty loosey' to figure shit out."

"Honey, we all do that," Willa said, finishing up a muffin and licking her fingers. "Ungh. If I were murdered right now, my chalk outline would be a circle. Keane won't be able to get his arms around me."

Muffins weren't on Colbie's diet either but she told herself that her New York diet could be different from her San Francisco diet. Her first bite of a blueberry muffin had her moaning. "Tell me this counts as a serving of fruit."

"Maybe we should go to the gym later and do some crunches or something," Willa said, sounding less than enthused about this prospect.

Kylie shook her head. "My brain just autocorrected the word *crunches* to *cupcakes*. And we all know that once you lick off the frosting, a cupcake is really just a muffin. Which is almost a serving of fruit, as Colbie pointed out."

Contemplating this, they all ate some more muffins.

"Listen," Willa said to Colbie. "I'm really sorry about what Daisy Duke did to you yesterday. She's usually such a good girl but that stray black cat is her nemesis."

"She's not a stray anymore," Colbie said. "She's sleeping on my bed as we speak."

"You were able to catch her?" Willa asked. "I've been trying for weeks. I wanted to find her a home."

"I didn't catch her," Colbie said. "She caught me." She took another muffin. "So who makes these little bites of heaven? I want to bow down before them."

"Tina. And she's currently spoken for," Kylie said. "If she's ever single again, we're all on a waiting list for her."

They all eyeballed the last muffin.

"How about we split it four ways," Kylie suggested.

Elle produced a pocketknife.

"What the hell is that?" Kylie asked.

"I always carry a knife," Elle said. "You know, in case of having to split a muffin into four pieces. And don't look so shocked. You carry dangerous tools yourself. Yesterday I watched you use a huge jigsaw like it was nothing."

"Yes, but that was for work," Kylie said. "Although you've got a point about being able to split a muffin. I bet I could do that with a jigsaw in an emergency."

Elle carefully and surgically split her muffin. "How's the elbow?" she asked Colbie.

"Fine." She'd had far worse injuries breaking up fights between her brothers. "Thanks again for taking such good care of me yesterday."

"That was all Spence."

"He was great too," she said.

"He's always great," Willa said. "He's one of the good ones, smart, super-sexy eye candy, and he doesn't even know it."

Elle shook her head.

"What?" Willa said. "I'm taken, not dead."

"What is it that Spence does for a living?" she asked.

Elle gave a little smile. "A lot."

"Such as?"

"Such as a lot."

Kylie and Willa, watching the exchange like they were at a tennis match, popped their quarters of the last muffin into their mouths in unison.

Colbie turned to them. "Is she being mysterious on purpose?"

Kylie choked on her muffin. Willa patted her on the back before answering. "Spence is our resident genius."

Elle gave her a look.

"Well, he is," Willa said. "He's the smartest person we all know. That's no secret."

"But what he does for a job is?" Colbie asked.

"Let's just say we're a little protective of him," Willa said. "For good reason."

"He seems like a guy who can protect himself," she said slowly.

"Oh hell yeah, he can," Willa said. "Just a few weeks ago, Kylie here was locking up late one night on her own and some guy started hassling her, and Spence —"

"Willa," Elle said in warning.

"What?" Willa asked. "He . . ." She mimed some sort of karate motion and straightened with a smile. "Kicked ass like a glasses-wearing superhero."

Colbie had no problem picturing Spence stepping in to help a friend in trouble. But picturing him using actual physical force gave her a ridiculous feminine flutter.

Kylie was hugging herself now and Willa's smile faded as she seemed to realize that she'd brought the vivid memories back too harshly. "I'm sorry," Willa said, hugging Kylie tight. "I shouldn't have —"

"No, it's okay. Really." Kylie gave a little smile. "He *was* my superhero that night. And he never even lost his glasses." She was wearing a heavy work apron and covered in wood chips. And Colbie realized that in one of her big apron pockets was a stuffed animal. A very small French bulldog.

But then it moved. It was real, and she laughed in delight because the dog was smaller than Cinder.

"His name's Vinnie," Kylie said. "He's a foster fail." She handed him over to Colbie and she and the dog eyed each other.

Vinnie's head was the same size as the rest of his entire body and his huge deep brown soulful eyes melted Colbie. "Oh my God," she said, snuggling the thing close. "How do you get anything done other than loving him up all day long?"

Kylie smiled. "That's why he practically lives in my pocket — well, unless I'm working the big table saw or the planer or anything dangerous like that. He's small because he was malnourished but I think he's still growing."

"I need a cutie like this to keep in my pocket," Colbie said. "No danger in what I do."

"Which is what again?" Elle asked.

Colbie met Elle's gaze. Friendly enough, but sharp as a razor. "I'm a writer."

"Oh, cool," Kylie said. "What do you write?"

"Yes, and how do you make a living while doing it?" Elle asked.

Again, not unfriendly, not at all. But the woman was definitely reserving judgment. "I write young adult," Colbie said to Kylie, still snuggling with the lovebug Vinnie. To Elle, she said, "And I do other stuff as well. Write short stories, waitress, retail, whatever comes my way."

Again, more of an omission than a lie, as she'd done all those things — just not since the royalties had started rolling in.

"You landed in a pretty amazing place to write," Kylie said. "This building's a fun place to be creative."

Exactly what Colbie was banking on.

Chapter 7
#WhatTheFrenchToast

That afternoon Spence was trying to apply himself to his computer. He needed to be working on the software for the security of the cargo on the drones he'd built but he was getting nowhere fast.

When Elle showed up carrying his first choice of poison — coffee, black and strong — he was grateful for the interruption.

He couldn't concentrate or focus to save his own life. Instead he kept picturing Colbie's fathomless green eyes and how they revealed her thoughts more than her words.

"You also got another present in the mail," Elle said. "One of the *Real Housewives* producers is apparently a fan and she sent a box of your favorite candy. Wants to know if you date cougars."

Spence slid her a look.

Elle laughed. "Right. I'll decline politely." She paused. "Your newest tenant's been busy," she said casually.

But here was the thing. Elle was never casual. "Yeah? Doing what?"

"Asking questions about you, trying to figure out what you do for a living."

Spence shrugged that off. "It's just a little game between us — relax. She's not press."

"As long as you know what you're doing. Oh, and check your e-mail. I sent you some things I need you to go over and get back to me on. I'll be in my office."

"Ah, don't go away mad," he said.

A little humor came into her eyes. "Just go away?"

"That'd be great."

She rolled her eyes. "Fine," she said, heading to the door. "Follow your heart, whatever. Just promise me you'll take your brain with you. Oh —" She stopped short and turned back. "I almost forgot the best part." She set her iPad on the desk in front of him, her browser opened to an article.

SAN FRANCISCO'S TOP TEN MOST ELIGIBLE BACHELORS

Jesus. "Tell me I'm not on this list," he said.

Elle didn't speak.

"Shit. Tell me I'm not number one on this list."

Elle let out a breath. "You're not number one."

"Number two?"

She grimaced.

He scrolled through the list and felt insulted. "Number four?"

She laughed at him as he pushed the iPad away. "So let me get this straight. You didn't want to be on the list, but now that you are, you want to be number one?"

"Well, yeah. Anything else just sucks."

"It's not a poker game you lost — you do realize that, right?"

He shrugged.

"Maybe if you went to more of the social events, you'd get bumped to number three," Elle teased because he'd gone to a grand total of zero society events.

"Elle."

"Yeah, yeah, I know, go away."

And thankfully, she did, leaving him alone. Just how he liked it. When he'd sold the start-up, it'd been a life changer. It'd given him the freedom to do what he wanted when he wanted. Buying this building, for instance. Then moving in and then filling it with people he cared about, allowing him to burrow in and create his first real "home," where he knew everyone and felt comfortable. He was grateful for that.

It'd allowed him to keep the real world at bay too. For a while he'd been hounded for interviews, but for the most part it'd been easy enough to dodge them. That is, until a month ago, when an old college roommate had surfaced, begging him for a sit-down.

College hadn't been a great time for Spence. He'd gone at age sixteen, which had put him at a big disadvantage on all levels. One of his roommates, Brandon, hadn't exactly been a friend but at least he'd allowed Spence to tag along to frat parties and drinking nights with him. Then Spence had graduated before Brandon, and Brandon had stopped speaking to him.

All these years later, Spence hadn't wanted to give the interview but . . . hell. Spence had been hired right out of college at age eighteen to a government think tank. He'd gone from there into business with Caleb, a kid he'd met in the think tank. Both adventures had been hugely successful, which meant that Spence had gotten lucky.

Brandon hadn't been nearly so lucky. Nothing had worked out for him after he'd finally graduated. He was a struggling tech writer for a second-rate online magazine. Feeling bad about that, Spence had very reluctantly agreed to an interview — on the stipulation that they talk only about

Spence's work.

But Brandon had used his personal knowledge of Spence from their college days to spice up the final piece. Deeply private stuff, including his screwed-up beginnings, not to mention his spectacular failure with media darling Dr. Clarissa Woodward.

Now the whole world knew things he'd kept private. Such as just how socially inept he was, how out of step with the rest of the world he felt, and how he couldn't seem to manage to sustain any sort of intimate relationship.

Worse, the article had turned his life into a living hell. The press had leapt on it like Christmas had come early. Spence still didn't understand why, but for some reason people were fascinated by him, the poverty-stricken kid turned *Forbes* Top 100.

Who was now one of San Francisco's most eligible bachelors.

Shit.

That was a joke in itself.

There really wasn't much that embarrassed Spence, but this. This did the trick. He was pissed as hell at Brandon and pissed at himself for letting it happen. Some smart guy he was . . .

His phone had been having seizures, which he was ignoring. But the sound was driving him crazy, so he turned it off. "Now maybe you'll shut the hell up . . ."

"Talking to yourself again?" Caleb asked.

His sometime business partner and one of the few people in the world who had access to this apartment strolled in. Spence narrowed his eyes. "Hey. You made millions on our last deal, where we sold the start-up."

"Yep." Caleb headed for Spence's fridge. "What's your point?" Without waiting for the answer, he helped himself to the refrigerator, which was stocked by Trudy, the building's housecleaning supervisor.

Trudy loved Spence. Trudy also knew Spence didn't cook — unless popping a Hot Pocket into the microwave counted — and she knew his tastes. He wasn't fond of vegetables aside from corn on the cob, hated anything green unless it was a gummy bear, and basically had the appetite of a tween.

"My point," Spence said, watching Caleb shopping his fridge shelves, "is that *you're* not being hounded by the press."

Caleb shrugged. "Yeah, well, I wasn't stupid enough to talk to them in the first place. Nor do I have a tragic background or fumble the ball with the ladies."

Spence scowled and slouched further in his chair. "I thought I was doing a friend a favor."

Caleb pulled out some Tupperware, and when he moaned, Spence knew he'd found Trudy's homemade lasagna. "Oh my God," the guy said. "I want to marry Trudy."

"She's twenty years too old for you and she's currently married for the third, or maybe it's the fourth, time — to her ex-husband. Luis would kick your ass."

"I don't even care." Caleb was eating right out of the container. "And we have no friends to do favors for, remember? Not real ones, you know that. Or you should by now."

"I have friends."

"Yeah. Me, and Archer and Finn and Willa." Caleb cocked his head and gave it some thought. "Oh, and possibly Elle, though I'm still not convinced she's human."

"*No one's* convinced Elle's human." Spence shrugged. "But you guys are all I need."

Caleb jabbed his fork in Spence's direction. "If that was true, you wouldn't be moping around like you have since you sold your start-up. Or maybe it's since Clarissa."

Getting up because the lasagna sounded good, Spence snatched the Tupperware from Caleb. "I don't mope."

"Like a baby wanting its mama." Undeterred, Caleb turned back to the fridge to see what else he could mooch. "I take it you're suddenly blocked on your drone project?"

"So."

"So you're blocked. It happens."

"When? When does it happen?" Spence asked. "Because more than anyone else I know, you're a lot like me and *you're* not blocked."

"First of all, we're not that much alike."

Spence just looked at him.

"Okay, so we're both smart and a little bit techy. Whatever. But on me, it's sexier."

Spence rolled his eyes.

"And second of all," Caleb said, "I don't get blocked as much as you because I get sex regularly. Sex is the answer, man."

"To what?"

"Everything," Caleb said. "Sex is always the answer. And I'm pretty sure you haven't had any in way too long."

All true, but he'd never been all that good at emotionless, unattached sex. Unfortunately, he was even worse at emotional sex.

Caleb didn't seem bogged down by the same baggage. Spence was pretty sure the rugged cowboy look didn't hurt much either. The guy was every bit as smart as Spence, but unlike Spence, he didn't struggle in social situations. He could talk to a five-year-old throwing a tantrum in the courtyard, the geriatric blue-hairs who spent their mornings in the coffee shop, or anyone in between and they all unequivocally loved him.

Caleb's phone buzzed. He pulled it out and frowned.

"What?" Spence asked.

"It's Elle. Which isn't fair. She told me to lose her number and yet *she's* allowed to contact me —" He broke off as he read the text.

"What?"

Caleb lifted his head. "There's a woman? Why didn't you say so? Now you can test my theory about the sexy times unblocking you."

"What are you talking about?"

"Elle said there's a new woman in the building and that you're going to be stupid about her and go for it, so I should babysit you so that you can't," Caleb said. "Except I'm all for you going for it." He deleted Elle's text. "Whoops." He looked at Spence. "So. Is she hot?"

Spence shut the fridge and gave Caleb a nudge that might've been more like a shove to the door.

"Let me guess. Visit time's over," Caleb

said dryly.

Spence opened the door.

"Fine." In the hall between the front door and the elevator, Caleb turned back to him. "Do me a favor. Don't give her an interview." Then, cracking his own ass up, Caleb got on the elevator just as Joe came out the stairwell.

Joe looked surprised to see Spence just standing there in the hallway. "Hey. What's up?"

Spence crossed his arms, no longer willing to even pretend to be having a good time. "You first."

As a rule, Joe was unflappable. Impenetrable. A virtual stone when he wanted to be. Always cool under pressure and usually make-a-joke-in-every-situation, and yet he rocked back on his heels, his hands shoved in his front pockets. Uncomfortable.

"Talk," Spence said.

"It's . . . nothing."

"Or . . . ?"

Joe blew out a breath. "She wants me to run the new girl."

No need to ask what "she." Elle, of course, being mama bear. Joe had access to some serious search programs. Once Spence had searched himself on the system and had learned he'd skipped both first and second grades, going straight to third — which he'd actually had no memory of doing. He scrubbed a hand down his face. "Why didn't she ask Archer to do it?"

"Because she knows Archer would've said no. He's not afraid of her like the rest of us are."

"You were Special Ops," Spence said. "You still have all your skills. You could just stand up to her."

"Look, no one says no to Elle, okay?"

"Well start," Spence said.

Joe pulled his not-ringing phone from his pocket and stared at the dark screen like he wished a call would come through and save him from this conversation.

"You're not going to research Colbie," Spence said. "It's no one's business if she's got secrets. And tell Elle that I'll fire her nosy ass if she doesn't chill."

Joe grimaced. "Aw, man, I can't tell her that. Why do you hate me?"

Spence shook his head. If Joe told Elle no, she'd just find another way. "Okay, new plan. Just find a way to put her off before you run her. Blame work, I don't care."

"I'll try," Joe said. "But it's going to cost you too. *Big.*"

"You're not going to fly one of my drones again," Spence said. "We never found the two you lost."

"Hey, those drones were faulty."

Spence rolled his eyes.

"Fine. What I want is an entire tray of Trudy's five-meat and cheese lasagna for myself."

Joe was constantly hungry, and constantly on the hunt for food. The guy was built like an MMA fighter, lean, solid muscle. Spence had no idea where he put all the food. "Seriously, you're a grown-ass man, one who's been trained in a million different ways to kill someone. Why do you let Elle terrify you?"

Joe didn't bite. He just pointed at Spence. "Forget it. Deal's off." And then he pivoted on his heel and headed back to the stairwell.

"Chickenshit," Spence called.

"Sticks and stones, man. You're on your own."

Which meant leaving Elle sniffing around, butting in, because that's what she did. Most of the time, Spence appreciated it. But for whatever reason, he didn't want her snooping around in Colbie's personal life. He wasn't trying to be stupid, but it felt wrong. "I'll pay you a thousand dollars to hold off checking into Colbie's background for at least a week."

Joe turned back, brows raised. "Okay, you

have my full attention."

"Are you serious? You'll get Elle out of my hair for money?"

"Hell yeah." Joe paused. "But when she finds out and kills me, I want an open casket. A week is all you want?"

"I'd ask for three weeks but even I know you can't put Elle off that long."

"True."

Spence shook his head and strode back into his apartment. He stared at the computer screens he was getting nowhere on and left again, hitting the stairwell too, needing to clear his head.

This drone project was really weighing on him. Work always did, since he put it first. But there'd been bonuses to that. He'd been able to take care of his family, for one. His mom had never had a penny to her name, so she hadn't wanted anything from him when he'd sold the start-up, but he'd bought her a house on the coast anyway. It was about an hour south of here, the perfect distance for the both of them, and she felt like she'd won the lottery.

Spence got to the courtyard and turned to look down the alley. The homeless man who lived in it was called Old Man Eddie by all. Too many times to count, Spence had tried to get him a safe, dry, warm place to live, and too many times to count, Eddie had told him where to shove it. The old man liked the alley as much as he liked the special brownies he'd learned to bake way back in the early seventies, and no one could tell him otherwise. He looked like Doc Brown from the *Back to the Future* movies — if Doc Brown had baked his brain at Woodstock — and was currently sitting on an upside-down crate twirling several coins between his fingers like a magician.

Or probably more accurately, like a con artist getting ready to find a new mark. His favorite were ladies of a certain age, several of whom lived in the building, and all of whom had crushes on him.

"I didn't do it," Eddie said at the sight of Spence.

"Do what?"

"Whatever you're going to bitch at me about."

Spence blew out a sigh. Last year Eddie had been caught selling mistletoe that had turned out to be weed. Last week he'd had to warn Eddie it wouldn't be tolerated this year.

It hadn't gone well. "I'm not here to bitch at you," he said.

"Well that's a change. Wanna play a game?"

The last time Spence had played cards with Eddie, he'd actually lost a hundred bucks because Eddie could count cards. "Do I look stupid, Grandpa?"

Eddie's smile widened. He was Spence's only other living relative besides his mom, except his grandpa wasn't nearly as easy to take care of. The man was nontraditional, incorrigible, and mischievous to say the least, and he couldn't be reined in.

Spence did the best he could to always have the old man's back, but Eddie made it more difficult than getting medical care to countries in need via his drones.

"I just wanted to make sure you're warm enough," Spence said. "The nights are getting cold."

"I'm good."

Not really an answer, which didn't make Spence feel any better. Eddie was a good guy, a smart guy, but he was also good at putting distance between himself and any sort of emotional attachment. He'd always said he was meant to be alone for the rest of his life, and Spence knew he believed it.

Spence knew the same thing about himself, which was ironically also his biggest fear — ending up alone. So far he'd made that a self-fulfilling prophecy.

But he knew without a doubt that he

didn't have the ability to love someone and give her everything she needed. He was an all-or-nothing kind of man and work came first because, well, that's who he was. "You know how to get ahold of me if you need anything."

"That I do," Eddie said. "And right back atcha."

Spence let out a low laugh.

Eddie's good-natured expression faded. "What does that mean?"

"Nothing."

"Bullshit," Eddie said. "You're saying this is a one-way street, that you help me but I don't do shit for you."

"I'm not saying anything."

Eddie stared at him and then blew out a breath. "You don't have to," he muttered. "Because it's true."

"Grandpa —"

"Go away, boy." And then instead, Eddie walked out the alley to the street and vanished.

Spence shook his head, went to the coffee shop, bought two cups to go, and two bags of mini muffins. He left one of the coffees and bags on Eddie's crate and took his breakfast back to the stairwell. He went straight up.

To the roof.

There, he strode across the rooftop to the far corner of the building. He hoisted himself up on the ledge and, as he'd been doing since he first bought this building, swung his legs over the side, leaned back, and then did what he had a hard time doing anywhere else.

Relaxed.

He let out a long breath and waited for calm to come over him.

But it didn't. Not this time.

He'd long ago learned how to compartmentalize each section of his life. But at the moment he had so much going on that his brain raced over each problem, touching down and bouncing back up, unable to settle on any one thing. Part of this was his ADD. He had some serious attention deficit problems, always had. He'd gotten pretty good at managing it.

Mostly.

But not today. Today his brain felt like he had a full dozen massive flat-screens on, each set to a different channel, all at full volume. It actually physically hurt and he rubbed his temples.

"Headache?" asked the soft female voice that had seduced him in his dreams last night. A new voice that belonged to the

woman he'd seen wet more times than dry.
  Colbie.

CHAPTER 8
#HolyChickenNuggets

Colbie had spent the day happily wandering the city. She'd written some pages while sitting with her laptop in the Castro District, loving the rainbow sidewalks and relaxed atmosphere. She'd bought a pretty LBD and a pair of killer heels in Pacific Heights and was wearing it all now because she wanted to break in the shoes. And okay, because she felt like she looked amazing for the first time in . . . well, recent memory.

She'd located the roof access to the Pacific Pier Building by accident but got excited at the prospect of watching the city as the sun went down. She could hardly believe her luck when she'd found that the stairwell went all the way to the top.

The sign on the door had given her a second's pause though. No Trespassing. We're tired of hiding the bodies . . .

Not that it'd stopped her. Truth was, not much did. She'd been sitting on the roof in the far corner, staring down at the incredible world she was so happy to be a part of for a little while, when Spence had stormed through the stairwell door.

His long legs had easily eaten up the space as he crossed to the far corner away from her and perched — to her near heart failure — on the ledge, legs over the side as he stared pensively out into the early evening.

She was trying to decide which was better, to remain quiet and give him time to himself, which he clearly seemed to need, or to announce her presence. In the end, her curiosity won. She'd made it to his side and asked him if he had a headache when from inside her purse, her phone went off with a call.

With a sigh, she gave Spence an apologetic smile, turned away, and dug out her phone, answering to one of her brothers.

"What's for dinner?" Kent asked.

She had to laugh. "I texted you. Yesterday. I had Janeen text you as well. And you've texted me. Why in the world don't you read my texts? I'm not home."

Home being the place she'd bought for them all to stay, a place that was meant to be a real home but instead felt like a burden, as she'd become the housekeeper, chef, and prison warden all in one.

There was a silence while Kent clearly, finally, read her texts. "You're on vacay?" he asked, sounding butthurt. "Without us? That sucks."

"Not a vacation . . . exactly. I'm working."

"You said you're on a break."

"Yes," she said. "From New York. From being in charge of you all. I'll be back on Christmas Eve."

"That's like three weeks away. I'll starve to death."

She would've laughed but he wasn't kidding. *Tough love,* she told herself. *You're tough on yourself — it's time to be just as tough on the people in your life.* "You're twenty-three, not five," she said. "You'll figure it out." When she disconnected, Spence was watching her.

He pushed his dark sunglasses to the top of his head. He wore cargo pants and a hoodie sweatshirt that said *I Can Explain It to You but I Can't Understand It for You.* "Husband?" he asked, tilting his head toward her phone. "Boyfriend?"

"Brother. One of two. Twin pains in my ass."

He nodded his understanding with a small smile. "How are you doing? The apartment okay? Your elbow bothering you?"

"Fine, great, and nope."

"You look amazing."

"Thank you." She knew she should be feeling at least a little uneasy over her impulsive decision to rent the apartment instead of going to a hotel. A hotel would have been more anonymous.

And she'd needed anonymity. Badly.

But she didn't feel uneasy at all. The thing was, this building put her right in the thick of things, and she loved it. When she'd left New York, she'd hoped this would do it. A few weeks away would fill up the well, unleash her creativity, and unblock her.

One day in and she was already well on her way. She'd actually written last night as well as today, late into the night, in fact, and it'd all felt great. The truth was, she really loved this building, the views, the people. She was having a blast, feeling like a kid on summer break. Not that she really knew what that was like. Her own childhood had been cut way too short.

The only thing she regretted with this trip was the little layer of guilt beneath it all. Apparently that old habit of feeling responsible for her entire world and everyone in it was harder to shake than her writer's block.

She looked at Spence, noticing a tenseness to his shoulders. "And how about you?" she asked. "Are you okay?"

His mouth curved in a small smile. "Almost always."

"Almost always, huh?" She cocked her head and smiled back. "That's quite the trick. Maybe you could teach it to me sometime."

He snorted. "You think it's a trick?"

"Yes, because you don't really seem all that okay."

"How would you know?" he asked. "We're strangers, remember?"

"Ha," she said at him using her own words against her. "Maybe I don't *know you* know you, but I consider myself a good read of character." She lifted a shoulder. "It's a hobby."

"Because you're a writer."

"Yes," she said, glowing with pleasure that he'd remembered that about her but also feeling the tiniest bit of dread. She didn't want to taint this — whatever *this* was — by getting into who she really was. It changed everything, every single time. And she loved being here as herself, Colbie Albright, and not CE Crown, number one *New York Times* bestselling author of the Storm Fever series. "Why are you on the edge?" she asked.

"I guess it's been a long few days." He paused. "But on a positive note, I haven't needed any bail money and haven't had to hide any bodies yet, so . . ."

"Actually," she said on a laugh, "I meant why are you on the edge, literally. Your feet are hanging over, Spence, which, I've gotta tell you, is making me incredibly nervous."

He let out a quiet laugh and shook his head. "I like this spot. It's where I come to think."

"Think about . . . your deep, dark secret of a job?" she asked hopefully. "Or maybe . . . the woman who so damaged your heart you'll never love again? Or just about what you're having for dinner?"

That won her a grin. "You think I'm damaged?"

She tossed up her hands. "Aren't we all?"

He shrugged. "And the 'never love again' part?" he asked.

"I thought if I threw that in there, you'd decide telling me what you do for a living would be the easiest response," she admitted.

"Blatant manipulation." He nodded approvingly. "Good strategy. Except for one thing."

"What's that?" she asked.

"I really am much more interested in talking about what might be for dinner."

She had to laugh. "I wouldn't mind cooking something. Cooking is relaxing."

"I accept," he said quickly and smoothly, his stomach growling its own acceptance. Not that this seemed to embarrass him.

She smiled. "You don't want to first ask me if I can cook?"

He got off the ledge and straightened with an ease of motion that said he was in even better shape than he looked. And he looked pretty damn fine . . .

"If you even *think* you can cook," he said, "you can cook better than me." He took her hand in his and, with yet another heart-stopping smile, led her off the roof.

He took her down one flight of stairs to the fifth floor using his special keycard.

"I thought this floor was just gym and storage," she said, confused.

"No, although most people think that." He studied her for a few long seconds. "I live here."

"In the gym?" she asked.

"Not exactly." He opened another door and she barely contained a small gasp. "Holy chicken nuggets." This was an apartment, and it was *huge,* with floor-to-ceiling windows. The furnishings were simple, almost spartan, but masculine and utilitarian. Huge L-shaped couch, massive TV, and a glass coffee table that was completely strewn with . . . well, a wide assortment of electronic parts, tools, and multiple sets of plans.

There was nothing else in the vast room. What seemed like a football field away was the kitchen, and beyond that another room she couldn't see. "This is your place?"

"Yes."

"Are you ruler of the universe? Is that your job?"

He made the sound of a game-show-loser buzzer. Still holding her hand, he led her past the coffee table, where she caught sight of what she thought might be a trio of . . . drones? "Is that —"

"I'm *starving,*" he said, his broad shoulders blocking her view as he pulled her into the kitchen.

Okay. So the man was starving. After years of feeding her brothers, she could fix that in her sleep. Looking around, she found herself completely smitten with his beautiful chef's kitchen, almost forgetting she was there to find something for dinner. When she turned to Spence, he gestured for her to help herself. So she opened the fridge. Pretty much empty.

"Damn Caleb and Joe," he muttered. "Try the cabinets."

She peered in one.

It was completely bare.

So was the next one.

The third contained two glasses and a pair of mugs, a salt and a pepper shaker, and a stack of takeout menus.

Huh. She looked at him. He was staring at the empty shelves, seeming just as surprised as Colbie, and she burst out laughing. "Are you sure you live here?" she asked.

"Pretty sure." He shook his head. "But with me, you never know." He paused. "I get immersed in a project and I forget to come up for air."

He said this like it was an admission that she wouldn't want to hear. But for her, it meant they were kindred souls and she saw him in a new light. "I get that," she told him, and when he looked at her doubtfully, she smiled. "No, really, I do. I write for hours and hours at a time and shut out everything else."

"Like what?"

"Like . . . my family and friends," she admitted. "Everything. I'm not easy to be with."

"Maybe it's that other people don't get it."

She looked at him. "You think so?"

Something interesting happened then. His eyes changed. Softened somehow. "I know so," he said. "You're just focused, that's all. There's nothing wrong with that, Colbie." And this time when he smiled, it went all the way to his eyes and practically changed the temperature in the room. It certainly changed *her* temperature.

Half an hour later, Colbie was sitting at Spence's kitchen island, eating a feast that she'd put together for them with the things she'd run downstairs to her own apartment for.

It hadn't been all that difficult, at least not for her, as she'd long ago learned to make do with what she had. She'd made turkey burgers and salad, and Spence shook his head in marvel as he finished up.

"I don't know what's more impressive," he said. "The fact that you conjured all of this out of almost nothing, or that you've got me eating a salad with beets and blueberries and . . ." He lifted his fork and stared at the glistening leaf. "I've got nothing."

"It's kale."

"Kale," he said with a shudder.

"You don't like beets, blueberries, or kale?"

"I'm not a fan of green stuff but . . ." He showed her his empty bowl. "Either you

119

have great skills or your distraction skills are amazing."

"I think it was probably the salad itself," she said.

"I think it was you. That husky laugh of yours," he said. "Or maybe it's your amazing eyes. They're beautiful." He waited until she met his gaze in surprise. "You're really good in the kitchen, Colbie."

Unused to compliments, she looked away and shrugged. "Survivor skills."

"On your own young?" he asked.

She bought herself a minute by carrying their dishes to the sink, but he grabbed their glasses and came to the sink as well, meeting her gaze.

"My mom was pregnant with twins when my dad walked off his job because his boss was a hard-ass," she said. "He spent a year on the couch with his booze feeling sorry for himself before he went out for a six-pack and never came back."

"Sounds rough."

"Sounds like a country song," she corrected.

He gave a low laugh. "Or that."

Her mom had rallied a few times, eternally in love with love, but she'd still managed to self-destruct every single relationship she'd had since.

A tendency Colbie had tried really hard not to inherit. Wanting to make a very long, boring story as short as she possibly could, she said, "My mom worked all the time. She had to. So as the oldest kid, I took care of everything else."

"Including the cooking."

"Yes." That'd been the easy part — when they'd had money for groceries, that is. Raising hell-bent-on-trouble twin boys had been the hard part.

"How old were you when your dad left?" Spence asked.

"Six," she said and turned on the water to rinse their dishes. "The twins had just turned one."

"Jesus, Colbie." Reaching past her, he turned off the water. "I don't know how it works at home, but here the cook never does the dishes. Especially since I imagine you've done more than your fair share over the years."

"Hey, without those years I'd not have been able to make you this amazing five-course first-class meal."

He smiled, as she'd intended for him to, and if he felt sorry for her, he was smart enough to hide it.

"You still close to your mom and brothers?" he asked.

121

She felt her own smile slip a little. "Sure." She turned the water on again.

And he turned it off. Again. "It's funny," he said, "how sometimes when you talk, your mouth says one thing but your eyes tell me another story entirely."

"Such as?" she asked, not liking where this conversation was going.

"Such as . . ." Not even a little scared off by her "back off" voice, Spence stepped in closer and cupped her jaw, holding her face up to his as he searched her gaze. "You like to put a good spin on everything."

"Well, I am a pretty good spinner."

"I bet." His mouth quirked on one side and it was disarmingly sexy. "I'm not. But I'm actually a pretty good listener when I'm focused."

Her breath caught a little bit. Or a lot. "And you're . . . focused now?"

"Very."

His stare rooted her to the spot as she tried to read the level of his seriousness, while something warm and dangerous slid into her belly and headed south.

"You joked about running away from home," he said. "But it doesn't feel funny."

She gave a slow head shake. "That's because it isn't."

They were standing very close in front of

the sink. She had one hand gripping the counter because she needed the balance, needed an anchor in a suddenly spinning world.

"Talk to me," Spence said and put his hand over hers.

She let go of her grip on the granite, turning her hand over so their fingers could entwine. Talk to him? She didn't know where to start. Or if she even wanted to. "There's a lot going on back home," she said quietly, meeting his gaze. A mistake, as one look into those curious light brown eyes and it all just came tumbling out of her mouth. "So many pieces to the whole puzzle," she said, "and they all depend on me keeping them in place. Personal *and* work." She closed her eyes. "It's always all on me, you know? *Always.* And I just felt overwhelmed and . . . tired. And that killed my muse." She opened her eyes again, knowing he'd be able to see the pain swimming in them but unable to hide it. "I need to find my muse, and to do that, I needed a change of scenery. A break. Even just for a little while. So I got on a plane. I wanted to go to a deserted Caribbean island beach but there was a big hurricane . . ."

"Never thought I'd find a reason to thank a hurricane," he said, making her smile.

123

"Your mom and brothers depend on you financially?"

And emotionally . . . "Yes. Kurt and Kent are twenty-three. The Peter Pan years, as it turns out. They don't want to grow up, a syndrome that's been ramped up since their twenty-first birthday."

"I remember being twenty-one," he said. "I'd just graduated Caltech with my master's degree in mechanical engineering. I had enough debt to sink an entire country and about twenty bucks to my name."

A mechanical engineer. That . . . fit him. Perfectly. "But you made something of yourself," she said, gesturing around her. "Kent always says he'd be more inclined to grow up if he saw that it actually worked out for anyone."

Spence smiled. "I just got lucky."

"I think I call BS on that. You worked your ass off doing . . ." she raised a brow ". . . mechanical engineering? Whatever that is?"

He smiled. "Still curious, huh?"

"Yes! Of course I am!"

He tugged a loose strand of her hair. "I ran a start-up with Caleb, my business partner. We created some technical back-end apps that Google found useful and when it suited us, we sold to them. That's when I bought this building."

She sucked in a breath. "Did you just kind of tell me what you do for a living?"

"It was never really a secret. I just liked hearing your guesses."

She laughed. "It's actually a relief to know. My next guess was going to be either a spy or a supervillain." Then his words sank in and she felt her eyes bug out of her head. "You own this *whole* building?"

Something shifted in his eyes. He wasn't comfortable telling her all this, but he nodded and she felt something shift inside her too, but in a good way. Because she realized that he too knew exactly what it was like to go from having nothing to extreme success.

She'd felt alone in this for so long she almost didn't recognize the emotion tumbling through her.

Relief.

CHAPTER 9
#SonOfABeach

"So other than being a real estate mogul," Colbie teased Spence, giving him a little hip bump at his sink, wanting to lighten the mood, "what else do you do these days?"

"I still do the app's updates as needed, but I'm also working on something new."

"The drones on your coffee table?" she asked.

"They're part of a big project that's due in January."

"How's it going?"

His gaze met hers. "I don't know. There's been a beautiful stranger tossed into the mix and I'm having trouble focusing."

The air between them seemed to crackle and she got the tummy flutter again. "You . . . think I'm beautiful?"

"I do."

The air crackled some more and then he stepped into her and then there seemed to be no air at all. He reached for her and . . .

from deep in her pocket, her phone vibrated twice in quick succession.

"Son of a beach," she muttered.

He laughed. "You ever going to answer any of those texts or calls you've been getting all night?"

"No." She hesitated, conflicted, worried. Everyone knew she was on a break, even her brothers. She'd checked in with Janeen and Tracy. She'd spoken briefly to her mom and Jackson when she'd been out in the city earlier, both of whom had wanted the usual. Her mom to complain about her life, and Jackson to get her to agree to some public appearances — an ongoing bone of contention between them because she tried to do the bare minimum when it came to those things.

Part of what had drawn her to writing — besides the fact that she absolutely loved the actual writing — was the simplicity of the life. She didn't want to be a public figure. She wasn't good at it, as proven by what had happened the last time she'd reluctantly agreed. She'd been sent to do the *Late Night* show and had tripped coming out onstage. On camera.

The YouTube video of her revealing her black lace thong had seven million views.

But that her phone kept going off made

127

her worry that maybe there'd been some kind of emergency.

"There's this little thing called the power-off button," Spence said. "Works like a charm."

"I thought about turning it off," she admitted. "But I'd know the messages were still there and worry about missing an emergency."

"Feel free to check in," he said easily.

"I know I shouldn't keep it on me like this, but I'm a hopeless control freak, apparently. Old habit from when the twins were minors and capable of unbelievable stupidity."

"It's okay, Colbie."

Reluctantly, she pulled the phone from her pocket. One look at the screen had her taking a deep breath. Kurt. No surprise there. And . . . Jackson. There'd been a time when just seeing his name would've made her heart leap like she was a teenager with a silly crush.

But he'd fixed that for her with one shockingly hurtful event, eradicating any romantic feelings she'd had in a blink, which didn't mean that she was ready to face him.

She pushed the thoughts aside and called Kurt back first. He was always the easiest to get things out of. "Hey," she said when he picked up. "What's wrong?"

Except she could hear what was wrong. "Why is the smoke detector going off?"

"Because I was making a cheeseburger and set off the alarm," he yelled.

"Again?" she asked, putting her finger in her other ear, as if that could help her hear past the wailing alarm. "Seriously? How hard is it to turn the vent to high when you're cooking burgers on the range?"

"What?"

"Turn on the vent!" she yelled.

"I can't hear you!"

She closed her eyes and shook her head.

"I can't remember how to get it to turn off!" her brother yelled.

"The broom! It's in the corner by the trash. Wave it at the smoke detector and then call the security company to let them know it's a false alarm —" She broke off. "Are you eating in my ear?"

"Hey, gotta eat the burgers while they're hot."

She pulled the phone from her ear and stared at it before punching disconnect and shaking her head. "I'm sorry."

"How old is he again?" Spence asked.

"Twenty-three going on twelve." Since she had the phone out, she went ahead and flipped through the unread texts. Kurt from earlier, wanting to know where her car keys were. Jackson wanting to know when she was sending a chunk of her manuscript. Kent wanting to know if she'd send him some money because he forgot to pay the electric like she'd asked and now there were extra fees to turn it back on.

She stopped and transferred some money but by then Kurt was contacting her again, wanting to know if she could get him tickets to *Hamilton* to impress a date. And last but not least, her mom wanting her to bring her some soup from her favorite deli, even though the deli was literally half a block from her mom and three thousand miles from Colbie.

Did no one read her texts? "I know you said the chef doesn't do dishes but I'd really like to," she said. "It calms my brain."

"How is that even possible?"

"I'll show you." She turned to the sink.

"Uh . . ."

She paused and he grimaced. "You should know something," he said.

"Okay. What?"

He grimaced again. "I've never done dishes in this place."

"Never?"

"I'm not even sure I have dish soap."

She stared at him and then laughed.

"But I swear I'm not like your brothers," he said. "I don't have a sister but if I did, I wouldn't call her for money or help. I'd take care of her."

Wishing that those words hadn't moved her, she found some dish soap beneath the sink.

"Not my doing," he said, lifting his hands. "Trudy. She takes care of this building and also me. I'll have to give her a raise."

Colbie made the water hot and squirted soap into the sink. "Put your hands in here and scrub a dish."

He did and then slid her a look.

"Is your brain calm yet?" she asked. "And empty of thoughts?"

"Does imagining you doing these dishes in those heels you're wearing and nothing else count as calm and empty of thoughts?"

Amusement and arousal vied for her current top emotion, which had never happened before. Having both those things barrel through her with equal fervor left her momentarily unable to decide what to do.

So her inner child came out and she splashed him.

Water dripping from his nose, hair, and glasses, he grinned — the kind of grin that felt like 100 percent trouble of the naughty variety.

Which, clearly, she was imagining.

"Now I'm imagining you *wet* and doing dishes in nothing but those heels," he said.

Okay, so she hadn't imagined anything and at the knowledge, her knees wobbled. "You're . . . flirting with me."

"I am. You okay with that?"

Oh boy. Her gaze dropped to his mouth. "I'm just not used to the feeling," she admitted. "I'm not sure what to do with it."

"Let me help you with that," he said and splashed her back.

This started a water fight that invoked squeaking — on her part — and swearing — on his part — and the most fun she'd ever had doing dishes *ever.*

After, he got them each a towel. "Are you cold?" he asked. "I've got some hot chocolate mix. I make a mean hot chocolate."

She met his gaze. He'd had to remove his wet shirt, and somewhere along the way, he'd also lost his shoes. His feet were bare and for some reason, she found this combination incredibly sexy. Maybe she just found *him* sexy . . . "I do love hot chocolate but it's getting late . . ."

"The hot chocolate comes with marshmallows," he said. "If that interests you."

"The freeze-dried marshmallows or real marshmallows?"

"Are you kidding me? Real, of course."

She smiled. "So you've got your priorities."

"Damn A straight."

Gah. That smile. But she needed to think and she needed to do so without him looking at her, because when he looked at her like he was right now, like to him she was pretty and sexy and interesting, *her,* Colbie, not CE Crown, she couldn't think at all. "Thanks for letting me in your space tonight." She got the feeling it was special that he'd done so, and rare.

"Uh-oh." His eyes locked on hers. "I sense both a 'but' *and* a blow-off coming."

She shook her head. "Just a 'but.' " She paused. "But . . . I really should go."

"Before dessert."

She bit her lower lip in indecision. "What?"

"I've never successfully resisted dessert."

He smiled. "A woman after my own heart. Sure, dessert is the base of my food pyramid." He opened one of the pantry drawers. It was filled with cookies, candy bars, and more.

"Holy cheese toast," she murmured. "It's the mother lode."

"Help yourself."

Said the spider to the fly . . .

133

He began plying her with an armful of cookies and the like. He added on one too many packages of cookies and it all fell out of her arms to the floor.

Laughing, she bent low to scoop them up, just as he did the same. They bumped heads, and not nearly as graceful as he, Colbie fell backward to her ass.

"Sorry!" they both gasped at the same time, and then their gazes locked and there was that crazy spark again, bouncing through Colbie's insides, touching down at all her good spots — of which she seemed to have far more than she remembered having.

Spence, still crouched low and easily balanced on the balls of his feet, dropped to his knees and pulled her up to hers. Brushing the hair from her forehead, he eyed the spot where they'd connected. "You okay?"

She started to say yes but his gaze slid to her mouth and she lost her train of thought, instead licking her suddenly dry lips.

Spence, watching the movement avidly, let out a rough breath. "Colbie," he said quietly, in a very serious, very low octave that sounded like pure sex.

She stood up. "Y-yes?"

Also standing, he slid his hands up her arms, giving her a very slow tug, almost as if expecting resistance.

There was no resistance. Hell, she nearly took a flying leap at him.

He laughed softly, sending a bolt of heat through her. Her knees wobbled and his arm wrapped around her waist, steadying her. Their gazes locked and they both froze in place, she from a sudden rush of emotions, Spence probably from watching them play out across her face. She once again started to say something — still had no idea what — but was silenced by his hot mouth covering hers.

Yes was her only coherent thought and she pressed up against him as he angled his head, taking the kiss even deeper. His arms tightened on her, pulling her in hard, and she squirmed to get closer still, suddenly desperate to feel as much of him as she could.

He kissed her long and deep, and she heard a moan. *Hers,* she realized, shocked at the neediness of the sound as well as the hunger and desire that flooded her at the same time. It'd have humiliated her to the core if she'd been alone in this but with Spence's arms closed around her, along with his rough groan, she knew he was right there with her.

When she was breathless — which took

135

shockingly little time — and on the verge of ripping off his clothes, she forced herself to pull back. Out of her comfort zone, with her heart threatening to secede from her chest, she stared at him as the battle raged inside her. Fear and lust were in mortal combat, the outcome uncertain. "Okay," she said breathlessly. "So now I've *really* gotta go."

Spence drew in a deep, shuddering breath that wasn't much steadier than hers and pulled off his now crooked glasses. "Hang on a second." He tossed them aside. "I need to check on something."

"What?" she asked warily.

Once again he slowly drew her in, his eyes heated and focused on hers, infusing her with some of his calm. "I want to see if this is how it's going to be."

"How what's going to be?" she whispered.

"This." His kiss started out just as slow and thoughtful as the first, all careful control. But when his tongue touched hers, control flew straight out the window. So did all good sense as they went at each other, desperate and hot. Suddenly, her back was to the wall and Spence was plastered against her front and she was trying to get even closer.

Good God.

When they broke apart rather than suffocate, they stared at each other, breathing unevenly.

"Okay," he said, stroking the pad of his thumb over her lower lip. "So that's definitely how it's going to be."

She didn't have words. Neither did he, it seemed, because he used his actions instead, lowering his mouth to her neck, nuzzling in.

"You smell so good," he murmured against her skin. "I want to eat you up."

She was all for that, she really was. But there were extenuating circumstances. Weren't there? Before she could do something stupid — like take off her clothes — she backed away. "Gotta go," she whispered and headed to the door fast as her feet would take her, which wasn't that fast, because her feet didn't seem to remember they belonged to the rest of her body. She took the stairs to the third floor and got to her door before she remembered.

She'd left her purse — with her keys — inside Spence's apartment. "Monkey balls," she said and thunked her head against her door a few times.

"Careful — you'll knock something loose."

Forehead still pressed to the door, she opened her eyes and found her purse dangling in front of her.

From Spence's fingers.

Spence watched — through blurry eyes because he'd left his glasses upstairs — as Colbie pressed her forehead to her door before slowly turning to face him with a wry smile.

"Guess that's what I get for running off like that, huh?" she asked and took her purse. "Thanks." She sorted through a mountain of what appeared to be notes to locate her keys.

Spence gently took them from her and unlocked the door.

The black cat came running with a chirpy greeting and wound herself around Colbie's ankles until she scooped her up and nuzzled her.

"Colbie," Spence said.

She looked up at him, her gaze guarded. "You're not wearing your glasses."

"I know. And I can't see shit."

She smiled a little. But only a little, because for whatever reason, he'd spooked her and she clearly didn't want to discuss it. "Rain check on dessert?" he asked.

She hesitated and then nodded.

" 'Night," he said.

" 'Night." But she didn't move. She nibbled on her lips and stared at his mouth, and under different circumstances he'd have nudged her inside for a repeat of that brain-melting, heart-stopping kiss they'd just shared upstairs.

It'd be fun. Hell, he had a feeling it would be explosive . . . But it wasn't going to happen.

Shouldn't happen.

It wouldn't be good, for either of them, and she'd just realized it before he had, that's all.

And yet she was still looking at his mouth like she wanted another taste of him. He let out a low groan and a rough laugh and then gently pushed her inside. "I'm going to shut your door behind me, Colbie," he said. "And then you're going to lock me out."

"Probably a smart idea." She met his gaze. "Thanks for tonight. It was . . . perfect. Everything felt perfect. Even you. I guess that's why I had that little momentary freak-out back there. I'm sorry about that."

He shook his head, waving off the apology. "Trust me, I'm not even close to perfect. If you were staying in San Francisco for any length of time, I'd prove that to you." He believed that, 100 percent. He would focus on work, prioritizing it over her without even realizing it.

"So you're saying . . . you're going to

disappoint me?"

He felt his smile fade. "I have no doubt."

She stared at him for another beat and then nodded. "Good to know."

Several days later, Spence had pulled his second all-nighter in a row in front of his computer and needed caffeine more than he needed his next breath of air. He left his office and blinked at the morning sun, feeling like a vampire. He'd spent months being frustrated at the press and at being followed around thanks to Brandon, at having everyone and their mother want him to invest in their crazy schemes. It'd fueled him to bury himself in creating the security program for the medicine delivery drones. And he'd been really getting somewhere too, on the verge of completing it . . .

And now nothing. The thermal imaging cameras he was using were necessary for medical care but they were heavy and wore on the batteries. Balancing those two things was taking more than physics.

There was a solution, he knew it. He just needed to concentrate but all his brain cells had been dedicated to bugging him to go find Colbie and finish what they'd started.

Which meant Caleb was wrong. Sex — or almost sex — had the opposite effect of helping him.

He crossed the courtyard and headed straight for the coffee shop. Tina owned and ran the place, and the dark-skinned six-foot woman in towering platforms flashed him a warm, welcoming smile. "Looking a little crazy there today, sugar."

"Feeling it too," he said as she made his usual without asking. Back when Tina had been Tim, there'd been only coffee here. Now Tina made muffins, croissants, and when she was in a really good mood, pie as well. Amazing pie.

Spence eyeballed the display hungrily.

"Haven't gotten to the pies yet today." Tina bent to a low shelf and came up with a to-go box. "But I saved you a slice of yesterday's key lime." She smiled. "To miss my key lime is a crime."

"Hey," a guy standing in the pickup line said. "You told me you didn't have any key lime."

"I don't," Tina said and winked at Spence. "Your girl was here earlier, working her very cute ass off at one of my tables."

His girl . . . It wasn't true but damn if he didn't feel a little bit like a happy caveman at the thought.

"She pounded away on her laptop like she was possessed," Tina said. "It was cute. And

141

inspiring. I have no idea what she was doing or working on, but she was happy doing
it."

Okay, so Spence wasn't the only one
working his ass off. And at that thought, he
realized something else.

Colbie wasn't like him. She *could* balance
a full life and work, and even, it seemed, be
inspired by it.

The knowledge did something to him,
deep in his gut.

It tapped into some deep-seated belief that
maybe he could do the same.

At least with her . . .

Out in the courtyard, he opened the box.
Two pieces. Two forks.

Tina knew him all too well, knew that Old
Man Eddie had the same food tastes — and
distastes — as Spence and that Spence
would share. With a sigh, he strode past the
fountain and peered into the alley.

And yep, there was Old Man Eddie, leaning against a Dumpster talking to someone.

The same petite, curvy someone he
couldn't stop thinking about.

CHAPTER 10
#MonkeyBalls

Colbie had come downstairs, seeking coffee after staying up late several nights running to write. She was getting into it too. It was wonderful. Amazing, even.

But she needed the company of some living and breathing humans instead of just Cinder and her own made-up fictional characters. She'd been hoping to find Kylie or Willa. Or even Elle.

Which meant she must be desperate indeed.

Actually, she secretly wanted to run into Spence.

It was odd to her how connected she felt to him. Odd and . . . amazing. He was so different from anyone she'd ever known. Quiet but not even remotely shy, incredibly smart, and shockingly intuitive . . . he was an enigma to her.

And she'd dreamed about his mouth on hers every night.

But she knew she needed to stay smart and cautious. She wasn't here for more of those amazing kisses, or even to let a man into her world at all. She was here to right her world.

And then move on.

She'd met Eddie a few days earlier on a walk through the courtyard, and she'd found him funny and charming — enough to finagle her cup of coffee and muffin from her within two minutes. He seemed to know everyone in the building, but when she mentioned Spence, he'd suddenly gotten very busy brushing crumbs off his chest.

Then Spence appeared, wearing another pair of wrinkled cargo pants and a button-down over another T-shirt that read *Trust Me, I'm An Engineer.* Most of his pants pockets were bulging with various goodies, although it was easy enough to see that not all his goodies were relegated to his pockets.

He gave Old Man Eddie a long, indecipherable look before turning his sharp gaze on her. "Hey."

She smiled. "Hey back."

They stared at each other until she forced herself to move. "Okay, well, have a good day," she said to Eddie and went to walk past Spence. "And you too," she said. "Happy working, yeah?"

Spence's mouth quirked a little as he stared down into her face. "Yeah."

Colbie flashed him one last smile and shifted clear but Spence caught her hand in his.

"You cooked last time," he said. "How about it's my turn tonight?"

She raised a brow. "You're going to cook?"

"Hell no. I'm going to buy. But I'll make sure there's something green and disgustingly healthy to eat, how's that?"

Eddie shook his head. "You're going about this all wrong."

"Am I?" Spence asked mildly.

"Yeah. You're supposed to wait a full week before you contact her after a date, and then you text. No one asks anyone out in person anymore. It's just not done."

"How would you know?" Spence asked. "You haven't dated since the seventies."

"Hey, I get around plenty. And the rules on dating are everywhere. Don't you Snapchat? Or Instagram?"

Spence looked pained and Colbie laughed, amused by their interaction, which on the surface was all sarcasm and cynicism, but she could feel a deep affection between them. They'd obviously known each other a long time. And there was something else. She could see a blanket of Eddie's peeking out from his crate and it was the exact same blanket that Spence had on the back of his couch.

Spence took care of Eddie, and that made her a sucker for him.

"You're playing it too easy," Eddie told Spence. "Women need to feel chased but not smothered, or it's over. And this one . . ." He smiled at Colbie, his whole demeanor softening. "She's a keeper. She deserves the best." He shook his head at Spence. "You millennials think you have it all figured out, but you don't."

Spence didn't take his eyes off Colbie, so she saw them flicker with good humor. "Should I wait a few more days, Colbie?" he asked.

"Well . . ." Far be it from her to settle this disagreement, but . . . "I'm only here until Christmas Eve. I don't think we've got time for games, or to be coy."

The smile in Spence's eyes spread to his really great mouth, and she was reminded of how that really great mouth had felt on hers.

"Is that a yes?" he asked.

"Make him wait, cutie," Eddie said.

Colbie smiled up at Spence when he sighed at Eddie's interference. "I just think it'd be more interesting if you *cooked,*" she said playfully.

Eddie barked out a laugh. "Darlin', you want him to burn down the building? The boy's a genius, but trust me, it's book smarts only." He pointed to his own brain. "It's all up here, see? Not in his hands, if you know what I mean."

Spence cut the old man a look.

Eddie cleared his throat. "Right." He lifted his hands in surrender. "Just trying to help."

"Maybe just run me over next time." Spence looked at Colbie. "I'll make you a deal. Have you started on your list yet? The one you made on the plane?"

Thinking of her list, specifically number ten, she blushed. She'd been out and about in the city, but only for short stretches at a time. She was looking forward to exploring. "Not yet."

"How about we knock something off your list and then eat?"

Her heart started to pound. By knocking something off the list, surely he didn't mean number ten . . . Somehow she managed to meet his gaze and found affectionate amusement all over his face.

He was teasing her.

Two could play at that game. "Sure," she said. "We'll play tourist and then eat something that you cook."

Spence laughed. "You're a stubborn one."

"Takes one to know one," Eddie said and lifted his hands when Spence sent him another long look.

"You gotta stretch yourself," Colbie said to Spence, mimicking his own words back at him.

Spence let out a rueful laugh. "Wow, I'm really an asshole."

"So is that a yes you'll cook me dinner?" she asked.

"Sure. What the hell."

"Oh Christ," Eddie muttered. "I better put the fire department on notice."

A little dazed, a lot excited, Colbie nodded and walked away, hearing Eddie say to Spence, "You told her stuff about you. Like you live here."

"Yeah."

"Huh," Eddie said. "That's new."

"Don't go reading anything into it," Spence said.

And then she couldn't hear anything after that, as she was beyond hearing range. Just as well, since no one ever overheard something they actually wanted to overhear.

"Don't go reading anything into it . . ."

She needed to remember that.

Spence hit the pub for lunch. As usual, Finn

had the far right side of the bar open for the gang. They were a close-knit bunch, forever sticking their noses into each other's business, fighting like cats and dogs, and yet always, without fail, having each other's back.

Archer and Elle were there. Archer was inhaling a huge plate of nachos while Elle talked. Which was a perfect picture of how their relationship went in general.

"She's cute, I'll give him that," Elle was saying. "But he's not ready for this, and besides, she's got an expiration date. And hello, she's not who she seems. She can't be."

"Babe, he's a big boy," Archer said. "And he's right behind us."

Spence rolled his eyes and leaned in to steal a nacho. "Your reflexes are creepy," he said to Archer before looking at Elle. "If you want to tell me I'm an idiot, do it to my face."

"You're an idiot."

Archer grinned at her. "I love it when you're mad at someone other than me."

"I can multitask," Elle warned.

"Don't I know it."

Elle stared at him and then let out a dopey smile that she never gave to anyone other than Archer. "I'm about to give the inquisition to one of your BFFs. How much do you love me on a scale from zero to burgers?"

"Burgers," Archer said without hesitation. "With bacon and cheese."

"I knew you were the one." She turned on Spence. "How are you doing? You've been working around the clock. You okay?"

He shrugged.

"You were doing really great until a few days ago," she said. "What happened?"

He shrugged.

She gave him a look that said they both knew exactly what had happened. And her name was Colbie.

"What can I do to help?" she asked.

The question was proof that no matter how much she drove him crazy, she was like family.

"Nothing," he said. "I'm working on it. Three nights ago, Colbie cooked me dinner and I'm going to return the favor tonight."

Archer high-fived him.

Elle blinked. "That's 'working on it'? And Colbie cooked you dinner?"

"Burgers and salad. It was great, even if it was turkey burgers and *salad*."

Elle wasn't amused. "You don't cook. In fact, you burn water."

"Hello, Pot," he said. "I'm Kettle."

Archer laughed.

Elle went brows up at him and Archer quickly returned to his food.

"I don't burn water," she told Spence.

"Okay. So I suppose that time you pretended to make Archer dinner but really you ordered out because you'd already burned your first efforts didn't really happen. Even though it totally did."

Archer snorted but then turned it into a cough as he caught Elle's eye again. "No worries, babe," he said. "You give *great* takeout."

Elle had the good grace to roll her eyes. "Fine, I'm being ridiculous, whatever. But you." She pointed at Spence. "You're the most private person I know, and you rented a place to a woman on first sight — without even knowing her last name, I might add. So you can see why I'm worried. If I did that, you'd kick my ass."

"Yes," Spence said. "But I got her knocked into that damn fountain," he said. "I feel responsible for that. I just did what anyone else would've done."

"No," Elle said. "Anyone else would've paid her dry cleaning and sent her on her way. Period. Look, you're not acting like yourself. I'm just worried about you."

"Well, don't be." Spence nodded at Finn

as he came over from the other side of the bar to steal a nacho. "Hey, I need a bottle of wine for tonight."

"For?" Finn asked.

"Dinner."

"I mean for what kind of food," Finn clarified.

"Whatever goes with Cheetos," Archer said, making everyone laugh because they too all knew Spence had the appetite of a twelve-year-old boy.

Spence's phone went off with an unfamiliar number and he hit ignore, knowing it was either a reporter or someone who'd hunted down his number wanting him to invest in some crazy idea.

"You're still being hounded?" Sean asked, refilling their waters.

Sean was Finn's younger brother and co-owner of O'Riley's. And an all-around troublemaker and chick magnet.

Spence shrugged. "I should probably reconsider changing my number."

"No!" Archer, Finn, and Sean all said at the same time.

Elle rolled her eyes. "Pigs. All of you," she said just as a text came through from that same unknown number.

Sure enough, when Spence opened it up, it was a marriage proposal — along with a picture of a pair of bare breasts. Pierced.

There was dead silence for a beat. Sean recovered first.

"See?" he finally said. "You can't change your number, man. You need this. *We* need this."

Late that afternoon Spence was in his office, two large screens working as he crunched some new formulas and numbers, when Clarissa called, giving him a blast from the past.

"Hey," she said. "Checking in on things."

Things being their project, of course. It used to be that she called just to hear his voice because she missed him.

Things changed.

"I'm not trying to apply pressure," she said when he didn't answer right away. "I really just wanted to see how you were doing."

They hadn't made it as a couple — 100 percent his fault — but they'd managed to maintain a friendship, even with all the baggage and miles between them. She was important to him. His relationship with her, the one they had now, where they supported each other through thick and thin without the layers required of a romantic relationship, meant a lot to him. So when she said she wasn't trying to apply pressure, he knew she meant it.

But he felt it anyway. He'd failed her, in a big way. The biggest way a man could fail a woman. He hadn't cheated on her with another woman, but he sure as hell had cheated on her with his work.

Work was and always had been his mistress, and she'd left him for it.

He couldn't go back and fix that. Even if he wanted to, he couldn't. And he didn't want to. She was so much better off without him.

And so was Colbie . . .

"Spence?"

"I'm here. I'm fine." He blew out a breath and shoved his hands through his hair. By some miracle, she'd forgiven him all his many mistakes and she still loved him.

In her own way . . .

In any case, it was her pattern to call whenever she was stateside for a few days, which in itself was rare these days. "Where are you?" he asked.

"DC." She paused. "What's wrong?"

"I've got some problems in the software, but it'll come."

"Maybe you're working too hard."

"No, I —"

"Spence." Clarissa let out a low laugh.

"Let me rephrase. You *are* working too hard."

"You've been overseas. You don't know what I'm doing or not doing."

"Wanna bet?" Clarissa laughed again, but there was something in the sound that said she wasn't actually amused. "I was with you, Spence, remember? For four years. I know exactly what you've been doing. Eating, sleeping, walking, and talking work 24–7."

"I've had to," he said carefully. "There're glitches in the —"

"There are *always* glitches, Spence. It's part of the process, part of the challenge on which you've always thrived. I have complete faith you'll figure everything all out."

This wasn't comforting in the least. It was actually the opposite of comforting and only served to make him all the more edgy because what if he didn't work everything out? What then? He'd have to tell her that once again he'd let her down —

"Stop," she said more gently now, all amusement gone from her voice. "Stop beating yourself up. You'll get this, Spence. You always do. Work always wins in the end with you."

"Ouch," he said but couldn't take offense, because it was true.

Work did always win.

Personal life always lost.

"You know what I mean," she said softly.

"Yeah."

"Listen," she said. "I'm thinking of skipping Christmas in Cali this year. My folks flew here to meet up with me for a few days, and then I'm thinking I might head down to Miami."

"What's in Miami?"

Another pause, and this one had him taking his gaze and hands off his laptop and pausing back. "What," he asked, jokingly. "You've got a guy in Miami?"

Her voice was regretful. "Spence . . ."

"Wow," he said. "You do." He nodded. "Okay, then. Well, good. Good for you."

"Do you really mean that?"

"Yeah." And he did. Even more than that, there was in fact a small surge of relief going through him. "Who is he?"

"A doctor in the Docs Without Borders Extreme organization I work with."

Shit. A noble cause, but probably yet another man who would put his work before her. "Clarissa —"

"Don't worry about me, Spence. I'm okay, I promise."

"I get that. But if something changes and suddenly you're not okay, then I'll —"

"— Kick his ass," she said with a smile. "I

know. I'll keep that in mind. How about you?"

"What about me?"

"You putting yourself out there at all?"

He thought of Colbie and could almost see her smile, hear her laugh . . . feel the touch of her mouth to his.

"You need to get back on the bike," she said.

"So I can hurt someone else?"

"Spence."

He closed his eyes.

"Spence."

"What do you want me to say?" he asked.

"That I didn't destroy you for all other women."

He had to laugh. "It wasn't you. It was me. We both know that."

"Bullshit. I was needy."

"And I was an oblivious, self-centered asshole. That hasn't changed."

"You were never a self-centered asshole," she said. "Oblivious . . . maybe. But it's how you're wired. You're programmed to concentrate on a problem until it's fixed, and until you do, you can't easily concentrate on anything else. You need to accept that about yourself. You're working your ass off on this drone project to get meds and personalized doctor care delivered to tiny corners of the world. It's a big deal."

"Other people have big-deal jobs and they can successfully manage to keep a relationship."

"You can too," she said.

But . . . could he really? He'd seen no proof of that. And yet there was no denying that he wanted to do just that with Colbie.

"Are you sure you're okay with me not coming home for Christmas?" she asked. "I know it's a rough holiday for you."

It wasn't rough so much as . . . lonely. His mom always flew back east to visit friends. He'd spent his last few Christmases right here with his friends. But he couldn't deny he'd felt something was missing. He scrubbed a hand down his face. Christmas was two weeks away. He had plenty of time to think about it later. "I'll be fine."

"Because you always are," she said.

That got a smile. "Yeah."

"I'll be there in January though," she said. "And I'm not rushing you, but . . . is there any chance you have a projected date for the prototype? We'd said January and I was hoping that was still the case. I've got some heavy-hitting investors interested in helping me fund the program once we get it up and running, and they're pressuring me for an estimated start date."

Tension set in Spence's shoulders. He could feel the burn across the back of his neck.

And in his gut.

"Yes," he said. "January works. But say end of the month." That gave him a cushion he needed — only until Colbie left, he told himself; then he'd get caught back up. Which in no way helped to alleviate the pressure he was feeling now.

"You sure, Spence?" she asked softly.

He got the question. Once upon a time he'd disappointed her. Was he going to do it again? "I'm sure."

"I have faith in you," she said. "You know that, right? You're the guy who can do anything he sets his mind to. Anything at all." She blew him some kisses and then was gone.

He tossed his phone aside and dove back into work. Normal habit for him. But then he stopped and looked at the clock.

Not normal habit.

Also not normal — he didn't have to stretch his brain to try to remember what else it was that he was supposed to be doing.

He had a date.

With Colbie.

He headed straight for the door and

yanked it open, only to stop at the sight of Caleb standing there, keycard in hand to let himself in.

"You got food?" Caleb asked hopefully.

"Yeah." Distracted, Spence waved to the kitchen. "Trudy restocked me. Help yourself."

"Where you headed?"

"Date," Spence said.

Caleb reached out and blocked Spence from leaving. "Whoa."

Spence gave him a look. "Come on. It hasn't been that long."

"Actually, yeah, it has. And that's not what I meant. You trying to get laid tonight? And before you bust out my teeth for asking, take a good look at yourself."

Spence looked down. He was in knit boxers.

Caleb grinned. "You know what? On second thought, by all means go just like that. But first . . ." He took out his cell phone and took a pic. "Looking good, man. That gym's really paying off."

Spence flipped him the bird and went through the door that took him directly into his apartment.

A two-minute shower and a quick toss of his closet later, Spence was on the third floor, knocking at Colbie's door.

She opened up and swept her gaze over him from head to toe. "Nice," she said. "But I preferred your first outfit."

She smiled when he just blinked, and it was the kind of smile that could light a guy up from the inside out, the kind of smile that also had her face coming alive.

"Kylie had me add her on Instagram," she said, "and she reposted a pic that someone named Caleb posted. Your business partner, right?" She leaned in. "Seems as though you really do put your gym to good use."

"Excuse me a sec." He pulled out his phone and hit a button on his security app. This would set off an internal alert that would go straight to his security company.

Archer's company.

In two minutes or less, Archer's men would storm Spence's apartment in full kickass mode and scare the ever-loving shit out of Caleb.

"Everything okay?" Colbie asked.

He smiled. Payback's a bitch. "Everything's great."

Chapter 11
#SonOfAMotherlessGoat

Colbie had to laugh at the look on Spence's face. Pained, but not even remotely embarrassed. And since he looked fantastic in his clothes — and now she also knew he looked fantastic *out* of his clothes — she wouldn't have been embarrassed either.

"I wasn't sure what we were going to do," she said. "So I didn't know how to dress."

He smiled. "I wouldn't mind if you wore the same outfit I wear when working."

"Ha," she said, giving him a small push to the chest.

He was solid enough to not be budged, and that, along with his assured stance and easy smile, did something to her.

The same something that getting away from New York and all her problems there had done.

It made her feel . . . alive.

Spence took her hand, looking her over the same way she had done to him. She'd

162

dressed for the weather, which she'd learned in her five days here was as unpredictable and moody as her muse. The one thing you could be sure of in San Francisco was that you couldn't predict the weather. So she'd worn layers: a cami, a sweater, a scarf, and dark jeans tucked into boots.

Spence's gaze lingered on the leather boots. "I like those as much as your heels," he said in a voice that gave her a delicious sort of shiver.

And for a moment she was torn between wanting to go sightseeing and tugging him into her apartment and stripping him down to his work attire.

And beyond.

He took in her expression and let out a low laugh. "The way you look at me is way too good for my ego." He shoved his glasses to the top of his head. Then he snagged her around the waist, pulling her into him, and kissed her until her toes curled.

The appetizer on the menu of Spence Baldwin's kisses, which only made her hungrier.

He grinned at the look on her face as he put his glasses back on. "Later," he promised. "We've gotta go. We're on a schedule."

"For what?"

"You'll see."

They left the courtyard through the wrought-iron gate to the street. As they did, someone came out of the shadows and started snapping pictures of them.

Colbie gasped in surprise, instinctively turning her head into Spence's shoulder, not wanting anyone to catch a photo of her and announce her whereabouts.

But then the guy's shouted questions penetrated. "Who's the woman, Spencer? How does she feel about you being nominated for San Francisco's most eligible bachelor?"

Okay, so this wasn't about her, she realized and began to lift her head because . . . *San Francisco's most eligible bachelor?*

Spence cupped the back of her head in a big hand, pressing her face into his shoulder as he tightened his grip on her, shielding her from the lens.

"Come on," the guy yelled at Spence. "Give me one sound bite, man. I make a living off this shit."

"You need a new job" was Spence's sound bite as he walked her past the guy without another word. "The truck's a block over," he told her as they passed a clothing boutique, a burger joint, and a . . .

"Bookstore," she said, the same thrill zinging through her that bookstores had brought all of her life.

"Do you want to go in?" he asked because she'd stopped, practically putting her nose to the glass window display. Reading had always been her happy place, a blissful escape, far before she'd become a writer.

"Can we?" she asked.

Smiling, he opened the door for her.

It was an independent store and to her delight, her books were prominently displayed. The first one in the series was front and center, thanks, of course, to the upcoming premiere of the movie on Christmas Day.

Spence didn't even glance at the display; he just headed straight back to the nerdy science book section, and she had to laugh. She ran a finger over her book and eavesdropped on the two readers standing there eyeing the display.

"I still like her writing," one said to the other. "But the third book didn't have the same heart as the first two."

Colbie put a hand to her own heart, feeling it tighten at the words, like someone was criticizing her firstborn or something.

"I completely agree," the second reader said. "Think she's doing it just because she has a big, expensive contract?"

Colbie took a deep breath. There was a

reason writers should never read their own reviews or, apparently, eavesdrop on readers. She started to walk away but a third woman joined the other two.

"I love the entire series," the woman said. "I'd read CE Crown if she copied the phone book. But she should've put Cria and Del together. They deserved their happiness too."

"Yes!" the other two women said at the same time, and then Colbie was alone at the display. She hunted down Spence, finding him nose deep in a book so thick it must've weighed twenty-five pounds. The title had a lot of words like *thermodynamics* and *applied elasticity.* "Hey," she said.

"Hey."

"So . . . most eligible bachelor?"

He shoved the book back on the shelf. "You're not going to give me grief about this, are you?"

"Oh, most definitely."

He grimaced and took her hand. "Save it until after I've had food."

Five minutes later, they were in his truck, a completely redone 1957 Chevy Deluxe cab, turquoise blue with whitewall tires. "Not what I pictured you driving," she said, running a hand along the dash, admiring the gorgeous beast.

"No?"

"No, I saw you in a sleek, fast sports car."

He shrugged. "This has sentimental value. It was my grandpa's. He abused it until he lost his license. I bought it off him and rebuilt and restored it a few years back."

He could've bought a new truck. He could have bought a fleet of new trucks. "You like old stuff?" she asked.

He glanced at her, his eyes hidden behind dark lenses. "I'm sentimental," he said without apology.

Their gazes held for a long beat as she absorbed that. He was brilliant. An engineer. An inventor. Good with money. And very hot in a sexy engineer geek sort of way with his perpetually finger-combed hair and glasses . . .

He flashed a smile, making her realize that she was still staring at him, so she cleared her throat. "Well, whoever did it for you did an amazing job." The interior matched the exterior paint job and was spotless.

"I did it myself," he said.

He was one surprise after another. "So you're a mechanic too?"

"I've been taking apart things and putting them back together my whole life." He gave a wry smile. "I was five when I rigged my mom's watch to count her steps. In hindsight, I probably should've grabbed the patent for that."

She choked out a laugh. "So you're a man of many talents."

At that, he slid her a look so hot she glanced down to make sure her clothes hadn't gone up in smoke. "How did your grandpa lose his license? He get too old to drive?"

"He had one too many homemade brownies last summer and got himself arrested."

She blinked. "Seriously?"

"Seriously. I was his one phone call because his daughter-in-law — my mom — would've killed him and left him to rot in prison."

She laughed, even though she suspected he wasn't kidding. "Do you have a big family?"

"No," he said. "Just the three of us."

"Are you close?"

"My mom and I, yes. This is the Embarcadero," he said, pointing ahead of them. "That's Coit Tower. And there's the Bay Bridge. And you can see Alcatraz out on the water."

She practically glued her nose to the windshield. "All of that is on my list!"

"I know." He turned in at Pier 39, lined with boats of all sizes, each so close to the next that she couldn't imagine how they could possibly get out of their slips without bumping.

Spence came around for her, taking her hand as he grabbed an old tattered duffle bag from the back, which he slung over his shoulder. "Come on."

"Where to?"

"Still a surprise," he said mysteriously.

They walked past a pier lined with sea lions lounging together, past groups of tourists wandering around. "The tour companies are shutting down for the day," Spence said. "This time of year they don't do night tours."

This was disappointing. She'd begun to hope that they were going out on the water.

Spence just smiled at her expression and walked up to a locked gate. He produced a key, let them both in, and locked the gate behind them. They walked down the dock and stopped at a slip in front of a sleek-looking ship.

"Other than the Long Island ferry, I've never been on a boat," Colbie said, still staring at it. "Until now, I've never even been away or on vacation." She'd never been anything but in over her head, both at home raising her brothers and her mom and also at work in the crazy surprising career that demanded so much of her time.

Spence cupped her jaw and turned her face to his. He brushed a soft but potent kiss across her lips. "I'm sorry for that," he said, "for all you've gone through, but I'm also glad I get to be the one to share this with you."

A woman stood on board, looking at her watch. "I'm impressed," she called down. "You're not only on the right day but on time too."

Spence laughed as he led Colbie on board. "Pru, meet Colbie. Colbie, this is Pru, Finn's soon-to-be better half. She's going to be our pilot and captain tonight. And she's not going to stick her nose in our business at all."

Pru grinned. "Wanna bet?" She gave Spence a hug and kiss, and then Colbie as well. Next was a quick tour of what looked like an amazingly well-kept and well-loved ship.

"It's beautiful," Colbie said. "Is it yours?"

Pru laughed. "No. I couldn't even buy the fuel for this lovely. It belongs to my boss's family. He let me rent it out for tonight." She eyed Spence. "Somebody I know wanted a sunset/moonlight tour of the bay."

Colbie could hardly contain herself and turned and gave Spence a huge hug.

He was quick to gather her in closer, wrapping his arms around her. "Might wait to reserve judgment until you see the dinner picnic I made for us," he murmured, his mouth at her ear, his breath warm, giving her a full set of goose bumps and all sorts of other reactions that she was pretty sure shouldn't be happening in public. "I'm not as good a conjurer as you are." Then he lifted her off her feet just enough that their bodies lined up perfect. Face-to-face, chest-to-chest, thigh-to-thigh, and . . . everything in between.

Colbie sucked in a breath.

And so did he.

"Alrighty, then," Pru murmured to herself. "Going to work now. I'd say relax and enjoy, but I think you've got those two things covered."

Chapter 12
#HolyGolfBalls

Ten minutes later, they were out on the bay and Colbie had her gaze glued to the horizon and a huge smile on her face. Watching her, Spence felt some of the pressures of his day fade away. It was hard to remain stressed when he was with Colbie, as he'd already discovered. She was like a warm spiked drink on a hot day.

A balm to the soul.

As for their view, it was that magical time between day and night. The bay was smooth and still beneath them, small swells slapping against the ship, the wind in their faces, the last of the light slanting sharply across the water, illuminating it with a soft blue glow. In the distance, they could see the Bay Bridge, which was also lit with thousands of small white lights, making it stand out against the night sky.

The two of them sat at the bow of the boat on a huge almost trampoline-like lounger that fit them both. Spence had packed the duffle bag for the weather and pulled out two down jackets and a wool blanket, then bundled Colbie in one of the jackets and covered them both with the blanket. They leaned back, the gentle jostling of the swells having nudged them up against one another so that they rocked together with each smooth rise and fall of the ocean tide.

Next to him, Colbie felt soft and warm, and he couldn't think of another place he'd rather be.

"It feels like we're birds," she said, tilting her face close to his. "We're flying low, skimming over the water. It's amazing. I feel like my heart's soaring as fast as the boat." She sighed in pleasure and he felt his body react. He wrapped an arm around her to keep her close, liking the way she snuggled into him way too much.

Pru took them out of the bay, where they caught sight of whales moving out in the distance, five of them swimming together, enormous and massive and gorgeous.

"Holy golf balls," Colbie said and clutched Spence tight. "Do you see?"

He never took his eyes off her. "Yeah. I see."

Turning to him, she laughed. "The whales, Spence! Don't look at me — look at the whales!" She went back to reverently watching them, so moved her eyes filled with unshed tears.

"You okay?" he asked.

"Better than okay." She blinked the moisture away and laughed a little at herself. "It's just that I realized that here, my life doesn't revolve around me getting everything handled and done on my own. Here, life revolves on its own axis. I'm just along for the ride."

He was getting that her growing-up years had been more than a little rough. Something they had in common. And that she'd clawed her way out of the gutter by her fingernails.

Something else they had in common.

She must have felt her phone vibrate because she pulled it from her pocket with a grimace of apology and accessed a text.

"Problem?" he asked.

"Kent. He says the emergency-only credit card I left him isn't working at the pizza joint." She rolled her eyes and thumbed in a response and shoved her phone away.

"What did you tell him?" he asked.

"That an emergency involves blood. And not just any blood either, but an *arterial* bleed."

When he laughed, she sighed and smiled.

"You know what I love?" she asked, her eyes back on the last of the sun as it sank below the horizon. "That I'm not important here."

"You're important anywhere," he said.

She shook her head. "I didn't mean it like that — I'm not having an existential crisis. It's just that here, away from home and work, I'm not the glue, you know? I'm not the one having to hold it all together."

He stared into her green eyes and felt himself lean into her, wanting to drown in them. "So the trick is to run away from home," he said. "Got it."

She smiled. "You need to run away?"

"Actually, this, here with you, is working wonders. I'm starting to feel like I'm not the glue right now either." Still holding her against him, he slid his hand into her hair. "You should know something, Colbie."

She licked her lips and nearly made him groan. "What?" she whispered.

"I want to kiss you again."

Now she dragged her teeth over her lower lip. "Why?"

No one had ever asked him that question before, but she'd tilted her head, waiting on his answer, and he had to laugh. "I want to kiss you again because you're a smartass. Because you're a little demanding too, and those things somehow really turn me on."

"Hmm," she said and he laughed.

"I also want to kiss you again because you're smart as hell. And also funny as hell. Not to mention *sexy* as hell."

Her breath caught. "You think so?"

"I know so. And you roll with life's punches and give it all you've got." He pushed his sunglasses to the top of his head and lowered his head so that their mouths were only inches apart. "And you're so pretty you make me ache."

"Can you see me without your glasses?"

"No, but I have a good memory."

With a laugh, she gripped the front of his jacket and tugged his mouth to hers. The aggressive move had him groaning and when she broke from the kiss, he had to take a long, unsteady breath and grapple for control. The only thing stopping him from letting her have her merry way with him was that they weren't alone. Plus it was fucking cold and when he had her, he wanted her naked against him. Not in a down jacket. "Colbie —"

She shut him up with her mouth in another kiss so hot he was surprised smoke wasn't curling from their bodies.

"You're a good kisser," she whispered against his lips. "Which you probably already know from previous relationships."

"Yeah, well, it's not like my life has lent itself to many relationships," he admitted. "And the ones I've had have all gone bad over time."

She looked at him for a minute and then gave a small smile. "Good thing that time is the one thing we don't have," she said. "So no one can read too much into this, right?"

He stilled and met her gaze. "You heard me say that to Eddie. Listen, I didn't mean —"

"No, I get it. And you're right." Her stomach growled and she pressed her hands to it, changing the subject. "The beast is hungry, apparently."

"Colbie —"

"Didn't you say something about dinner?" she asked.

"Yes, but —"

"I'm starving, Spence."

He looked at her for a second, trying to ascertain if she really wanted to change the subject. She did, so he nodded. "I've got you." And once again he reached for his old duffle bag.

"Did you really cook?" she asked.

"Sort of," he said.

"Did you burn water?"

"Funny." Relieved to hear the laughter in her voice, he took her hand in his, brought it up to his mouth, and playfully nipped at her fingers. "I put together a picnic."

"Ingenious," she said. "Also cheating."

He had to laugh. He'd totally cheated, even more than she knew because he'd had Trudy put it all together for him. "We've got wine, cheddar cheese, salami, crackers, grapes, and chocolate chip cookies," he said, citing the list he'd given Trudy. "Because everything goes better with chocolate chip cookies." He pulled out the goods and Colbie stared down at it all and laughed. She laughed so hard she tipped over.

"Can't wait to hear how you explain this," she finally managed, swiping a tear of mirth from her cheek.

He'd unloaded Gouda cheese, a beef stick, red apples, a still warm foil-wrapped loaf of garlic bread, and sugar cookies. He shook his head.

"You did get the drink right," she said, nudging the bottle of wine. "So, who did this for you?"

"Trudy, my housekeeper." He gestured at the garlic bread. "Why would she add garlic bread?"

"Because it's delicious?"

"Yeah, but . . ." He scratched his jaw, thinking it might hinder any further kissing action, and he'd *definitely* planned on more kissing action.

Colbie grinned. "I think it's okay if we *both* eat it."

He locked eyes with her, liking the look on her face, the one that said she was remembering exactly what it felt like when they kissed, and that she liked the memory very much. "Maybe we should test that theory," he said, and leaning over her, he brushed his lips along her jawline.

And then the side of her neck.

She moaned and tilted her head in invitation, which he took, rolling with her, pushing her to her back, his hands pressed on the canvas on either side of her head.

She sucked in a breath, and it assured him that she liked the move. As did the way her legs shifted, making room for him between them.

Her hair was spread out over his hands and forearms like a halo as she whispered his name.

Another invitation that he gladly took, along with her mouth. She kissed him back eagerly, the kind of kiss that pretty much guaranteed a guy was about to get laid and it was going to rock his world.

Except they were still on the boat. With Pru, who probably couldn't see them from where she was controlling the boat but knew they were there. With regret, he broke the kiss and lifted his head.

Colbie's eyes were filled with straight-up lust and she was breathing just as hard as he was. She smoothed out the nail marks from where she'd been clutching his jacket. "I think we're supposed to actually eat the bread first," she said on a rough laugh as Spence's phone went off.

Looking pained, he pulled the phone from his pocket.

Pru:
Coming up on Alcatraz, under a full moon. Rare sight. If you're lip-locked, might want to lift your head. And if you're not lip-locked, do you need pointers?

Spence shook his head and put the phone away.

"Emergency?" Colbie asked.

"Nope. No arterial bleeds," he said, and together they took in the sight of Alcatraz lit by the full moon. It was both spooky and stunning, and Colbie seemed transfixed by the sight.

"Wow," she whispered, breathlessly. "Tonight's the best night ever."

Spence thought so too.

CHAPTER 13
#MOTHERTRUCKER

After they docked and helped Pru lock things up for the night, Spence took Colbie on a long walk along the Embarcadero. The pylons, the benches, the streetlights . . . everything had been decorated for the holiday and she loved the look of it. It'd rained earlier for long enough that everything felt clean and shimmered with condensation. For the first time in years she was excited for the season, even though she knew she'd be gone by Christmas Day.

She hoped to bring the holiday cheer home with her. "It's so beautiful here with all the decorations," she said, her breath crystalizing in front of her face. "I've never seen anything like it."

"New York doesn't do it up for the holidays?"

"Yes, but I mean . . ." She broke off, not sure what she meant at all. "It just seems . . . nice. Really nice. And like it could all be true. Santa Claus and all that."

He smiled. "You don't believe in Santa?"

"Well . . . let's just say I have mixed feelings about the holiday."

"A cynic in a sweet package."

She rolled her eyes, but he reached for her hand and pulled her into him. "Talk to me," he said.

"For as long as I can remember, I've been Santa."

He looked at her in surprise.

"I told you my dad left us when I was little," she said and then paused. "It was on Christmas Eve."

"Seriously?" Spence tightened his arm around her. "What the hell's wrong with him?"

She shrugged. She didn't know. "He wasn't made for being a family man. And actually, he was right. My mom said we were better off and I have to believe that."

"I'm sorry," he said quietly. "That's a shitty memory to carry around."

Colbie didn't like to talk about this. Correction: she *never* talked about this. So why she was suddenly opening up, and to a man who lived three thousand miles away from her, was a big unsolved mystery.

Or maybe it wasn't. There was still something about this place *and* Spence that made her want to be something she'd never been.

Open and carefree.

But maybe . . . maybe to be those things, she had to let go of her past. "Not everyone's cut out to be a parent."

"I agree." He paused. "I got lucky with my parents. My dad didn't have it easy. My grandpa was a hard-ass but a brilliant inventor, a tough act to follow." He smiled a little wryly. "So to the everlasting frustration of Grandpa, my dad didn't even try. He was a family man to the end."

The tone of his voice had her heart squeezing. "You lost him," she said softly.

He nodded. "A few years ago. Cancer."

"It must've been hard on your mom."

"Very," Spence said. "But she's taken up something she couldn't do when my dad was alive. Traveling."

"Why couldn't she travel with your dad?"

"They didn't have the means, but even if they had, he hated flying." Spence shook his head. "Always said that if people were meant to fly, we'd have been born with wings."

She laughed and he smiled at her, bringing their joined hands up to his mouth, where he brushed a kiss to her fingers before taking a look around them. "You're right. It is pretty amazing out here. I guess I forgot to see it anymore."

"How long have you been here?" she asked.

"All my life." He was still looking around as if trying to see the city from her eyes. "I grew up not too far from here, actually."

"In Fisherman's Wharf?" she asked, having studied online maps of San Francisco's famed neighborhoods. She was dying of curiosity about this man who was so private.

"The Tenderloin."

An area, she now knew, that had once been one of the toughest and most degenerate places in all of San Francisco. "Does your mom still live there?"

"No, these days she lives on the coast about an hour south of here."

He didn't mention his grandpa again. Maybe he'd passed away too. Or maybe they weren't close. She didn't want to pry. Okay, she totally *did* want to pry but she didn't want to open it up in a way that would require her to do the same back. She'd told him all she'd planned to. In fact, she'd told him more than she'd planned to. And in any case, she was here to *not* think.

He was watching her. "So if there was a Santa Claus, what would you ask him for?" he asked.

You, she nearly said. She'd want him for Christmas and no take-backs. "I'd like my book to write itself," she said instead.

He smiled.

"And you'd want what?" she asked. "Maybe your project to invent itself?"

"That would be high on the list."

When she yawned, they headed back, stopping for dessert at a cupcake shop.

"Did you know that once you lick the frosting off a cupcake, it becomes a muffin?" she asked. "And muffins are healthy." She leaned in and took a lick of his frosting. "You are welcome."

He laughed and so did she because she loved the sound of his laugh.

When a sprinkle got stuck in the stubble of his jaw, she had some fun with him, playfully misdirecting him as he tried to get it.

"Maybe you should shave," she teased.

"You have no idea how lucky girls are that they don't have to shave every day," he said. "You've all got it easy."

She choked on a laugh. "Says the guy who's never had to navigate a razor around his kneecaps or . . ." she paused ". . . any other specific areas."

He laughed.

"Not funny," she said. "It's a suicide mission."

185

He guided her into the cobblestoned courtyard of the Pacific Pier Building. It was midnight and the place looked like a holiday dream with the strings of white lights and each of the potted trees lining the walkway decorated with colorful ornaments.

"Elle went overboard this year," he muttered.

"So she works for you?"

"More like she allows me to pay her to be bossy."

She laughed. "They say friends and business don't mix."

"She's family," he said simply.

She nodded, thinking that sounded . . . lovely. Really lovely. "So what are your holiday plans?" she asked. "Will you spend Christmas with your mom?"

"Probably not."

She glanced up at him, startled. "No?"

"She went back east to see friends. I'll probably spend it at the pub with Finn, Elle and Archer, and the others. We're a sort of misfit ride-or-die self-made family."

Coming from a family that was close only because she'd kept them together by sheer force of will, she envied the whole family-by-choice thing in a big way.

"How about you?" he asked.

She shrugged. "I'll spend it at home with

my brothers and mom, like always. We'll fight, also like always, but old habits die hard."

He cocked his head and studied her. "You do know you're allowed to do whatever you want, right? It's the only perk to this whole adulting thing."

She let out a small laugh. "Never mind me. Christmas sometimes makes me a little . . ."

"Hollow?"

She met his gaze. "Yes. How did you know?"

"Let's just say I've been there."

A little off her axis, Colbie looked at the pretty fountain. "Do you really not believe in the legend?"

He lifted a shoulder.

She turned to him. "How about love? Do you believe in love?" And for some reason, she held her breath for his answer.

He paused. "I believe it's out there for most."

"Gee, that's only a little cryptic."

He gave a rough laugh. "Here's the thing. My family . . . when it comes to work and love, we tend to only do one of them well. Not both. So we choose."

She raised her brows. "And you chose . . . work?"

He shrugged again. "It's what I do best."

"So you've tried love before, then," she said. "And . . . failed?"

"Big-time."

"Do you think you could possibly explain that with more than two words?" she asked.

A smile touched his lips. "I told you about my grandpa. He was a workaholic. His entire life was the job — to the detriment of his family, which he completely ignored. My dad learned a lesson from that. He chose love. I was raised by two loving, if not a little baffled-by-me, parents who did the best they could. They had each other, if not always the rent money. But I always knew that what they shared wasn't going to be for me."

"Why not?"

"Because I'm shitty at love." He paused. "And I hated being poor."

"You really believe you can only have one or the other?" she asked in disbelief.

"I know it. In college, women would give me their phone numbers and I'd forget to call."

"Forget?"

"Well, I was sixteen," he said.

She raised her brows. "At that age, you'd have been both physically and emotionally behind everyone else."

"Yeah. I definitely preferred labs over women, which didn't help me out any."

She grinned. "That seems to have changed."

His smile was wry. "Yes, but not by that much. My last girlfriend, Clarissa . . . she was positive she was going to be the one."

"And she . . . wasn't?"

"We met when I was working for the government," he said. "She was in medical school at the time, and just as busy as I was. At first, everything was fine between us because we didn't ask much of each other. Though in hindsight, I think I asked nothing of her because my head was always in my work and she didn't ask anything of me because she knew that and didn't try to compete. Which really meant that I shortchanged her at every turn, even though I really cared about her. I tried to put her on my radar, I really did. We moved into an apartment, the theory being that at least we'd sleep together every night."

Colbie was working at not feeling the teensiest little bit of jealousy. No one had ever tried that hard to keep her. She got that the point to this story was that Spence had shortchanged Clarissa, but all she saw was that he'd at least given it everything he'd had at the time to give. "What happened?" she asked.

"We stayed together for several years. She began a charity organization that brought meds and doctors to remote corners of the world, desperate remote corners, which meant she was gone a lot. Which worked for me. It became easy to forget her needs, to forget to put her first. I got out of the habit way too easily. And then came a huge fundraiser she'd cochaired, and it was incredibly important to her. As it was the only thing she'd asked of me all year, I promised to go." He shook his head. "She reminded me every day for two weeks and I brushed off her concerns that I'd forget."

"And . . . you forgot," she guessed.

"I did." He looked pained. "I didn't show up and she went without me, and I didn't realize I'd forgotten the most important night of her life until she got home late that night dressed to the hilt, steam coming out her ears."

"She dumped you," she said, surprised. Up until that moment, she'd assumed he'd been the one to break it off.

"Oh yeah, she dumped me," he said ruefully. "She said I was going to end up a lonely old man someday. Actually, she yelled that part, right after chucking a shoe at my head. Then she packed her things and moved out, leaving my sorry ass in her dust."

"Ouch."

"Yeah, well. I deserved it. I was a self-absorbed, selfish dick."

"You don't seem self-absorbed or selfish to me," she said.

"Like I said, give me some time."

She didn't believe this. Or more accurately, she didn't want to believe it. The thing was, he said only what he meant, and she knew he meant this, to his core. He'd warned her from the beginning that he would disappoint her.

She just didn't want it to be true.

"The truth is," he said, "I'm busy all the time and no woman's going to be okay with that for the long term. So undoubtedly, I'm going to end up a lonely old man, just like Clarissa so aptly predicted."

"I don't believe that," she said. "I've seen you engrossed in work. You've still always made time for your friends. And me."

"That's because you're a welcome distraction." He tugged her hair. "Beautiful, funny, smart . . . but a definite distraction nevertheless."

She stared at him, torn between melting at what he thought of her and wanting to cry at the knowledge that this would never

be anything more than an amazing inter-
lude. "Good thing, then, that I'm just a
temporary one," she said with more cheer
than she felt. Because what she felt was a
hollow pit in the depths of her gut that she
didn't want to name. She pulled a quarter
from her purse and turned to the fountain.

"What are you doing?" he asked.

"Making a wish." She tossed the quarter
into the water and closed her eyes.

"For . . . ?" he asked, sounding worried.

Silly man. Although he *should* be worried.
"For true love. For you." She opened her
eyes and grinned at his horror. "See, you do
believe."

"You're a scary woman," he said.

"Now you're catching on," she said as
from inside her pocket, her phone went off
again.

She sighed.

"You should probably make sure the
house is still standing," he said. "Here, let
me." He took the phone and looked at the
screen. "Do you have a third brother named
Jackson?"

"No." She took the phone back and stared
at it before hitting ignore.

"Problem?" Spence asked.

She took a deep breath, realizing with a
shock that she'd so thoroughly distanced

herself from her life for the past week she'd actually forgotten about Jackson. "He's my agent."

Spence looked surprised. "You must be close to being published to have an agent. That's great, Colbie."

His encouragement was sweet, but it also made her feel guilty for not telling him about this part of her life. *You've only known him five days,* she reminded herself. And this escape was private. And extremely important to both her mental health *and* her career. And whether they knew it or not, it was also important to her family, staff, and editorial team, all of whom counted on her. And in fact, just thinking about it, she felt the familiar smothering pressure to sustain the franchise her life had become sink into her chest.

She looked into his eyes and knew she couldn't do it — she couldn't, shouldn't, keep secrets from him. He was private, incredibly so, but honest. She needed to be the same. At least as much as she could be. "You know how you're bad at love?" she asked. "Well, so am I. I picked Jackson as my first love and it wasn't reciprocated."

His eyes were sympathetic but not pitying, which was a good thing. A nice thing.

"Since the past sucks," he murmured,

slowly pulling her into him, kissing her jaw, "maybe we should stick to the present."

Good idea. *Great* idea. But she wasn't done coming clean. "Spence?"

"Yeah?" His mouth was on her throat now, so erotic and sensual that she felt her eyes roll back in her head.

"There're things about me that I still haven't told you," she whispered. "Things I'm not ready to talk about, at least not yet. Are you okay with that?"

He met her gaze and held it. "I want only what you're willing to give me, Colbie. No more."

For a moment, that stopped her. He wanted only what she was willing to give, meaning he didn't need anything more than that. Which meant he really was fine with this being whatever it was until she left. And after that, the end.

And as she'd said that was what she wanted too, she had no business even thinking about it. None at all.

But she *was* thinking about it, a lot.

She was thinking how nice it would be if they decided to take this wherever it took them, even past their Christmas Eve expiration date.

Unfortunately, he wasn't, and she swallowed hard past the disappointment before she spoke. "Given what I just told you, and how *I'd* feel in reverse, meaning if *you* were telling *me* that you were holding something back, I wouldn't blame you if you want to walk away," she said softly, and it was with mixed feelings that she watched him crane his neck to look around them, certain he was about to do just that.

"We're alone out here," he said instead and pulled her in closer. "Pretty rare."

"Spence —"

"We all have secrets, Colbie," he said and kissed her gently, his passion clearly in check. "And we laid out our line in the sand from the beginning."

"That being . . . that this thing between us is temporary, right?" she said. "Because I'm neither relationship material nor geographically desirable, and you're . . ."

"Bad at this," he helpfully filled in for her.

She nodded and then she shook her head. "Except you're *not* bad at this, Spence."

"I am," he insisted. "And that's a promise."

"So you're saying that it's a *good* thing we don't have time?"

He gave her a small smile.

Yeah. That's exactly what he was saying. That it was a good thing they didn't have time. Again, she worked to shove the disappointment deep but wasn't entirely success-ful. Time to pull back and regroup, she thought. "I had fun tonight," she said. "Thanks for the date. It was pretty incred-ible."

"You're more than welcome. I had a great time too." The warmth in his gaze, the heat from his body . . . Even with what they'd just discussed, it was all heady stuff. More so when he wrapped his hand around her ponytail and used it to bring her face closer to his. And then he gave her what she was pretty sure he'd intended to be another quick kiss — but wasn't. Not by a long shot, and when it ended, she had to lock her knees to keep from slipping into a puddle of longing on the ground.

With a gravelly groan low in his throat, Spence drew himself away from her. "That's getting harder to do," he said.

"Kiss me?"

"*Stop* kissing you," he corrected. "The fountain must be taking your wish seri-ously."

She saw the teasing light in his eyes, swirled in with a good amount of heat, and managed a smile in return even though she thought maybe the fountain was taking her wish very seriously indeed.

CHAPTER 14
#GODBLESSAMERICA

When Spence got home, he was far too keyed up to sleep. Thinking he'd work, he went to his office and logged on to his computer. But his concentration was even more shot tonight than it'd been all week.

He gave up and went to bed, telling himself he'd get back at it tomorrow.

But he didn't. Not that day or the next three. That was because for three straight days he pulled Colbie from her apartment and knocked something off her list. He took her shopping in Union Square, for dim sum in Chinatown, and wine tasting in Napa Valley.

But not the nights. The nights he worked. Not full throttle, because his brain felt otherwise occupied with one sweet and sexy Colbie, but he did try. And as he stared at his screens, he realized that he was actually making a very real, very serious attempt at balancing Colbie and work.

As for whether he was successful at it, the jury was still out. But three days in, he sent what he had to both Caleb and Joe — who was consulting with them on the security end — hoping one of them might be able to put a finger on what he was missing. Then he dragged his exhausted ass into bed. It was three a.m. and he looked at his phone for the first time all day.

Three new marriage proposals. One request for a picture of his bare feet. That was a new one. He deleted everything, including a stack of e-mails from investors wanting him to come in on their ideas and bankroll them. He deleted three e-mails from Brandon.

Done, he tossed his phone aside. Then he stared at his window, where the building's holiday lights were blinking, making his eyes rattle in his head. He texted Elle.

Spence:
Your lights are giving me a seizure.

The Ruler of Your Universe:
Do what the rest of us do in the middle of the night — shut your damn eyes.

Spence:
Seriously. Wake up and shut off the lights.

The Ruler of Your Universe:
I'm not sleeping. I'm doing one of your best friends.

Spence:
Overshare! Shut off the fucking lights, Elle.

The Ruler of Your Universe:
Okay, Grinch, sheesh . . .

Spence tossed his phone aside. Grinch. He wasn't the Grinch. And just because he chose not to use it didn't mean that his heart was two sizes too small. He handled the holiday season just fine. He looked around his place. Not one holiday decoration, not so much as a single strand of tinsel. Okay, so maybe the holidays tended to get to him. His mom was already back east and would be there for weeks. His only other blood relative preferred a damn alley to a perfectly nice, warm apartment. And yeah, he had his friends and he was grateful for them but . . . Well, he still didn't feel into the spirit. Especially knowing that by Christmas Day, the one person he'd love to celebrate with would be gone.

Shaking his head, he rolled over and closed his eyes. He was deep into the best dream of his life, doing things to Colbie that were making her cry out for more, when he heard something.

"Spence . . ."

Yeah, that's right, he thought, *say my name, scream it —*

"He's smiling in his sleep," came Joe's voice. "Why is he smiling in his sleep?"

"Maybe he's making a breakthrough," Caleb said. "Don't wake him up in case he's solving all our problems."

"I bet he's dreaming about a woman," Joe said. "Not work."

Caleb snorted. "With this problem unsolved? Not likely."

"He's only human."

"But that's the thing — he's not human," Caleb said. "He's a machine and he's on the job. That's all that matters to him. Right, Spence? Wake the fuck up and tell him you're solving our problems in your sleep and not hooking up."

"Why are you in my bedroom?" Spence asked without opening his eyes.

"Uh, because we have a meeting," Caleb said, sounding ticked off.

"Had," Joe said. "You missed it."

Shit. Spence sat up. Daylight was streaming into his bedroom. "What time is it?"

"Time for you to tell us if you were bit by a vampire or a woman," Joe said, eyeing Spence's neck. "I vote vampire, because when you're this deep into a project, you can't remember your own damn name, much less enough niceties to get laid."

Spence didn't bother to cover the hickey on his neck, the one Colbie had given him yesterday after he'd taken her for the dim sum in Chinatown. He loved that hickey. Instead he gave them each a shove off his bed and slid out from beneath the covers to head into his bathroom.

"Jesus," Caleb said, shielding his eyes. "Warn a guy, would you? Put some fucking clothes on."

A pair of pants hit Spence in the back of his head.

Joe's doing. Caleb couldn't throw worth shit. Spence let the pants fall to the floor and headed straight into his shower.

"Think he got laid?" he heard Caleb ask.

"Hope he did," Joe said. "He's been pissy as hell."

"I'm not pissy!" Spence yelled, turning on the water.

"Nope," Caleb said. "He didn't get laid."

■ ■ ■ ■

That morning Colbie sat in the coffee shop with her laptop. Her fingers were moving on the keyboard, always a good thing. She was writing something new and she had absolutely no idea if it was any good. But she figured she could fix crap on a page. What she couldn't fix was a blank page.

The important thing was that she'd been in San Francisco for nine days now and her rough draft was coming along with shocking ease, thrilling her heart. She was several pages in when she recognized the battered athletic shoes that came into her vision. She let her gaze run up a set of long denim-covered legs, past a jacket and an untucked, unbuttoned shirt over a T-shirt that said *Ride or Die,* and felt all her good spots tingle.

"Hey," Spence said. He had a black Lab at his side on a leash and was holding a coffee to-go cup and a brown bag that smelled amazingly delicious.

"Hey back." Her stomach growled, reminding her that she'd had only coffee and she'd missed breakfast hours ago now. "Something smells like heaven on earth."

"Thanks."

"You're welcome, but I don't think it's you," she said. "It's whatever's in your bag."

Willa just happened to be walking past her table with a tall, good-looking guy. Keane, her boyfriend, Colbie assumed. They kissed and he got in line for them while Willa stopped to talk. "Don't even bother to ask Spence to share," she told Colbie. "He never shares his muffins. Ever."

Spence gave the bag to Colbie and Willa sputtered. "Are you kidding me?"

Spence just smiled at her and handed *her* the black Lab's leash. "I've got to get to work, but he's done his business."

Willa pointed at him. "I could tattle on you for sharing your muffins with her and not us — you know that, right? Your life as you know it would be over."

"You really want to tell stories, Willa?" He gave her a long look that obviously meant something to Willa because she sighed and rolled her eyes.

"You fight dirty," she muttered.

"Remember that," he said, and when Willa moved off with the dog at her side, Spence reached for Colbie's hand. "Break time."

"But you just told Willa you had to get to work."

"And I do. But this first. Get up, Colbie.

We're going to do this and it's going to be good."

Oh boy. Butterflies danced low in her belly as she shut her laptop, slipped it into her bag, and stood up. "Um, I feel like I should warn you, I haven't done laundry yet, so I'm not in my best lingerie —" She broke off at the wide grin Spence flashed her. "God bless America," she said on an expulsion of air. "You didn't mean sex at all, did you."

"Hey, I'm nothing if not flexible," he said. "We can work it into the plans. If you're a very good girl." He leaned in and put his mouth to her ear. "But being bad works too."

When he pulled back, she had to blink away the sensual fog he'd put her in, seemingly with no effort at all. "You're talking like we're going to . . ." She broke off and bit her lower lip. "Like it's for sure going to happen."

His low laugh was sexy as hell. "Oh, it's going to happen." Since she couldn't feel her legs, she sat back down.

With a laugh, he took her heavy bag from her shoulder and slung it over one of his. Then he pulled her back up and tugged her along with him across the courtyard.

They went out the gate to the street and

down half a block, where he shepherded her into that beautiful '57 Chevy of his.

"Where are we going?" she asked as he pulled out into the street.

He just smiled.

"Are you kidnapping me?" she asked.

"Eat your muffins."

"You mean *your* muffins." But she opened the bag and happily busied herself eating them.

Twenty minutes later, they pulled into a huge parking complex for some biotech company. Spence flashed his ID at the guard gate.

"Where are we?" she asked.

"Mission District." He pulled to a far corner of a vast parking lot and got out of the truck. Before she could figure out what he meant to do, he came around, opened her door, unbuckled her, and lifted her, then dropped her behind the wheel.

"I don't know how to drive," she said.

"We're going to change that. Number nine on your list, remember?"

She blinked, even as a surge of excitement barreled through her. She was going to learn how to drive! "I hope you have good insurance."

CHAPTER 15
#SonOfABiscuit

Spence had thought it'd be fun to teach Colbie how to drive. Turned out *fun* wasn't quite the right word.

Terrifying would've been a better one.

Or here were two. *Living. Nightmare.*

She stomped on the brake and he practically kissed the windshield. He was still peeling his face off the glass when she hit the gas, knocking the back of his head into the seat rest . . .

"Whoops," she said and jammed *both* feet on the brake.

Shaking his head from the whiplash, he put a hand on her arm to stop her.

"I'm sorry," she said. "Your pedals are a little touchy."

Uh-huh. "Try sweet-talking it into doing your bidding," he suggested. "Ease it gently into following your whim. You do that and it'll give you a helluva good ride."

Colbie slid him a look. "Are you aware

that sometimes the things you say sound dirty? You want me to sweet-talk what exactly into giving me a good ride — your truck or your favorite body part?"

He grinned. "Honey, you can sweet-talk my favorite body part anytime you want. Now put *one* foot on the brake and then the truck back in drive."

She put her left foot on the brake pedal.

"Other foot," he said.

She switched to her right foot. "I've always thought that seems dumb," she said. "Why not use a foot for each pedal?"

"Because it works out better for the engine — and my neck — if you don't try to use both the gas and the brake at the same time."

"Oh," she said. "Good point." She paused. "You do know that I have no idea what I'm doing, right?"

"I'm getting that," he said. "Didn't you ever ride the bumper cars at the fair? Or Autopia at Disneyland?"

"No. But one time my brother stole an ATV. He joyrode it home and I had to drive it back."

"And how did that go?"

She didn't answer.

He glanced over and grinned at the flash

of guilt on her face. "Let me guess. Not good."

"I hit the gas too hard, did a wheelie, and fell off the back," she said and winced. "Got a concussion."

He had an arm stretched out along the back of the seats and slid his hand up the nape of her neck to palm and cradle her head. "We're not going to do that today," he said.

"Thought you didn't make promises you couldn't keep."

"I don't. Now hold the brake down and put it in drive," he said again. "You're going to be fine."

His voice was purposefully low. Authoritative. Calm.

Which in turn appeared to calm her. She held a foot down on the brake and put the truck into drive.

"Now slowly let off the brake," he said, "and ease on the gas. Emphasis on *ease.*"

She didn't exactly ease, but hey, she didn't stomp either, and then they were making their way across the empty lot, weaving because she was checking out the complicated-looking GPS system on the dash.

"You've got this thing rigged for a Mars excursion," she said.

"Watch the road, not the screen," he warned, eyeing the planter along the parking lot, the one lined with full-grown trees.

"No, but seriously, what are all these gadgets for?"

"I'll tell you later." They were getting closer to the trees. "Honey, watch the road."

"I'm not on the road. We're in a parking lot."

"Which is a good thing considering you're taking up the equivalent of four lanes. Going to have to lock it down to graduate to the road."

"How's this? Better?"

He paused.

She risked a look at him.

He grimaced. "Yes?"

"Wow," she said, shaking her head. "You're a really bad liar."

"Maybe because I'm distracted by the planter you're heading for. Trees, Colbie. Lots of trees."

"Son of a biscuit!" She swerved wildly, then slammed the brakes so that they both came up against their seatbelts hard enough to rattle some teeth loose.

"Huh," she said. "You know, this really isn't nearly as easy as it looks."

"Some people aren't meant for driving," he said. "Some people maybe have other talents."

She had to laugh. "Like ordering an Uber?"

"There's no shame in that."

On her fifth time around the lot, she'd gotten the hang of things. Somewhat. Sure, she'd mistakenly driven up and over a concrete planter and maybe killed a few daisies while she was at it. And okay, so she'd also left a good amount of rubber on the asphalt when she'd accidentally executed a burnout, but she hadn't crashed into anything.

Yet.

She was working on controlling her speed, going too fast into a tight turn, when a whoop of a siren and a flash of blue and red lights came from behind them.

"Uh-oh," she said, looking wild — and wide-eyed.

The security guard came to the driver's side window and bent down to look at first Colbie and then Spence. "What's with the Indy 500 act?"

"I'm learning how to drive," Colbie told him.

"Are you sure?" the cop asked.

"Yes!" Colbie sighed. "I'm just not all that good at it yet."

"You broke about ten driving laws just now."

"She's not on the street," Spence said. "We're on private property."

"True enough," the security guard said. "But someone called it in from the building. Said there were two stupid teenagers in the lot acting crazy and probably smoking pot." He lifted a brow and eyed Spence. "You in charge here?"

"Yes."

"Actually," Colbie said, "I'm in charge of myself."

Spence produced a badge and the officer took it, studied it, and then returned it. "I'm sorry, sir," the guy said. "I didn't recognize you. Have a good one." And then he left.

Colbie looked at Spence in disbelief. "What was that?"

"What was what?" he asked.

"He acted like you own this place."

"That's because I do."

She stared at him. "You're like one of those really great cinnamon twists we had the other day in Union Square. Lots of surprising layers I didn't see coming."

"Right back at you," Spence said. "And I bet, like the rolls, you're also sweet and good to eat."

She squirmed in her seat and blushed.

"You don't know that."

He smiled. "I have a good imagination."

At Spence's words, Colbie's face felt like it was having a hot flash. Then Spence — smiling because he seemed to know exactly what he did to her — leaned in excruciatingly slowly, until his lips just brushed hers.

Colbie's hot flash spread to every single inch of her body. The anticipation of his touch was enough to galvanize her into reaching up and tearing off his glasses.

His smile widened and he finally kissed her, making her moan in pleasure. And he kept kissing her too, until they'd steamed up the windows and had gotten their hands on each other in ways that made it hard to breathe, when Spence pressed his forehead to hers.

"Not here," he said, voice so low as to be barely audible.

She heard herself give a little mewl of protest and then another in pure pleasure when his hands, one inside her shirt and the other up her skirt, caressed bare, heated skin.

"I'm not taking you in a parking lot," he said and nipped her lower lip. "Not for our first time."

So many things to quiver over. One, that

he clearly assumed there'd be more than one time. Two, that she was bad off enough that she started to argue the point. "But —"

With a husky laugh, he put his finger over her mouth. "There's security on the property, including cameras. The last thing either of us needs is a sex tape on YouTube." He lifted her out of the driver seat, put his glasses back on, and took over.

She barely remembered getting back because he had his hand on her thigh and that was all she could think about, that and also the way the rough pads of his fingers felt on her skin as he stroked it while driving.

After he parked at the Pacific Pier Building and came around for her, they collided and kissed right there on the sidewalk, Spence pressing her up against the truck until his phone buzzed.

He straightened his glasses and ripped the phone from his pocket. "What?" His gaze slid to hers, his mouth very slightly curved as he listened and then disconnected.

"What?" she asked.

"I have tight security on this building too. Joe's on the monitors and got worried that I might actually swallow your tonsils."

She smiled. "I don't have any tonsils."

With a laugh, he took her hand and they

moved through the courtyard and into the elevator. She stood next to him and tilted her face to his, looking at his mouth.

He groaned. "Stop."

"Cameras in here too?"

"Yeah. Remind me to rethink that," he said, cupping her face, running the pad of his thumb over her lower lip, his eyes heavy lidded.

Somehow they got to his floor, where he tugged her off the elevator, his stride so fast that she nearly had to run to keep up with him.

They tumbled inside his place, where he pressed her up against the foyer table and kissed her. She got his jacket off his shoulders but it caught on his forearms because he was simultaneously divesting her of her coat and scarf. Giving up on his jacket, she started pushing up his T-shirt, laughing breathlessly when they both went to kick off their shoes and tripped over each other, crashing into the wall.

"No cameras in here, right?" she asked against his mouth.

"Not a one." He was down to just pants now, and since he'd left her dress puddled on the floor, she was in her bra and panties when he stilled, his eyes glazing over as he took in the midnight blue see-through lace.

"You're the most beautiful thing I've ever seen," he said roughly, catching her hands, holding them out at her sides. "I could look at you all night."

The fire in his eyes did things to her. As did the telling bulge behind his zipper. "Me too. I mean" — she grimaced at herself — "I could look at *you* all night too."

He flashed a grin. "You're nervous."

"What? Of course not," she denied and then closed her eyes. "Okay, yes. I'm incredibly nervous. It's . . . been a while."

"Don't be. Maybe I'm really bad at this."

She laughed helplessly. "You're not."

"You don't know," he said. "Maybe I'm the one who's nervous. Go easy on me, okay?"

"Okay," she whispered, not buying this for one second but finding it incredibly sweet that he wanted her to be at ease.

Sweet and incredibly sexy. Needing a moment, she turned away, grasping the foyer desk, dropping her head, struggling to control herself.

Spence came up behind her, his hands skimming up her arms. She was so turned on by the feel of him surrounding her that she pressed her bottom into him, and this time it was his groan to echo in the apartment as he slowly circled her waist with his hands.

Using his jaw to sweep her hair aside, he brushed a kiss to her ear and then to the sensitive spot just beneath it as he pressed a hand flat to her belly to keep their bodies lined up.

She wanted him so bad that she had a death grip on the desk as she ground into him. When his hands slid north, her head fell back against his shoulder, her body trembling for his touch.

Her bra hit the floor. His hands came up to cup her freed breasts in his warm palms, his thumbs sliding slowly over her nipples, making her shudder. She was panting, unable to get control, and she was torn between embarrassment at her reaction to him and sheer lust. Sheer lust won when she felt his mouth on the nape of her neck before he turned her in his arms and captured her mouth in his.

She kissed him back, slow and deep, feeling more turned on than she'd ever felt in her life as he lifted her up against him and started walking.

The next thing she knew, she was flat on her back on his bed. "Um," she said, and he stilled, a question in his eyes. "I'm so nervous I might forget my moves," she said.

"I feel like this is my first time."

His lips curved in a dark, sexy smile. "This is going to be better than your first time," he promised.

"How do you know?"

He finished stripping and she stopped breathing as she watched. He grabbed something from a drawer. A condom. Good. At least one of them was thinking. She reached for him, pulling him down over top of her, wrapping her legs around his hips.

"Not yet," he said. "You're not ready —"

She reached down and guided him home. He said her name in protest, in pleasure, in surprise . . . She understood that last one because nothing surprised her more than the feel of him taking over, filling her to the hilt, and moving inside her so exquisitely that she came almost instantly.

"Not any good at this, huh?" she managed when she found her tongue.

Spence buried his face in her throat and both laughed and groaned. "Christ, Colbie." His voice was guttural and strained. "You feel so good. So fucking good that I don't want to ever stop."

"Then don't." She matched him thrust for thrust as they moved together, and she knew the truth, that it was *him* that felt so good because she didn't want to ever stop either.

"Colbie."

She managed to look at him as he took her hands in his, entwining their fingers on either side of her head, pressing her into the mattress as he moved inside her, taking her places she'd never been. His eyes held hers prisoner, watching, coaxing, his voice a low sexy murmur as she came again, or still. Their gazes were locked as her third — or was it fourth? — orgasm triggered his so that he came with her, her name on his lips as he finally let himself go.

It was the most erotic experience of her life.

CHAPTER 16
#HairyGoats

For several nights, Colbie slept better than she had in . . . well, forever actually. And not just because in the deep, late, quiet hours between midnight and daybreak, Spence always came to her after he was done working, sliding into her bed, pulling her into his strong, warm arms.

That's when all her problems faded away, replaced by an erotic, sensual hunger and desire for him such as she'd never known.

She always woke up alone, with a smile on her face. She had no idea why he never stayed. Maybe actually sleeping with her was one step too intimate for him. Maybe she snored.

Maybe it was just sex.

She told herself she didn't care, that he was still the best, most exciting thing that'd ever happened to her.

One morning almost two weeks into her stay, she sat all bundled up on one of the benches in front of the fountain and wrote.

And wrote.

She was painfully aware that the book she was writing wasn't the next book in her Storm Fever series.

It was something entirely different. But she loved it.

She also knew that Jackson would have a fit. On top of wanting her out there in public supporting the movie in a very visible way, he also wanted her to do what her publisher wished and expand her series.

Problem was, *she* didn't want any of that.

She'd closed up the series in her head and her brain just wouldn't go there. So she let her writing take her where it wanted to go, and she was completely lost in the world when someone plopped down beside her.

"Longest day ever," Kylie said and slumped on the bench, tilting her head against the wrought-iron to stare up at the sky. "Today alone I messed up a table I'd been working on for four months, said no to a date with a hot customer, and ate my boss's stash of candy bars. I think I'm going to hell."

"Why did you say no to the hot customer?"

"Because he's married."

"Then you're not going to hell," Colbie said.

"But the candy bars —"

"Hey, you did your boss a favor, saved him from getting fat."

"The top button on my jeans won't close." Kylie groaned and closed her eyes. "But thanks. You're sweet. Got anything for me on the table I messed up?"

"Nothing other than it sucks big-time."

"Yeah." Kylie opened her eyes and sat up. "All this crappiness has got me starving. I need sustenance."

"Did I hear someone mention food?" a twenty-something woman in a white lab coat asked, stopping at their bench.

"This is Haley," Kylie told Colbie. "She's an optometrist on the second floor. She's the one responsible for Spence's hot geeky glasses, and also for being the voice of calm reason in our group."

"We're going for food," she told Haley. "Coming?"

"Can't. I've got patients waiting. Have some wings for me, would ya?"

"Will do." Kylie stood and pulled Colbie off the bench, tugging her toward the pub. "Chicken wings. Life won't be complete until I inhale a platter of Finn's chicken wings."

The pub was packed and Finn was pulling out his hair. "Down a waitress," he called to them. "I'll get to you soon as I can."

Colbie watched him and Sean struggle to keep up with the crowd by themselves and stood up.

"What are you doing?" Kylie asked.

"I can't watch."

"I can." Kylie took in Sean bending to pick up a pallet of clean glasses, the muscles of his shoulders and back bunching beneath his T-shirt, not to mention his jeans going taut over a first-class ass.

Colbie waved Finn down, and he came over, looking distracted.

"Let me help you," she said. She slid behind the bar and pulled on an apron. "I've waitressed before."

Gratitude and worry warred on his face. "Are you sure —"

"Yep. Now go cook . . . whatever it is you're cooking." And she hit the tables. Delivering the drinks turned out to be easy. It was remembering to check if the food orders were ready that was a problem. Mostly this was because she found herself busy eavesdropping on conversations, fascinated by the slices of life she heard.

". . . And so he admitted he had an extra

testicle . . ."

". . . Apparently, doing the boss's boss is the only way to the top . . ."

". . . Remember that time we took out the wrong colon?"

Colbie kept stopping to write down notes for herself so she wouldn't forget anything. Problem was, she was using her order pad and stuffing the notes into her pockets and getting them mixed up with actual orders.

"Hey," Finn called when she dropped off two new orders in the kitchen. "What's this?"

"Um . . . two orders of sweet potato fries?" she asked.

"No, it says 'extra testicle.' " He looked up at her, brows raised.

Horrified, Colbie snatched back the note and stuffed it into her pocket while pulling out her other notes to try to find the missing order. A cascade of slips fell from her pocket. *"Hairy goats!"*

Finn stared at her. The entire kitchen staff stared at her.

And then they all burst out laughing.

"Tell me the truth," Finn said, grinning. "You've never been a waitress a day in your life, have you?"

"Hey, I was so a waitress!" She sighed. "For a while. Before I got fired . . ." She turned to get back out there and came face-to-face with Elle.

Who stood there looking killer in an ice blue dress that outlined her very outline-able curves.

Spence came in behind her and flashed a grin at Colbie. "Waitressing?"

"Helping out Sean and Finn." She grimaced. "And not doing a really great job of it."

"Are you kidding?" Sean asked. "You've been more entertaining than anything we've seen all season. You're great," he said, giving her a one-armed hug before moving out to the bar.

"Hey," Finn called out from behind the grill, waving another order. "Who's doing the boss's boss? Is that code for something actually on our menu?"

Colbie grimaced again, snatched the paper back, and headed to the tables. She served Spence and Elle and Kylie, and afterward, when she'd cleared their dishes, Spence stood up and wrapped his fingers around her wrist. He tugged her in and gave her a goodbye kiss so hot that she nearly self-combusted on the spot, and while she was trying to remember her name, he walked off, but not before leaving her a tip.

A huge tip.

This gave her a flash of something she hadn't seen coming — guilt. He'd left her so much cash because he thought she needed the money. Which reminded her that while they'd grown closer over the past two weeks, very close, she'd left out a big piece of herself by not telling him who she was.

But the truth was she'd not intended to tell him. This had started out as a diversion, on both their parts, so it hadn't been necessary.

But it'd become more for her, much more, and suddenly, she *wanted* him to know. "Spence?"

He turned and met her gaze.

"Dinner tonight?" she asked.

"Sure," he said. "I'll come get you at seven."

"No, *I'll* come get *you,*" she said. "It's *my* turn to cook."

His mouth curved and the smile was in his voice as well. "I'll be ready."

When she was done pitching in, Finn and Sean handed her an envelope of cash.

"Wow," Colbie said, counting through it. "Can I come work here every day?"

"Hell yeah," Sean said.

"I'm sorry but hell no," Finn said. "You're great to look at and my customers loved you, but please, God, don't come back to work tomorrow."

Chapter 17
#HolyMacAndCheese

Colbie left the pub and walked across the courtyard. She had an hour to rejuvenate herself for her date with Spence, figure out how exactly to tell him about her pseudonym, and worry about if by doing so, she was about to blow the best thing that had happened to her in forever.

After all, ruining one's life did run in her family.

What was it that made some people good at loving those in their lives and others self-destruct those same relationships — as her mom had with every relationship she'd ever been in? And though Colbie had always assumed she was nothing like her dad, she was starting to fear that wasn't true at all. That in spite of herself, genes were genes.

She was thinking how much she hated that as she walked by the alley and Old Man Eddie flagged her down with a wave.

"What's up, dudette?"

"Nothing much," she said.

He shook his head. "No use lying to Old Man Eddie." He tapped a finger to his temple. "I know all. And I know you're . . . off."

She had to laugh. "If that's true, then you tell me why."

"Simple," he said and stared into her eyes. "You're hiding your true self."

"What?" she asked, startled at the truth of that statement.

"Yeah, you're walking with your shoulders up to your ears and your eyes are on your feet when you walk. That tells me you're closed off, not wanting to share yourself. You're hiding from the world and probably yourself."

She blinked.

He smiled. "So what did you think I meant? I've got a feeling whatever you're hiding is better than that bullshit I just made up."

Ha. He hadn't been all that far from the mark. "Nothing. I'm just . . . tired. And maybe a little stressed." Or you know, a lot. "I'm not hiding anything. At all. Why would I? Hide anything, that is."

"Hmm. Say it one more time and maybe I'll believe you." His smile was kind as he patted the bench next to him.

She sighed and sat. "You're deceptively laid-back, but you're not really laid-back at all, are you?" she asked. "You're sharp as a knife."

He laughed. "Here," he said, and held out a clear plastic bag filled with brownies. "You need one."

In the very worst possible way. So she took a brownie and dove in.

"So," he said, smiling as she inhaled it and licked her fingers. "About that thing you're hiding . . ."

She waggled a finger at him and eyed the baggie of brownies again.

"Not yet," Eddie said. "Let the first one settle another minute first. These are a rather potent batch."

She swallowed and stared at him as his meaning sank in. "You mean . . ."

He smiled.

"But . . ." She trailed off, a little horrified. She'd smoked a few times in college. She'd been a total and completely embarrassing lightweight who'd spent the rest of the day giggling and eating everything in sight.

Old Man Eddie shrugged.

Colbie narrowed her eyes. "Eddie, did I or did I not just eat a . . ." she lowered her voice ". . . 'special' brownie?"

"It's actually more like a space cake."

She just stared at him.

"It's cooked with cannabutter, see, which is butter that's been heated in a pan with —"

"Holy macaroni and cheese!" She covered her ears. "Don't tell me."

"It's okay." He pulled a lanyard from beneath his sweatshirt, with his laminated medical marijuana card attached. "It's legal. I've got a card and everything."

She dropped her hands. "But *I* don't have a card!"

"This is California. You won't need one soon enough."

"Okay," she said, taking a deep breath. "It's going to be okay." She gave herself a mental checkup. "And besides, I don't feel weird at all." Which, she could admit to herself, was the teeniest, tiniest bummer. She took another breath and nodded. Yep, she was fine.

She looked at Eddie, who also looked fine. Ish.

How had he gone from whatever life he'd led to living in the alley? she wondered. Did he have a family he'd left behind, like her dad? "I've got a question," she said.

"No worries. The only real calories come from the butter —"

"No, a question about *you,*" she said.

"Research?"

"Yes," she said. "But it's personal." She paused. "My dad's not in the picture. By choice."

"Ah." He nodded. "And you're wondering if I have a family whose picture I'm not in."

"I know a lot of homeless people are homeless because they have mental illness, mostly untreated. But you seem . . ."

His mouth quirked. "Normal?"

"Well, not entirely," she said and made him laugh.

"An honest woman," he said. "I like it. And yeah, I've chosen to live like this and not because of mental issues. Although I can't claim to be entirely sane." His smile faded. "The truth is, I wasn't so good at being a father and husband. And when I say I wasn't good, I really mean that I was bad."

The brownie suddenly felt like lead in her gut. "Did you hurt them?"

"Not like you think, not physically." He shook his head. "Never physically. But . . ." He closed his eyes. "I'm not proud of this, dudette. I worked around the clock, away from home. Traveled all the time. And the few times I wasn't gone, I was still in my head, exhausted and grumpy." He paused. "I was a self-centered, narcissistic asshole who didn't give my kid or my wife the time of day."

"Did they leave you?"

"No. I left them." He looked at her then, and she tried to swipe away the judgment that she knew was all over her face but she was pretty sure she failed because he gave a slow head shake.

"I wasn't this laid-back then," he said. "I was . . . uptight. Stressed out." His eyes flickered with guilt. "Derisive. I came home and my son was in the yard riding his bike without a care in the world. I went off on his lack of drive, the ridiculousness of time wasting, and how life was too short to waste it doing jackshit where he could be out there changing the world for the better like I thought I was doing." He shook his head and closed his eyes. "I didn't realize I was yelling and screaming until my wife tried to pull me inside. I turned on her as well. I had them both in tears and shaking in fear when I came to my senses and realized what I was doing."

"What happened?" she whispered.

"I left that night. I walked away, leaving them better off." He closed his eyes. "Most of my family never forgave me. Just my grandson, whose big heart has a lot to do with the fact that he never saw me at my very worst."

"He sounds like a good guy."

Eddie looked at her. "He is. I live here because of him. He thinks he's taking care of me, but the truth is, I'm here watching over him because, of all the people in my family, he's the most like me. The most likely to follow in my footsteps and ruin his life. I can't let him do it. He's a lot of things, including way too smart for his own good and thinking he's always right, but . . ." he smiled ". . . he *is* always right. And he deserves more than following in my foot-steps."

She stilled. "Spence. Your grandson is Spence."

"Yeah." There was pride and fondness in Eddie's eyes, but also more.

"You're worried about him," she said, and when he nodded, she asked, "Is that why you stay here? In the alley?"

Eddie laughed. "You sound horrified. I like it out here, you know. Spence has kept an apartment open for me since he bought this place, and though it's filled temporarily at the moment . . ." he gave her a knowing wink ". . . I know he'd find me something else if I needed. But I don't."

"Because . . . you're punishing yourself?"

He met her gaze, his own unusually solemn and serious. "You've got to understand just how much I royally screwed up my life. At every turn, I made bad choices — until a few years ago. Somehow I managed to turn things around, at least a little, and Spence brought me here. He's surrounded himself with a nice, cozy community here in this building. He's trying, you see."

"Trying . . ."

"To not be me," Eddie said.

Colbie stared at him as things started to click into place. About who Spence was, what he wanted out of life, and how, no matter what he said, he *didn't* want to be alone. That, in fact, being alone was one of his biggest fears.

"He's the closest now to getting what he needs than he's ever been," Eddie said. "Because of you."

"Me?"

"Yeah, you. You're the one who's shown him he can love."

"Oh, but you're wrong," she breathed softly, the air escaping her lungs. "We're not . . . I'm not the One."

"But you are."

"No," she said. "I'm not. I'm a writer. I'm . . . flighty. Quirky. Odd. I got on an airplane to San Francisco because I couldn't get to the Caribbean. I'm disorganized and more than a little crazy."

He smiled. "You're perfect."

"You've eaten too many of your own brownies."

"True. But you're still the right one for my Spence."

Colbie shook her head. "I'm going home soon. In a week, actually." The words, spoken aloud, made things seem far too real, and sadness welled up inside her chest. "Wow," she whispered. "Time went by so fast here."

"So stay," he said simply.

"I can't. I have people counting on me."

"No one can make you do anything you don't want to do," he said. "Well, except for maybe a prison warden."

"Or family," she said.

He laughed wryly. "Touché. I'd do anything for my grandson, including watching him make a big mistake by letting you go, simply because his only stipulation to me being here was that I not interfere in his life. I gave my word."

Colbie was undoubtedly high as a kite because that actually made some sense. "I'd think he'd be proud to be like the man you are now, loving and caring."

"You're very sweet," Eddie said softly. "But I didn't tell you what made me turn things around. I fell in love again. Me and Mati had six great months before I lost her."

"Oh no," Colbie breathed. "She passed away?"

"No, she left. I'd finally met someone more screwed up than me." He smiled wryly. "The wanderlust took her and she had to go. I could've gone with her but . . ."

"But what?"

"It was time for me to be here, with my family." His eyes were fierce with love and memories, and shiny with pain. "So I had to let her go. Just as my family had let me go all those years ago. It's what you do for those you love. But for the first time, I knew their pain. Still, those six months were the greatest months of my life. For once, work wasn't the focus of my world. Love was. And I promised myself I'd stick by Spence until he learned the same thing."

"But sometimes people have to make their own mistakes," she said, knowing this from personal experience. Because she'd walked away from her family. Same as her dad, same as Eddie.

But she now knew what Eddie also knew, that family was family. Even if you got stupid and walked, you went back. No matter what. And that's what she would do too. Go back. Even if she didn't want to. Suddenly sad, and just as suddenly ravenous, she put her hands to her stomach. "I've gotta go."

"Where to?"

"To eat. I'm starving."

He smiled and held out the bag. "I've got ya covered."

Chapter 18
#FudgeADuck

When Colbie didn't show up at Spence's like she'd said she would, he figured she'd gotten caught up in her pages and lost track of time.

Something he understood all too well.

He waited another half hour before losing patience. He wasn't a good waiter. He took the stairs down to her place and knocked on her door, but she didn't answer that either.

He stood there for a few minutes, wondering for the first time if maybe he was being stood up.

Ten minutes later, he decided that, yep, he was definitely being stood up.

Which sucked. They'd managed to spend a fair amount of time together in spite of the fact that they were both working a lot — which he often gave thought to deep in the night while holding her in his arms.

And something else he'd spent a fair

amount of time doing? Arguing with himself whenever he left her bed. It was getting harder and harder to walk away. He'd been telling himself all along that this expiration date of theirs was a good thing.

But he no longer believed it. The truth was that he wasn't ready for her to leave and was pretty sure he'd never be ready for her to leave.

He made his way to the courtyard and poked his head into the alley to ask Eddie if he'd seen her.

And there she was, sitting with the old man, junk food wrappers scattered all around them like the living dead.

"What the hell?" He looked at his grandpa. "Tell me you didn't get high and rob a convenience store with my girlfriend in tow."

Colbie gasped at the sight of Spence and jumped up. "Fudge a duck!" She looked at her watch, squinting to read it. "It's seven forty-five? How did that happen?"

"Well," Eddie said. "The earth revolves around the sun, see, and —"

"I was supposed to pick Spence up at seven!" she whispered furiously to Eddie. "I'm late! I'm never late! Should I call him?"

Eddie grinned. "Or you could just turn around and talk to him."

"Wait — he can see us?" she asked, horrified, eyes nearly bugging out of her head. *"We're not invisible?"*

"Christ," Spence said.

She whirled to face him. "I'm so sorry! I don't know where the time went!"

He looked into her stoner red eyes and had to laugh. "I do."

She flushed. "We got caught up . . . talking."

"Uh-huh." Spence looked over her head at Eddie and his mouth tightened. "You butted in."

Eddie shrugged, the gesture apparently so Spence-like that Colbie clapped a hand to her mouth. "I see it now," she said behind her fingers. "The similarities."

Spence added disbelief to his anger. "You told her?"

"That you're way too smart for your own good and you think you're always right?" Eddie asked. "Yeah, I told her, but I don't think she was all that surprised."

Spence was not amused, but Colbie put her hand on his arm. "I think it's incredibly sweet that you have your grandpa here, taking care of him like you do."

"Darlin', you've got that backward," Eddie said with a grin at Spence.

Colbie slipped her arm in Spence's and

looked up at him with sweet worry. "I really am so sorry," she said. "I never do this, forget the time. Or a date. Well, okay, so I forget dates when I don't wanna go, but this wasn't one of those times." She paused. "I got hungry."

Spence eyed the empty candy and chip wrappers. "I see that." He turned and met Eddie's nonsheepish gaze. "We'll talk later."

Eddie sent him a mocking salute.

"Oh please don't be upset with him," Colbie said earnestly. "It was my idea to have the second brownie —"

"You had more than one?" Spence asked and looked at his grandpa.

Eddie had the good grace to look slightly shamed. "She was really hungry."

Spence shook his head, trying to let it go. The fact was, he and Eddie rarely saw eye-to-eye, and actually, that was all on Spence anyway. He'd never completely forgiven his grandpa for basically deserting his dad and grandma.

The resentment was in direct opposition to Spence's need to still keep Eddie safe, but since the guy insisted on living on the streets, it was an unfulfilled need. It'd taken him a long time to accept his grandpa's unconventional lifestyle, or so he'd always thought. But the truth — the rather appalling truth — was that Spence was far too much like Eddie for his own comfort.

"I'm sorry," Eddie said quietly, and Spence stared at him in shock. He'd never heard those words from him before. He didn't want to be moved, but like Spence himself, Eddie never said anything he didn't mean. Spence nodded his appreciation of the statement and took Colbie up to her apartment. He had no idea what she'd planned for them but whatever it was, she was going to need a minute.

Or a few hours . . .

"I can't find my key," she said at her door, head bent, searching through her mess of a bag.

Spence took her hand and looked her over. She seemed okay. Her hair had fallen in her face, which was flushed because she was overheated and probably dizzy as hell. He gently pushed it from her eyes. "I can't believe you ate the brownie."

"Brownies," she said, emphasis on the *s*. "As in plural. And I knew better too, but . . ." She trailed off guiltily.

"I know. He can be deceptively sweet and persuasive." *And a menace . . .*

"Yes!" she said. "He's so wonderful!"

Not the exact word Spence would have used. He took her purse and tried to find her keys, but all he saw was her wallet and notes upon notes. "Come on," he said. "I'll get you another key, but for now we'll go to my place."

"But I went grocery shopping to make you dinner," she said. "I went on an empty stomach too, so I'm now the proud owner of aisles three through twelve."

He laughed because damn, she was a really cute stoner. "We'll figure it out." He took her up two flights, opened his door, and ushered her in.

"I like this place," she said. "It's serene and quiet. But you really need some pictures and personal stuff. Hey, are my feet touching the ground or am I floating?"

He sighed and she laughed. "Okay, never mind. I only float after a few margaritas. Hey, do you have any idea how lovely I think it is that you take care of your grandpa like you do?"

"Says the woman who takes care of her entire family," he said.

She pointed at him. "Touché. I like him, by the way. A lot. Is he a secret?"

"No," Spence said. "I just . . ." He shook his head. "I guess I feel like I've failed him by not getting him off the street."

"No," she said, shaking her head. "Do you want to know why I love your grandpa so much? Because we're kindred spirits. Like him, I always truly believed I'd be happier alone. It was actually a huge fantasy of mine all my life. When I was growing up, all I wanted was to *not* live with two brothers and my mom in that teeny, tiny one-bedroom, one-bathroom hovel we grew up in, where I never had a single inch of space to myself. Being alone has always sounded like heaven, just me and my computer and my imagination. But this trip . . ." She shook her head. "I had it all wrong, Spence."

He ran a finger along her temple, tucking a loose strand of hair back from her face. "Yeah?"

"Yeah." Stepping into him, she ran a hand up his chest. "And you've got a lot to do with that. I learned some things from you."

He pulled her into him and nuzzled his face in the crook of her neck. "I learned something too," he admitted. "Something I didn't see coming."

She slid her hands into his hair. "What's that?"

It took him a moment to find the right words. "For most of my life," he finally said, "I wanted to change my grandpa. Make him . . . I don't know, normal, I guess. Then when I bought this place and coerced him into moving here, I expected him to take an apartment. I had no idea how to help him, how to keep him safe. I just did the best I could. And in the end, he's the one who helped me. He taught me acceptance."

"Acceptance?"

"Letting people be who they need to be," he said. "Including myself."

She nodded. "I like that. I've always micromanaged my mom and siblings, setting up their lives how I thought best. They let me but . . . I haven't done them any favors."

"It's never too late to change."

She met his gaze, hers open and sincere, and nodded. "Why don't you have any Christmas decorations?"

The abrupt subject change reminded him that she was pretty toasted. "I do," he said. "You just can't see them because you're stoned."

She laughed. "You're funny. Hey, do you have food?"

"I have anything you want."

Her eyes were big and luminous. "Anything?" she asked, whispered really, looking very intrigued.

He smiled. "Are we playing?"

She bit her lower lip.

Yeah. They were playing.

"I need to get ready to feed you. But I

need a shower first." She sidled up to his front, giving him a very inviting smile, her eyes seeming to strip him naked.

Which he was totally okay with.

She ran her hands up his chest and around the back of his neck, lightly scraping her fingernails up into his hair, giving him goose bumps, among other things.

"Can I use your gym shower?" she asked. "Or am I allowed in your personal space now that you've had your merry way with me? Many times over now . . ." She brushed her mouth across his earlobe, laughing softly in his ear when he tightened his grip on her hips.

And then suddenly she had like eight hands and they were *everywhere.* "Colbie —"

"Colbie," she said, mimicking his lower tone. "You sound very serious now, Spence. Have I been bad? Am I in trouble?"

Jesus. He nudged — maybe pushed — her into his bedroom.

"Ooh, the man cave," she purred.

— And then into his bathroom. He gave her another nudge toward the shower and tried to step out.

"Where are you going?" she asked.

"To order food."

"What kind of food?"

"All the food," he said. "Unless you have a preference. What are you hungry for?"

She smiled a man-eating smile and he groaned.

And got harder.

He pointed at her. "Behave." And then he left the bathroom, shutting the door behind him. He leaned back against it and swiped his forehead. "I'm fucked."

"Yes. I'm pretty sure that's her plan."

Spence turned his head and found Caleb standing there, eating out of another Tupperware that Spence knew damn well had come from his fridge. "What the hell?"

Caleb shoved in a bite of what looked like Trudy's famous chicken enchiladas and groaned in pleasure. "Turns out that Colbie's not the only one who's hungry."

"How long have you been here?" Spence demanded.

"Since before you. Neither of you even noticed me. And why are you standing here griping at me for eating your food instead of getting into the shower with the Stoned One? She's hot."

Spence opened his front door and jerked his chin toward it.

Caleb blew out a breath. "Fine. But I'm taking the enchiladas with me." He turned back. "And you're an idiot if you don't go take what that woman is offering you."

Spence shut the door on Caleb's nosy nose just as Colbie came out of his bathroom. She was wearing the bathrobe his mom had bought him a couple of Christmases ago that he'd never worn — and bright blue toenail polish. That was it. He watched with a mix of lust and wry amusement as she sauntered straight to his pantry and helped herself to not one but three bags of chips.

She hopped up on the counter, opened all three bags, and began a smorgasbord, stuffing her face for a few solid minutes before going still, a handful of chips paused in the air halfway to her mouth. "I think I'm a little stoned."

He smiled. "You think?"

"No, I mean . . ." She shook her head. "I was sure I wasn't. I didn't feel anything."

"Honey, you're about as high as my drone can fly, which is nearly out of the stratosphere."

She ate a few more chips, closing her eyes and groaning. "Oh. My. God. Where have . . . ?" She straightened out one of the bags and read the label. "Salt and vinegar. Where have salt and vinegar chips been hiding my whole life?"

Spence took a bottle of water from the

fridge, removed the top, and handed it over to her.

She downed it and then went back to the chips. "You don't by any chance have any dip, do you?"

"No. But . . ." Spence pulled out a stack of takeout menus and handed them to her. "Take your pick and I'll order."

She tossed the menus aside and grabbed him by the shirt and hauled him in close. "I want to order *you*. You smell so good, Spence. You always smell so good."

He planted a hand on either side of her hips to keep an arm's length between them, but she had a good grip on his shirt with one hand, her other placed precariously low on his abs. Wrapping her legs around his waist to further trap him, she crossed her ankles at the small of his back.

"Colbie." He both laughed and groaned. "You said you're hungry."

"Yes, but not for food." She pressed her face against his throat and inhaled him like he was a ten-course meal.

His entire body went on high alert, sensing action within its grasp. He slid his hands up her arms to take ahold of her wrists, bringing them down to her sides.

"Mmmm," she said, taking a lick of him as she wriggled. "I don't remember feeling this . . . trembly with anyone else. You'd think I'd remember, right? I mean, sex is always nice and all, but this, with you, it feels a lot more than nice." She lifted her head, her eyes guileless and a little worried. "Do you know what I mean?"

He did, although he felt like he was eavesdropping on her personal thoughts, letting her tell him things like that when she was under the influence. "Colbie —"

"Uh-oh," she said. "You *don't* know what I mean. Well, that's embarrassing." She tried to shift away but he caught her.

"No, I do," he said. He knew exactly. "But, Colbie —"

She wriggled against him some more, during which time he kept a tight grip on her because if he let her go, he was afraid of what she'd convince him to do. "You're not yourself," he said. "I don't want to take advantage, but I'm only human —" He broke off on a groan when she squirmed some more, humming when she came in contact with the proof of what she did to him, cradling him in the wedge between her thighs.

God help him. She was sexy and cute and sweet all in one package, and she had some moves too. "Honey —" He broke off when his phone buzzed an incoming call.

Colbie pulled back, eyes at half-mast as she smiled up at him. "You taste really good. You should answer your phone, Spence. Maybe your mom or grandpa needs you."

He didn't bother to point out that his family wasn't like hers. The Baldwins didn't need each other. They worked very hard to be independent. Stupidly so. Plus they'd just seen his grandpa. The man was a menace but fine.

"Seriously," Colbie said, her eyes so deep and earnest that he did what he'd told himself not to do again — he pulled out his phone and answered without looking at the screen. "Baldwin."

"Spence," a male voice said. "Don't hang up."

Spence stilled at the sound of Brandon's voice, then backed away from Colbie and turned from her.

"We need to talk," Brandon said.

"Sure. When hell freezes over."

"Seriously, man. My boss wants a follow-up, and I know what you're going to say but think about it. It could be really great for you too."

"You've got to be kidding me," Spence said.

Brandon dropped the charm. "Look, I did

you a favor with that article. I put you on the map with all the exposure."

"We were friends. You *knew* I didn't want any of it."

"If we'd been friends, I wouldn't have had to beg for the article in the first place. Look, you were the golden boy. A's in every class. All the teachers loved you, whatever. You were untouchable, man, never needing anyone or anything. So yeah, you threw me a bone and then gave me a boring interview that you could've given any Joe Blow, big fucking deal. The real sign of friendship would be you giving me a follow-up."

Spence actually laughed. "Do us both a favor, Brandon, and lose my number." He disconnected the call and then, for shits and giggles, blocked Brandon's number. When he shoved the phone away and turned back to Colbie, she was walking down the hall, clearly trying to give him privacy.

Which at the moment was the last thing he needed.

CHAPTER 19
#SonOfASeacock

Colbie walked into Spence's bathroom. The brownies were starting to wear off, leaving her tired and feeling bad about Spence. She'd gotten accidentally high, and possibly a little obnoxiously sexually aggressive, and she'd forgotten their date.

"Son of a seacock," she said, disrobing and then bending to pick up the clothes she'd left on the floor. They were wrinkled but they'd do, she thought, just as she heard Spence speak, his voice low and gravelly, like how it sounded whenever he was aroused. "And *cock* isn't a bad word?" he asked.

Whirling to him, she caught the slow scan of his eyes, making her incredibly aware of what she was wearing.

Or rather, not wearing. "Body parts aren't bad words," she whispered.

His expression made her hot in very specific places that she now knew he could

253

make *very* happy. He scooped up the robe and handed it to her.

"Sorry," she said, clutching it to her. "I was just going to get dressed."

His gaze locked in on something behind her and he groaned before coming toward her.

"The mirror," he said, his voice still a full octave lower than usual, which meant it was almost inaudibly gruff as he pulled the robe from her fingers to wrap it around her shoulders, waiting while she slid her arms into the sleeves before he belted it for her.

She craned her neck, caught sight of the full-length mirror that had most likely afforded him a hell of a view, especially when she'd bent over, and grimaced. "Holy Hostess."

He chuckled but his eyes were heated. Very, very heated.

"I left to give you some privacy for your call," she said. "It seemed . . ." *intense* ". . . private."

"Forget the call." He stroked her hair from her temple. "You still hungry?"

She nodded, suddenly a lot sober and also a little unsure of herself and her footing here. She'd come on pretty strong, and yet he hadn't made a move.

But in the times that they'd been together,

it'd all been magic and she wanted more of that magic. She'd hoped they'd continue to enjoy her last week in town to full capacity, but maybe he didn't feel the same way. She didn't realize she'd spoken that last part aloud until he spoke.

"Colbie. Look at me."

Nope. She didn't want to do that.

He pulled her in against him, slid his fingers into her hair, and tugged her face up to his.

She tried to pull away but . . . *"Oh,"* she breathed, feeling him hard as a rock against her.

"Yeah, proof positive. I want you so bad that I no longer have any blood left in my brain. By now you know that I'm not any more experienced at this navigating relationship stuff than you are, right? So maybe you could have some mercy on me for being a fumbling idiot. I was trying to be a good guy tonight."

She found a laugh and he stared at her, the corner of his mouth quirking slightly. "You think my condition's funny?" he asked.

"No, I think we're *both* idiots." She went up on tiptoes and kissed him. "I understand your restraint and while it's admirable, there's something you should know."

"What's that?"

"I *want* you to take advantage of me." She wrapped her arms around his neck and pressed into him. "And I want it bad too. I get that the proof of my wanting isn't as . . . *evident* as yours, but I'm quite certain you could find it if you searched hard enough."

She was pretty sure he stopped breathing at that. And so did she. A moment ago, he'd taken a call that had plummeted his mood about a hundred degrees. She was hoping to turn that around for him. Slowly, she slid her hands beneath his shirt, feeling the hard planes of his abs, which made her quiver. Yum, and she paused, thinking *north or south? Both,* she decided, but once again he sucked in a breath.

"You're still under the influence," he said, voice very strained.

Poor baby. "So heroic and gentlemanly," she murmured. Sweet, but not necessary. She was a big girl, and she was also a careful girl. But she needed this. Needed him. "I'm running at full capacity, Spence," she promised, humming in pleasure when his hands went to her hips to rock them against his.

"How do you know?" he asked, voice not quite steady when her fingers continued to map his body . . .

"Well," she said thoughtfully, "I could

prove it by walking a straight line or singing the alphabet or . . ." she ran her fingers down the front of his button-fly Levi's ". . . getting you to talk about the phone call that seemed to bother you."

"Okay," he said, catching her hand in his. "So you *are* sober."

"Yep." Again, she went up on tiptoes, putting her mouth to his ear. "And extremely turned on. Take advantage of me, Spence? Pretty please?"

He held on to her hands and met her gaze. "By my count, you have one week left here in San Francisco."

This surprised her. He'd been keeping track. "Yes."

"And we've knocked out everything on your list. Except for number ten."

She stilled, her body quivering. "Number ten?" she asked, like she wasn't clear what he was talking about.

His hot glance said *nice try.* "You remember. The wild, passionate, up-against-the-wall, forget-your-own-name love affair that makes you weak in the knees when you think about it." He smiled. "But a short love affair, really short, because you don't have time or energy to keep that level of sex up, much less maintain a relationship."

She stared at him. "You remembered it

word for word."

His eyes were badass sexy as he let go of one of her hands to reach for the bow he'd just tied at her waist, slowly pulling on it until it gave. The robe loosened and her nipples went hard.

"Be sure, Colbie," he said, his mouth against hers. "Be real sure."

She slid her hands into his hair. Having this man inside her again? Knowing that these memories would have to keep her warm in the months ahead back in New York? She'd never been more sure of anything in her life. "One hundred percent," she said and shrugged out of the robe, letting it fall to the floor.

"Oh, Colbie." His voice was like velvet as he pulled her in closer, his hands skimming down her back to cup her ass. "Missed this."

"It's been like twenty-four hours."

"Felt like a lifetime. You're so warm and soft."

"Soft?"

"It's a good thing," he murmured, dipping his head, letting his hot open mouth skim along her throat, her shoulder. "The very best thing. You're gorgeous."

She squirmed. "Are you going to talk all the way through this?"

He huffed out a soft laugh and took a bite

of her shoulder. "Yeah. I think so. Look at you." One big warm hand skimmed up her ribcage and cupped a breast. "You're perfect."

"Not . . . perfect," she managed.

"Perfect to me."

The words melted her. It was also hard to argue with him with his hands caressing her so deliberately. She was about three inches from coming and he hadn't even lost his clothes yet.

That had to change and quick. She got his shirt open and shoved it off his broad shoulders so that she could touch him skin-to-skin. He shucked his pants and when he was as naked as she, he snaked an arm around her waist, lifting her up against him so that her legs could encircle his waist. Then he took them on the move.

"Where are we going?"

"My bed," he said. "The bathroom counter isn't going to do it for me."

"Too hard?"

"Too cold." He took a couple of long strides and threw them both onto the bed. "You're not going to get cold on my watch," he said in a thrillingly rough voice.

"No? What am I going to get?"

"Lucky. Very lucky." He lowered himself over her until every part of them was touching and then finally, he kissed her. And not the light teasing kisses from before. This kiss was raw and shattering and intense, the kind of kiss that stopped hearts and melted brains, as his hands roamed her body, igniting fires everywhere they touched. He urged her thighs open, skimming a light touch over her heated flesh, and she nearly burst into flame right then.

"Spence."

He slowed. Pulled back the heat with deliberate control and she almost cried. She tightened her hands into his hair and tried to direct him but he just gave a low knowing laugh.

He knew what he was doing, and then to prove it, he did it again, taking her to the very edge before pulling back.

"I hate you," she finally gasped.

"No, you don't. I'm heroic and gentlemanly," he said, giving her back her own words.

Not that there was anything gentlemanly about what he was doing to her with his mouth. And especially when the more desperate she became, the more patient he became. He'd memorized her body, or so it seemed. He knew exactly where and how to touch her to make her putty in his hands. And where to *not* touch, apparently determined to make her beg to be finished off. "Son of a bumblebee, you're missing on purpose!"

With a deep laugh, he dragged his mouth along her body again, slow, hot, deliberate kisses, his systematic torment of her body leaving her writhing against him until *finally* he let her go, let her come apart at the seams, shattering into a million pieces.

While she was still panting and staring up at the ceiling in shock at how out of control he'd had her, he crawled up her body and brought his lips back to hers.

"You still coherent?" he asked, pushing her hair off her damp forehead.

"No," she said, gasping for air. "But don't let that stop you."

At some point he'd found a condom. Then the mouth that had just taken her to heaven slowly curved as he made himself at home between her legs, the question in his eyes.

Because she couldn't speak, she nodded and tightened her grip on him. *"Yes."* God, yes. Now. Yesterday. Tomorrow.

Always . . .

Shoving that thought deep, she gathered him into her arms, arching up to meet him halfway. He didn't close his eyes and neither did she, so they stared at each other, their breath blending as he entered her.

261

"How about now," he murmured. "Still with me now?"

"Stop asking questions and move!"

His shoulders shook with laughter, but he did as she asked. He moved. And sweet mother of pearl, how the man moved. In a shockingly short time, he had her crying out for him, sensation and emotions slamming blissfully together as their bodies did the same. And this time when she lost control, he finally did too.

After, when he went to shift his weight off her, she tightened her grip on him, not ready to let go. With a wordless comforting murmur, he slid an arm beneath her, rolling until he was on his back and she was all but poured over him.

Get up and go downstairs to your place, her brain said. *Before you get used to this.*

Oh please just one more minute, her body said.

And her body won.

CHAPTER 20
#SonOfABumblebee

Spence opened his eyes when Colbie's phone went off with multiple texts in quick succession.

Facedown on his bed, sated and still panting, she just groaned. "I'm going to kill them," she muttered into the mattress. "Unless they're in jail. If they're in jail, I'm going to leave them there." She sighed. "But I really hope they're not in jail."

"Hey." He turned her face to him, not liking the worry and guilt in her eyes. "They're legal adults. For that matter, so is your mom. You're not responsible for them."

"I know. But it's the life I've made. I take care of them. Always have."

Ever since her dad had left. It was her ugly past rearing its head and oh how he understood that.

"Maybe it's time to make a life for *you,*" he said.

She shrugged. "The thing is, when the

writing's good, I'm happy. I really don't need much more than that. The truth is, I'm fine with my life because I'm naturally introverted and actually pretty boring."

"Introverted, maybe a little. But boring?" Spence gently tugged on a loose wayward strand of her silky hair, dipping a little to look into her eyes. "Never."

"I am," she said on a laugh.

"Honey, the woman in my bed is the furthest thing from boring I've ever seen."

She blushed a little. It was cute. She snorted too. Also cute. "That was all you," she said, poking him in the chest.

"No." He caught her hand. "I've been with just me." He shook his head and laughed. "Trust me. You're the necessary ingredient and wild card." Utterly true. And something else he hadn't seen coming — she'd distracted the hell out of him but he'd still managed to work, disproving his theory that he was all work and no play.

Which wasn't even the biggest problem. Nope, that honor went to the fact that she was leaving soon, something he wasn't ready to face.

Her gaze dropped to his mouth. "As it turns out," she said softly, "you're my necessary ingredient too. I've been writing like I haven't been able to in . . . forever. You unblocked me."

He smiled and lifted her onto his lap so that she was straddling him. "So I'm your muse, huh?"

She slid her fingers into his hair and he nearly purred like a cat. "It would seem," she murmured.

"Well then, by all means feel free to use me anytime you need, creatively or otherwise," he said.

She wriggled a little, giving out a soft hum of what he hoped was pleasure as she felt him harden beneath her. "Now?" she whispered, the excitement unmistakable in her voice.

"Now."

Spence was wrapped in warm, sated woman and feeling pretty damn good about the evening as he dozed off, when suddenly Colbie stirred and murmured his name.

It was one a.m. and she'd been out for at least thirty minutes. He'd put her into a pleasure coma and it'd made him feel more than a little smug. He stroked a hand down her back. "You okay?"

"Who's Brandon?" she asked, voice thick with sleep. "I meant to ask that before but you distracted me."

"He's an old college roommate."

"And . . . ?" she asked, running a finger over his chest, an unbelievably soothing touch.

". . . And," he said, "he's also someone I stupidly gave an interview to when he asked."

"Hmm . . ." Her fingers danced lightly over his ribs and abs, which he liked way too much. "I take it that the interview didn't go well," she said.

"He works for a tech magazine and he needed a story. I agreed, as long as the article was business only, nothing personal. He promised."

"And then . . . he broke the promise?" she asked, her hand stilling.

"He gave my life story," Spence said. "Most of it pieced together from what he knew of me in college, the rest from gossip he'd dug up."

"Ah," she said. "And the next thing you knew, you were on San Fran's most eligible bachelor list, getting marriage proposals via texts with NSFW pics to go with," she guessed.

He groaned, which got a smile out of his bedmate. "Well you are pretty eligible . . ." she teased.

He sighed and she laughed, but it faded as she slid her hand up his chest to cup his jaw, her eyes sympathetic now and full of understanding. "I get it," she said. "No one's built for this kind of public scrutiny."

The thought that she understood him should've been comforting, but it wasn't.

Because in one week she'd be gone . . .

"He had no right to do that," she said, "to play on your friendship. I haven't known you very long, but even I know that your privacy is super important to you. He shouldn't have asked you for the interview in the first place."

"And now he wants a follow-up interview."

"I hope you told him where he could put it," she said, voice tight with anger for him.

That she was worked up over this for him was the sexiest thing he'd ever seen. He covered her hand on his chest with his own. "I did tell him."

"But it still sucks," she guessed. "So . . . how can I make you feel better?"

He slowly nudged her hand southbound.

Colbie laughed. Her eyes were that dark jade green they got when she was unbearably aroused and she reared up so that her mouth could brush against his, her lips soft and sweet. When her tongue touched his, his control snapped and he moved his hand to the back of her neck, closing his mouth over hers, drinking her in.

He should've been sated, but the kiss was deep and going deeper by the second. Her hands were running over his body, stopping at all his favorite parts. Ripping his mouth free, he rested his forehead against hers for a few seconds, listening to the both of them breathe like lunatics.

"This is a little bit insane," she whispered.

"Completely insane."

"I think about you too much," she admitted.

"Yeah?" He buried his fingers in her hair and met her gaze. "What do you think about?"

"This. You."

His heart skipped a few beats at the longing he saw in her face. He pressed her into the bed, needing to feel as much of his body covering hers as possible. He shuddered as her long legs wrapped around him, and he captured her lips in another mind-bending kiss, drinking in the little noises she made deep in her throat.

Then she pulled back, studying him, and he wondered what the hell she saw when she looked at him like that, like maybe he was the best thing that had ever happened to her. Which was gratifying since he was starting to come to terms with the fact that he felt the same. She was definitely the best thing to ever happen to him.

Something he thought about every morning when he dragged himself out of her bed and left her before she woke and saw it all over his face.

As he thought this and let it sink in, it suddenly took everything he had to not tell her. But he wanted her to be the one to make the decision about where to take things next, if they took things anywhere at all. He was starting to realize what his feelings were, but she needed to do the same — in her own time.

He thought maybe he'd see it in her eyes, but he wanted the words, and then, as if she could read his mind, she opened her mouth — but what came out wasn't anything he expected.

"Oh my God, *wait!*" she gasped and wriggled out from beneath him.

"What's wrong?"

"I forgot!" She sat up. "I forgot to tell you something. I can't believe I forgot but there were the brownies and then you naked . . ." She tugged the sheet up to her chin. "Sorry, I'm so sorry."

Since her voice was very serious and also very panicked and he couldn't see enough in the dark room to suit him, he reached across her and turned on the small lamp by his bed.

She'd been wearing a soft, warm glow when she'd first drifted off but right now her eyes were wide, dark, and full of haunting secrets.

Shit.

With his gut sinking hard, he watched her slide out of bed and grab the first thing she came to on the floor.

His shirt.

It looked good on her, falling to her thighs, open to expose a strip of creamy skin he knew tasted like heaven. He caught a glimpse of some whisker burn between her breasts and low on her belly before she yanked the shirt closed and started buttoning herself in.

"I'm really so very sorry," she said, head bowed to her task, her fingers fumbling. "I meant to tell you before we . . ."

Because her fingers were shaking, he got up and moved her hands aside, first undoing what she'd done since she'd lined the buttons up to the wrong holes, before starting anew. As the backs of his knuckles brushed over her flesh, she trembled.

Which killed him. What the ever-loving hell?

When she was buttoned from throat to

thigh, he let out a breath and stepped back and pulled on his jeans. "What is it?" he asked quietly.

She chewed her bottom lip. A tell. She did it whenever she was trying to hide an emotion, be it humor, arousal, or in this case, dismay.

"Okay," she said. "But I want you to know that I promised myself I'd tell you before we . . . we were intimate again. I was going to tell you tonight at dinner, only . . ."

"You ate brownies instead, got high, and then jumped my bones."

He meant for her to smile, but she didn't. She looked unsure of herself, kind of the same way she'd looked right after Daisy Duke had sent her swimming. It'd melted his damn heart then, and it did so now, even if he didn't want it to.

"I may have left you with the wrong impression of who I am and what I do," she said and hugged herself.

He stared at her and then sank to the bed. "Tell me you're not a reporter."

"No." She paused. "It's . . . worse."

Shit. Elle had been right, and oh how she was going to love that. "I need a minute."

"Now?"

"Yeah." He shook his head and got to his feet, walking out of his bedroom. Only there wasn't enough air in the living room either, so he went out the front door with the intention of going up to the roof, where he could sit in peace and quiet on the ledge and stare out at the world until he felt his blood pressure come back down from stroke level.

But he'd forgotten his keys.

Instead of going back inside his place, he pounded the elevator button with enough force to hurt his finger. It opened immediately. He stepped on and hit the basement floor.

Twenty seconds later, he walked into the large room and halted an ongoing poker game. Sitting at the table were Elle, Caleb, Joe, Archer, Finn, and Pru.

They were all smoking cigars, the ones that Luis — Trudy's three-time husband — had brought back from his trip to Cuba.

The entire table froze at the sight of Spence. Finally, Archer pulled the cigar from his mouth and jabbed it at Finn, sitting across from him. "Hey, remember the time you came out of the dumbwaiter with that same look on your face?" He jerked a thumb at the wall behind him, where the dumbwaiter door was currently closed. "Only you were in just your skivvies."

Pru grimaced. "That was my bad. I shoved

him in the dumbwaiter after we —"

Finn grinned when she broke off. "Oh, do finish that sentence," he told her. "But make sure and tell them how I rocked your world —"

"I just needed a minute to think," Pru said, blushing. "I never thought you'd end up down here. And besides, this is about Spence, hello! He's standing there in just his jeans. Where are the rest of his clothes?"

All heads swiveled back to Spence.

"Tell me you just got some," Joe said.

Elle went brows up in question.

Spence ignored them both. "It's freezing down here. Someone give me a jacket."

"Maybe you're freezing because your button fly's undone," Pru said casually and laid out her cards. "Flush."

"I've got a *royal* flush," Elle said.

Everyone groaned while Spence buttoned up his Levi's.

Pru sighed at her loss. "Damn. Well, back to Spence. Does he have another hickey?"

Spence slapped a hand to his neck.

"Bite marks, because sometimes it's important to mark your territory," Archer said.

Elle smiled and blew him a kiss as she gathered up her winnings. She scooped it all into her bag before pushing back from the table and moving across the floor to the far end of the room. Next to the washers and dryers was a closet. She pulled it open and rifled around in there before coming back toward Spence, holding out something pink.

"From the lost and found," she said. "It's only a medium, but that's the best I've got."

"It says *Princess* on it." The cold concrete floor was seeping up through his bare feet and he was shivering, but he stared at the sweatshirt dubiously.

"Put it on," Joe said. "Your nipples could cut glass."

Spence shot him a look that threatened death and Joe mercifully shut up. Not, Spence knew, because he actually feared death, but because Spence had stuff on the guy. He'd kept Joe's secrets but he wasn't feeling all that charitable at the moment.

Elle waggled the pink sweatshirt.

Swearing, Spence pulled the damn thing on. It was too short in the arms and bared a strip of his stomach, and he felt like an idiot, albeit a slightly warmer idiot. He needed to get back upstairs, because no matter what Colbie had to say, he'd been a real dick for walking out on her like that.

But Elle stopped him. "What happened?" she asked quietly, for his ears only. "Do I have to kill her?"

"Not discussing it."

But Elle was like a dog with a bone. She just crossed her arms and stared at him.

He blew out a sigh. "She said she may have misled me about who she is and what she does."

Elle stared at him. "Dammit, Spence."

"Yeah, you were right — not something you're going to hear every day, so don't get used to it."

She refused to let him joke this away. "So you . . . bailed."

"Yeah."

"After you slept with her," she said.

"Actually, there was very little sleeping involved."

Elle shook her head. "Why can't men think with two body parts at the same time? Is it in your blood? Is it just in the genes? What?"

"Actually, it's a combo," Archer said from the table with his superhuman hearing. "Don't blame us — we're born this way."

Spence rolled his eyes and started to head out but Joe stood up.

"Hey, man," he said. "Take my spot. I'm going to bed."

"Because he's losing," Caleb said.

Joe pointed at him. "Just for that, *I'm* staying."

Spence shook his head. He couldn't stay. Although . . . by now Colbie was surely long gone from his apartment and the thought of going back up there to an empty place made him feel . . . colder. "I don't have any money on me."

Elle sat back down at the table, in Archer's lap, leaving her seat open for Spence. "I think I can spot you," she said, pouring them all another round of what looked like Jameson.

"We're not supposed to play together," Spence reminded her, reaching over and taking Joe's shot, which went down nice and smooth. "We ruin it for the others."

Elle poured him another shot. "And?"

And . . . Spence thought about what was waiting for him upstairs. An empty apartment and way too many mocking memories, both of which would make him sad. Not to mention the consequences of his actions and Colbie's emotions over being deserted before she could tell him whatever it was she needed to tell him.

But he wasn't ready, and self-preservation kept him right where he was. Knowing that it was a complete dick move and utterly unable to save himself, he accepted the fact that he was a selfish asshole, tossed back shot number two, and blew out a breath.

"Deal me in."

It was four in the morning by the time Spence got back upstairs, a little drunk and three hundred bucks richer. Either Elle had been off her game or she'd felt sorry for him. In either case, the money in his pocket weighed him down and made his pants sag.

He didn't really want to go home and face the apology he owed Colbie, or his empty bed. Nor did he want to think about her not being whom she'd represented herself as — because when he wasn't drunk anymore, that one was really going to hurt.

A lot.

But right now, the Jameson had presented him with a nice cushy buffer. He walked into his place and then stopped short because it smelled *amazing,* like someone had just cooked up a mountain of bacon. He turned on the light in his living room and stared in shocked surprise as Colbie unfurled herself from his couch and stood, looking a bit unsure of herself. "Hey."

He held on to the doorjamb. "You . . . cooked?"

"Just bacon. Found it in your freezer. I saved you some but then I got pissed and ate it." She shook her head. "I really should've left after you did, but I wanted to talk to you and thought you'd be right back."

"Colbie —"

"No." She put a finger in his face, nearly taking out an eye. "You didn't come right back and that's when I realized. I was the mature one." She let out a hollow laugh. "God, if only you knew how funny that was. I'm pissed off, Spence, and I'm going to spell it out for you because you're just dense enough to not get it unless I do."

He opened his mouth and then closed it again but chances were, she was right.

"You've been telling me it's a good thing we only have three weeks together because you're not capable of more, blah blah. I didn't want to believe it but you proved it to me by leaving my bed after sex each night before I woke up." She was hands on hips now, her hair practically crackling from the spark of her temper.

And she wasn't done.

"I thought that what I had to tell you might change things," she said. "Might show you that if I of all people could open up to you, then maybe you could open up right back, but then you ran away for a couple of hours." She looked at his pink sweatshirt. "I'm not even going to ask where you've been for hours getting drunk while I was waiting on a grown-up conversation. I'm just going to tell you my truth whether you want to hear it or not."

He put his hands in his pockets rather than reach for her, which was exactly what he wanted to do seeing her all soft and sleepy — even as his stomach clenched over what was coming next.

"First," she said, "I'll apologize for not telling you sooner. But I thought we were both on the same page with our limited time restraint. And then when I realized I was aching for more and had to tell you the truth about me, I mistakenly thought it might change things, but now I see that you were honest with me — you really aren't capable of more." She took a deep breath. "Have you heard of the Storm Fever series?"

He blinked at the quick subject change, his thought processes more than a little impeded by the alcohol. "Uh . . . the movie doesn't come out until next week."

"I know. I've already seen the movie. I got a special preview a month ago." She paused, and he couldn't figure out why they were talking about this when —

"I wrote the books," she said. "I'm CE Crown."

His brain was having trouble connecting the dots. "You're not Colbie Albright?"

"I am. But I write under the pseudonym CE Crown."

He paused. This wasn't what he'd expected, although he couldn't have said what he did expect.

She was watching his reaction very carefully. Only he wasn't sure what his reaction was supposed to be. Hell, he wasn't sure of anything at the moment, other than he was wearing a way-too-small pink sweatshirt that pronounced him a princess.

"I came to San Francisco because I've been having trouble writing," she said. "I was hoping to pull myself out of my rut." She gave a small smile. "Which did happen." She paused, looking even more unsure of herself now as she met his gaze. "I didn't intend to tell anyone who I was. It's not this huge secret or anything, I just wanted to get away from my crazy life and all the responsibility for a bit and find the joy in writing again. But I just . . . It didn't feel right not telling you anymore. After the past two weeks with you, I wanted you to know the truth. Especially after we . . ." She looked toward the bedroom. "You know."

Struck dumb by her news, which was nothing even close to what he might have imagined, he nodded inanely.

"So." She clasped her hands together.

"Now you know my big, dark secret."

"Yeah."

"Yeah," she mirrored back softly, and then headed for the door. She lifted her gaze to his and searched his eyes once more. There were more questions there, questions she clearly wanted to ask, but after a long hesitation she didn't. "I was feeling really bad for misleading you," she said instead. "But I'm not feeling bad anymore. Especially since the truth is that I wanted you to know me as myself, as Colbie Albright, not CE Crown. That's all anyone sees these days when they look at me. But CE Crown isn't real. I'm real."

At that, his chest suddenly felt too tight and it wasn't the damn sweatshirt. "Colbie, I'm sorry. I'm so fucking sorry I vanished on you."

"I don't want to hear it." Her eyes were shiny bright when she turned away and walked out the door.

It took him a beat to acknowledge that either he was having a heart attack or the sweatshirt was just that tight. "You really are an idiot," he told himself and started to go after her. But then he caught sight of himself in the foyer mirror and stopped short.

Wow. Not only was the sweatshirt pink

with *Princess* on it, it was bedazzled. And here he'd thought it couldn't get worse. He ripped it off over his head, tossed it aside, and then headed out. He took the stairs to the third floor and knocked on Colbie's door.

No answer. He knew it was late. No, scratch that, it was early, *very* early, but he knocked again anyway, slightly harder.

Mrs. Winslow from 3D stuck her head out her door. She took in the sight of Spence standing there in just his Levi's and nothing else and put a hand to her heart. "Oh my saints alive."

"I'm sorry," Spence said. "I didn't mean to wake you."

Mrs. Winslow tilted her head up to the ceiling. "Nice work," she whispered.

Spence sighed and turned back to Colbie's door.

"Even better from the back," Mrs. Winslow said.

Spence closed his eyes and thunked his head on Colbie's door. "Go back to bed, Mrs. Winslow."

He heard her door shut. But what he didn't hear was Colbie opening hers. He could feel her though, just on the other side of the wood. "Look," he said. "Clearly I was telling you the truth when I said I was bad with women. I don't know jack about making them happy or keeping them."

Nothing.

"Colbie, open up so I can apologize properly. You deserve that much at least."

More nothing.

He decided to try to appeal to her warm, nurturing side, hoping she wouldn't be able to resist. "My feet are cold," he said.

And bingo, she opened the door to reveal two females staring at him, one human, one feline. He quickly stepped into the human one, nudging her back so he could get inside.

"Maybe I didn't want to let you in," Colbie said a little pissily.

"Yeah, well, right back at ya, honey."

CHAPTER 21
#BALLS

Colbie didn't give herself a pep talk about staying mad, because she was so mad she thought the pep talk wouldn't be necessary.

But she wasn't prepared for the sight of the six-foot way-too-good-looking Spence Baldwin standing in front of her wearing only a pair of dangerously low-slung Levi's and an even more dangerous smile.

"You're cold because you're not wearing a shirt or socks," she said, pointing out the obvious. And then she paused, her head kicking up a notch as she took him in from head to bare sexy toes and back again, lingering on the parts of him she now knew intimately . . . "Or underwear," she added.

He blinked at that, slow as an owl, reminding her that he was tanked. But even so, his usual calm and easy control was still in play, with or without his usual reflexes.

"How do you know I'm not wearing underwear?" he asked.

Mostly because the jeans were so low that if he took so much as a halfway-deep breath, he'd lose them altogether, no matter how lovingly and intimately they cupped him. All she could see were muscles and skin, along with those sexy vee muscles that made women stupid. No cotton or knit undies peeking out from his waistband, nothing but Spence. "God-given talent," she murmured.

He smiled at her, an open, warm smile that caught her off guard. She rolled her eyes, but it was to her shock that she found herself having to fight a return smile. "Why are your pants half falling down?"

"Because I'm the current Pacific Pier Building poker champion."

"Hmm." She cocked her head. "So on a scale of sober to several pot brownies, just how intoxicated are you?"

"I don't know," he said. "Which of the three of you are asking?"

A part of her softened and wanted to laugh but the rest of her, still hurt, held it together.

He looked at her for a long moment. "I'm sorry, Colbie. I heard you say you weren't who you'd claimed to be and . . ." He shook his head. "I'd just had that call from Brandon and I lost it. I wasn't thinking and I should've listened to you before leaving like that. I just needed a minute and then that minute turned into a poker game because I'd convinced myself I'd fucked up and you'd be long gone."

"I should have been."

"I'm glad you weren't," he said. "Because I think you're amazing. What you do, what you've accomplished . . . truly amazing."

She let out a tiny smile. "Yeah?"

"Yeah." He took her hand and slowly reeled her in.

She fought him for about a second and then let her hands come up to his chest like it was the most natural thing in the world.

"Admit it," he said. "The *Princess* sweatshirt was hot, right?"

She fought a laugh and lost.

"Right. And you thought I was sexy as hell in it."

"I think you're something," she said. "Not sure what though."

"Maybe we should figure it out from a horizontal position." His voice was the same one he used to whisper naughty nothings in her ear when he was busy taking her straight to heaven and back.

She'd like nothing more than a repeat, but they had problems. One, he hadn't trusted her. And two, if she was being honest, she hadn't trusted him either. She'd been wrong, she knew that now. She could trust him with anything.

Except for maybe the one thing she *wanted* to trust him with — her heart. "We don't tend to talk when we're horizontal," she reminded him.

He smiled a mischievous, wicked smile. And that's when she realized it was too late to protect her heart, because he already had it.

So you should just enjoy what time you have left, a little voice inside her head said.

But she was still confused. On the one hand, she knew he liked her. A lot. And not for the fame or the money she represented but for *her.*

On the other hand, something shockingly amazing had happened to her in his bed earlier, and then only a few hours later, whatever that shockingly amazing thing had been, it'd been over.

And that made her . . . Well, she didn't know exactly. But sad topped the list.

Not that it mattered. Whatever he made her feel — a complicated mix at best — she was writing again, and that was the whole purpose of being here. Not to fall for a guy who lived three thousand miles away who was already in a relationship — with his job.

She'd left his place with the intention of

forgetting him and going to write. She'd already put out more pages in the two weeks she'd been here than she'd written in months, and *that* felt amazing — even if she'd taken her new book in a direction she hadn't seen coming. It would fulfill her, she told herself.

It had to.

But now she stood there in front of the incredibly sexy man who'd helped her out of her crisis, and he looked like the best diversion she'd ever seen. And he was giving her the sexy, half-lidded bedroom eyes, a look so hot it singed her skin and gave her thoughts. Dirty thoughts. Especially since she knew now that he could back up that look with actions.

And oh good Lord, his actions . . .

He took her hand, using it to tug her into him. The minute her hands landed onto his hot bare chest, she knew she was sunk, that she was taking him to her bed. "I don't know why I try to resist," she murmured.

"Me either." He added an eyebrow waggle that made her laugh and then they were tumbling to her bed.

And then, not two seconds later, he was out cold.

Spence came awake in slow, excruciating

degrees. He was facedown, sprawled out in a bed that wasn't his. Naked. And his aching head might or might not be attached to his shoulders. He couldn't tell for sure.

With a groan, he managed to lift his head — oh good, it *was* attached, then — and open one bleary eye. He was in Colbie's bed.

Alone.

Well he deserved that, he supposed. And he had to say, he wasn't fond of being the one left behind . . .

No, wait a minute. He wasn't completely alone after all. There was a weight on his calves. A moving weight. Something on four feet walked up his legs and back and put its wet nose to his ear.

"Meow."

"Not the woman I was hoping for." Rolling to his back and dislodging the unhappy cat — who glared at him — he stared up at the ceiling as the night came back to him in flashes. "This isn't good."

Apparently coming to the same conclusion, Cinder jumped down off the bed and stalked off, tail straight up in the air, quivering with disapproval.

Spence shook his head and tried to put the flashes of memories in order. Colbie, in *his* bed, blowing his mind, amongst other things . . .

Then her mentioning that she wasn't who he thought, and him completely overreacting. Playing poker. Having those evil shots. Winning everyone's money including Elle's and then ending up on Colbie's doorstep, pockets heavy, heart heavy . . .

Things got a little fuzzy after that.

He was definitely alone in her apartment, as the place was completely empty of the vibrant, warm, sexy, fun energy that she always brought into a room with her.

Somehow he managed to crawl out of bed and into her shower, though he groaned and bitched like an old man the whole time. Using her soap and shampoo was an exercise in torture because they smelled like her, which gave him a painful erection that told him whatever they'd done once he'd gotten into her bed last night . . . it hadn't happened again this morning.

After, he pulled on his jeans and prowled through the apartment. Still no Colbie.

His phone rang and he looked hopefully at the screen, letting out a breath of disappointment at Joe's name. "Talk," he said.

"Mornin' to you too, sunshine."

When Spence didn't say anything, Joe went on. "Okay, so you're not caffeinated yet," he said, and that's when Spence started to clue in to the fact that Joe's voice was missing its usual smartassery and good humor.

"What's wrong?"

"This needs to be in person," Joe said. "I'm at your office. Where are you?"

"Two minutes," Spence said and then made it upstairs in one.

Joe took one look at him and shook his head. "You lost your shirt *again*?"

Spence ignored this and strode directly toward the coffeepot that Trudy kept here due to his inability to work without caffeine.

"Man, you're spoiled rotten," Joe said, working on his own cup. "This coffee is better than Archer's, and Archer demands good coffee."

"What's going on?" Spence asked him.

"I don't know. I think Trudy must fly to Colombia for this shit."

"I meant what don't you want to tell me?" Spence asked with barely there patience.

Joe flashed a grim smile. "I know. I'm stalling."

Spence stared at him. "Spit it out."

Joe sighed. Joe never sighed, so this wasn't a good sign. "Okay," he finally said. "But I need you to promise me that everything I'm about to tell you stays between us."

"Or?" Spence asked.

"Or I'll have to kill you."

Spence didn't laugh, because he was pretty sure Joe wasn't kidding. "Many have tried, no one's succeeded," he said. "But yeah, we're in the cone of silence."

Joe paced around the office, looking more than a little edgy. Normally he was fun, at times hilariously inappropriate, and usually pretty easygoing when he wasn't on the job. Today the easygoing was nowhere to be seen.

"Joe, I've got a bitch of a hangover. Speed this up before I croak, cuz I'll be worthless to you then."

"Okay, okay," Joe said and turned to face him. "You know Elle asked me to dig into Colbie. And you said I should go ahead."

"I did," Spence agreed. "After stalling as long as you could."

"Which I did. I was actually too busy to get to it. Until this morning."

Spence nodded. "Thanks."

Joe studied him for a few seconds. "That's it? Thanks? You don't want to know what I found?"

Spence shook his head and then seriously regretted the move.

"You already know," Joe said. "You know what I found."

"I do."

"Pretty cool, right?" Joe asked with a good amount of genuine marvel. "And impressive."

It really was. Spence still couldn't believe it, but he wasn't surprised. Colbie was special. And also, it seemed, especially talented.

"You knowing makes this a whole lot easier," Joe said. "But you do realize that if I tell Elle what I've found, the whole beehive will know. And frankly, I think it should be Colbie's decision what we tell anyone."

"I agree." But Spence understood Joe's problem. He was in an untenable situation, as he worked for Archer, who was sleeping with Elle, among other things. "Colbie will be okay with Elle knowing. Elle can keep a secret when she wants to. And knowing the truth will make her understand Colbie's secretive nature. Hell, it might even make her nicer, if not outright protective of Colbie." He smiled grimly. "We all know she's like a mama bear when it comes to anyone hurting those she cares about."

Joe nodded. "But I can probably buy you another few days." His phone went off. He looked at the screen. "Gotta go."

And then Spence was alone. He stepped to the window, looking to the courtyard below, and felt something go tense inside him.

A guy in a suit had Colbie by the arm and was steering her toward the street gate. She didn't look happy about it, but it was fairly obvious that whoever he was, he and Colbie were more than a little familiar with each other.

As if she could feel him the way he could always feel her, she glanced up and their gazes met. He lifted a hand but she didn't acknowledge him, though he was positive she'd seen him because she stilled for a beat.

Her eyes were hidden behind sunglasses but he knew her now and read her body language clear enough. Uncertain. Unhappy. Her clothes hid her luscious curves but it didn't matter. He knew every inch of her by heart. Knew how she felt. Tasted. Knew what it was like to have her pressed against him with nothing between them, to be buried so deep inside her they were one, her limbs wrapped around him like she was afraid to let him go.

So he also knew she didn't want to be walking with this guy. Not that *that* stopped her, as after another heartbeat, she turned away and picked up their pace.

Colbie was furious with Jackson for hunting

her down. Not only had he tracked her phone, he'd also used her chief research source from the NYPD to do it.

When he'd shown up at her door, she refused to make a scene. Instead, acutely aware that Spence was asleep in her bed, she'd gone with Jackson downstairs to find a place to talk in private. She'd figured the coffee shop would do it but Elle, Kylie, and Haley had been in there, so she'd quickly turned away. Jackson said he only wanted to talk, but she had a feeling he'd really rather fight, so she allowed him to guide her out of the courtyard because she didn't want witnesses for this.

The Pacific Pier Building was everything she loved. Interesting, quirky, cozy . . . a community within a community. But all those things also made it something she hadn't realized until that very moment — basically, a very small town, complete with the small-town clichés.

There were no secrets here.

She and Jackson had nearly made it across the courtyard when she'd caught sight of Spence at what she was pretty sure was his office window, watching them. It'd been impossible to read his expression from that distance and that was probably just as well. She rushed Jackson along. They crossed the street in silence and stepped into another coffee shop, one where she, thankfully, didn't recognize another soul.

"What can I get you?" Jackson asked, gesturing to the menu on the wall.

She crossed her arms. "The reason why you're here."

Apparently deciding that she wasn't playing, he sighed. "Sit. I'll be right back."

He returned with a hot Earl Grey tea and a banana nut muffin, both her favorites — which was not going to fix her mood. "What are you doing here, Jackson?"

"At least sip the caffeine so I have a chance of surviving this meeting," he said.

She blew out a sigh and sipped her tea.

"We were worried about you," he said quietly. "Me. Your family. Janeen and Tracy."

"I sent you all daily texts assuring you that I was fine, that I'd come home by Christmas Eve. You had no right to go all Sherlock on me and hunt me down and just show up like this."

"No right?" he asked in disbelief. "Okay, forgetting everything else for a minute — including why you're mad at me — you're two months late on delivering a manuscript. Who do you think your publisher is hounding every day? Me, the agent!"

"So that's why you're here?" she asked.

"To see how your investment is paying off? To make sure I'm working? I told you, Jackson, God, for months and months I told you that I was in a bad place, that I needed a break. You kept saying it was okay for me to take one, that you agreed I needed to get away."

"I meant me," Jackson said. "I agreed you needed to take a break from your feelings for *me.*"

She stared at him and then let out a breath and leaned back in her chair. "Wow."

"Colbie —"

"No, hold on. So you think this is about *you*?"

"Are you going to tell me it's not?"

"H-E-double-hockey-sticks yes!"

He sat back and shook his head. "Listen, I get that you're butthurt about what you saw that night, and believe me, I'm sorry you saw it at all."

"But not that it happened," she noted with far more calm than she felt.

He looked away for a beat and then met her gaze again, his own deep and dark with regret. And temper. "Keeping this about business for a minute. You realize that you're not the only one on the line here, right? This is my career too. And I'm expected to get you to interviews, signings, and other appearances to coincide with the movie release, Colbie — which is premiering in a week."

"You think I don't know that?"

"I don't know, you tell me," he said. "You've refused any appearances at all, saying you'd only do e-mail interviews and posts."

"That's not so rare, you know. Writers write. Let the actors push the movie. No one needs to see or hear the bumbling author of the books that the movie is based on. What you're not getting and not hearing is that I was in real trouble. I couldn't write a damn chapter, much less a whole book."

His expression softened and he reached across the table to cover her hand with his. "See, that's why you shouldn't be all the way across the country from your support team. Too many outside stressors."

"The stressors came *from* my support team," she said. "All I asked for was a few weeks away. I just wanted, *needed*, things to go back to where it all started for me, okay? To before I was too stressed to be creative." She stood. "Coming here to San Francisco was the best thing I've ever done for myself. And actually, it's the only thing I've done for myself in . . . well, ever. I just needed to go back to being that writer who was in love with writing, instead of my stomach churning in knots with tension and dread every time I turned on my laptop or got an e-mail requesting another live interview."

Jackson stood and grabbed her hand before she could walk away. "Look, I know it's been a whirlwind —"

"No, you're not hearing me. You don't understand —"

"Then help me understand," he said. "You walked away from everything when you left, not just your work. You have responsibilities, Colbie, and —"

"Wait, are you kidding me?" she asked, tugging her hand free as anger spiked hard and hot inside her.

"Your mom called," he said. "She wants to get the house ready for Christmas but doesn't know how to do that without you. And Kent didn't want to tell you, but he banged up his car for the third time and needs to know whether he should notify the insurance, or do you want to pay for it and avoid a claim? Oh, and Janeen and Tracy are on pins and needles wondering about their usual Christmas bonus but don't want to ask you directly."

No. Hell no was he doing this here, now, bringing guilt into her secret getaway. "I'll deal with it," she said. "All of it. Go home, Jackson."

"And what about us?" he asked. "You going to put us on hold to deal with later too? I used to be more important to you than that."

She whipped back and pointed at him. "There is no us, not like that. And even if there was, how dare you try to use our past like that, reminding me how I felt about you as if maybe it would turn me back into that sweet, quiet yes-girl. The one who was so excited about her career under your care that she'd do whatever you ask of her. Because she's not here anymore, Jackson. You don't run my private life or get to lecture me on what you think are my responsibilities. You lost all those privileges after you —" She broke off and shook her head. "You know what? Never mind. Because this isn't about you. None of this is about you."

"The hell it isn't," he said. "It's about what happened between you and me."

"Oh, you mean when you led me on, letting me think that you liked me too?"

"You had a crush," he said. "We both knew that's all it was."

"No," she said. "*We* didn't."

He sighed and scrubbed a hand down his face. "Look, okay, yes. Yes, I knew you had a crush on me, and yes, I let it go on too long. I thought you needed the crush to write."

She gaped at him. "And the reason for sleeping with me for three whole months?"

His face softened. "Maybe I had my own little crush for a while."

"Stop." She closed her eyes. "You weren't sleeping with just me."

"Wrong," he said. "I absolutely was sleeping with just you. Until you decided you wanted a break. You wanted to spend time apart. Your idea, Colbie."

"Yes, you're right, it'd been my idea. I meant a few days, Jackson. I was trying to get into my book and you were being insane with demands on my time. I needed a break. I buried myself in work for, what, four days? And then came to your office to explain why I needed the rest of the week, only to find you bending your co-agent over your desk. Not a good angle for either of you, I might add."

He shoved a hand through his hair. "You and I were on a break."

"Oh my God," she said. "You sound like an old *Friends* episode." She shook her head. "Look, forget about you and me. Forget about trying to guilt me back to New York. I'll come back when I said I would."

She turned to walk away and bounced off a hard chest.

Spence's.

He caught her and kept her from falling. "Hey," he said, his eyes on Jackson. "You okay?"

"Fine," she said and started to move around Spence, but Jackson said her name again and she looked back.

His expression was suspicious. "Who's this?"

"Get on a plane, Jackson," she said. "We'll talk when I'm back."

"Is he your get-even-with-Jackson guy?"

Colbie wished her tea wasn't so hot so she could toss it right into his smug face. "Goodbye, Jackson," she said and started out.

"Colbie, wait."

She didn't and she heard him swear and kick a chair out of his way to get to her. But when he didn't grab for her, she looked back.

Spence had stepped into his path, looking like a superhero in glasses.

Jackson slid his gaze to Colbie. "Seriously?"

"If you tell anyone where I am," she said, "I'll start tacking on extra weeks to my vacation." She grabbed Spence's hand and tugged.

Spence held his ground for an extra-long beat, his gaze still locked on Jackson's.

Jackson looked away first and finally Spence let her pull him away.

Once outside, the man she'd left in her bed that morning turned to her.

"Not here," she said. "Anywhere but here."

Chapter 22
#SomeDitch

Spence could feel Colbie shaking as they got back to the courtyard of his building. He turned her to face him. "You didn't answer me before, so I'm going to ask you again. Are you okay?"

She nodded. And then slowly shook her head no.

Shit. He took her hand and led her across the courtyard to the elevator. He bypassed the third floor. And then the fifth floor.

"The roof?" she asked quietly.

"The roof." He brought her over to his stargazing lounger.

"It's daylight," she said.

"I know."

"It might rain."

"I know that too." He nudged her down and checked his phone. "Ten seconds," he said.

In half that, the roof door opened and Caleb appeared, holding a big brown bag.

"I got everything that even remotely resembled comfort food," Caleb said. "It wasn't hard — Trudy had just loaded your fridge."

"The mac and cheese?" Spence asked, taking a peek.

"Yeah. And you don't know how bad I wanted to pretend I didn't find that one. I know it's morning and all that but . . . *homemade,* man. Crispy golden brown cheesy crust, and she added bacon. *Bacon!* That makes it breakfast."

"Thanks," Spence said, noting that he'd even included utensils.

"Sure." Caleb glanced at Colbie, who was unnaturally still, staring out at the city. "She okay?"

He had no idea. "She will be."

Caleb nodded and Spence took in the guy's ridiculously ugly Christmas sweater. "What is that?"

"Trying to get into an acceptable festive spirit," Caleb said.

Spence shook his head. "Christmas sweaters are only acceptable as a cry for help."

"Says the guy who wore a pink *Princess* sweatshirt to poker last night. Oh yeah," he said at Spence's surprise. "There are pics. Don't worry — none of us tagged you, but they're good too."

When he was gone, Spence sat next to Colbie. He opened the bag and started pulling out the food. She watched, silent, until he had everything opened.

Her nose wriggled, like she smelled something enticing. "Is that mac and cheese?" she asked.

"With bacon. I hope you don't have anything against eating nonbreakfast food for breakfast."

"No. And I smell bacon. Bacon is breakfast food. Bacon is every-meal food."

They were in perfect accord there. He handed the container to her and watched while she ate it in silence, her expression going from way too beaten down for his comfort to . . . less beaten down.

"Are you trying to bribe me into a good mood with food?" she finally asked.

"Is it working?"

"Yes." She sighed and leaned back. "But only because I'm easy that way."

"Only that way, huh?" he asked in a teasing tone, picking up her hand, bringing it to his mouth, smiling when she choked out a rough laugh.

"Well, with you," she said, "I might just be easy in all ways."

He smiled. "Who was the guy?"

"My agent."

"And . . . your ex," he guessed.

"Yes," she said. "And since I ran away with nothing more than a few notes, on some level I can't even blame him for being pissed off and tracking me down."

"You're not a minor, Colbie. You're a grown woman who's got the right to come and go as you please."

"I'm the head of my family, and they depend on me."

"Financially, I get it," he said. "I do. But emotionally? That's going over and above with their expectations."

She met his gaze. "Says the man who bought his mom a house and keeps his grandpa in sight and takes care of him. So tell me how exactly we're different?"

"My mom was always there for me," he said. "Always. I had to practically drag her out of her rundown dump into the house I bought for her because she didn't want me to spend my money on her. She never does. Two years ago for Christmas, I gave her something she never had, something she always wanted — a retirement fund. What did she do? She changed it into my name." He shook his head. "So last year I tried to outsmart her. I bought her something I knew she'd always secretly dreamed of — an all-expenses-paid vacation cruise to a bunch of Greek islands."

"I take it she didn't go."

"Nope. She cashed it in and donated the money to my favorite charity."

She stared at him and then laughed a little. "I think I'd like her."

"And she'd like you," he said. "But my point is that she spent most of her life dirt poor. She's never had it easy, but at no point in our lives has she ever dumped her entire life on me and made me responsible for her. I don't have siblings, but knowing what I know about her, she'd never let me take on responsibility for them either."

She closed her eyes. "I wasn't going to let you in," she whispered.

"I've had my mouth on every inch of your gorgeous body," he said. "And vice versa." At just the memory, his glasses fogged up and his voice fell an octave. "So it's a little late for that."

She blushed and bit her lower lip. "You know I didn't mean physically. I meant . . ." She tapped her temple.

Yeah. He knew. And he'd been sure of the exact same thing. But when it came right down to it, his brain wasn't always in charge. His heart was.

And no matter what, watching her walk away was going to suck.

"Your mom sounds like she's a really strong woman," she said.

"She is."

She shook her head. "My mom isn't like that. For as long as I can remember, she's been the victim, and she enjoys the role. I stepped in early because she needed me and . . . well, she's never stopped needing me. Emotionally, financially, mentally."

Her mom, who should've known better, had early on handed over her reins to Colbie, who'd been far too young to take it all on. But take it on she had, giving up her own childhood in the process. Spence was starting to understand the depth of her sense of responsibility, as a woman, a daughter, a sister, a writer. "Not your job," he said.

"I know. And I never meant to create a codependent relationship, believe me," she said. "I just wanted to help."

"And you have. And more than with just your family."

"You mean Jackson."

"He cheated on you?" Spence asked, trying to get a bead on what she might still feel for this guy.

She blew out a breath. "I made more of what we had than it was. I had a very longtime crush on him and mistook friendship and business for love. It wasn't."

"And now he's using that friendship and business to manipulate you into returning before you're ready."

She shrugged.

"Colbie . . ." He took her hand. "Don't let it do a number on you."

She laughed softly. "Baby steps."

"Baby steps," he agreed and kept ahold of her hand.

They ate, and when they were done, Spence pulled Colbie up.

"Where are we going?" she asked.

"Your list."

"We did everything on my list," she said and finally gave him a real smile.

He returned it. "There's something you forgot to put on the list. Trust me?" he asked, not sure she would or why he wanted her to so badly.

But when she looked at his outstretched hand, nodded, and put hers in his, he felt like he'd won the lotto.

"What are we doing?" Colbie asked as Spence pulled the '57 Chevy truck into traffic.

"You'll see," he said enigmatically.

Okaaay. Her phone buzzed.

Spence glanced over at her.

310

She sighed and pulled out her phone. "It's a text from Kent. He wants to know how to run the washing machine."

"Better late than never."

She typed out a response and put her phone away. "Hope he separated his colors from his whites."

"Rite of passage, making that mistake — which he'll only do once." Spence took a street that was a straight-up hill, the likes of which she'd never seen before, even in San Francisco, and that was saying something. They parked in a large lot that appeared nearly empty and then . . . they took a trail.

In the middle of the city. It was boggling.

She looked at Spence ahead of her, leading the way in his wrinkled cargos that fit across his very nice ass. He craned his neck and caught her ogling, flashing her a smile. He wore a backward baseball cap and his prescription aviator sunglasses lenses were dark.

The sexiest, hottest geek she'd ever seen.

"Where are we?" she asked, mesmerized by the 360-degree vista they had at the top, as well as the huge white concrete cross protruding out of the ground.

"Mount Davidson," he said. "It's the highest point in the city, which at 938 feet isn't all that high compared to the rest of the planet but it's what we've got."

"And the cross?"

"People come here at Easter for an annual prayer service. They illuminate the cross." He'd grabbed his beat-up duffle bag from his truck and worn it on a broad shoulder to walk up here. Now he opened it up and took out a small drone, along with a control panel.

It took him no more than two minutes to have the drone in the air, broadcasting to an iPad fitted to the controller. Colbie didn't know what to look at first, the drone rising and dipping in the sky like an eagle, the tablet sending them the dizzying, glorious images in real time, or the man himself at the controls like he'd been born to it.

He stood there, feet spread to brace against the wind, concentrating on the tablet screen, monitoring the craft's progress through its onboard camera.

And then he handed her those controls.

"What? No —" She tried to take a step back but he just shoved the controller in her hand and let go, so that if she didn't take it, the thing would've fallen to the ground. And so would the drone, and she couldn't even imagine how expensive it might be. "Some ditch! *Spence!*"

His head was tipped back, his gaze on the

drone in the sky. "Going to want to accelerate between now and five seconds from now," he said casually.

He was crazy. "I know your brain can handle like fifty things at once, but mine tops out at around two. Anything over that and it all shorts out." She waggled her fingers beside her head in a gesture to indicate her brain was frying.

He laughed.

The drone pitched violently and she gasped in horror. "Help me!" She actually felt her legs wobble with anxiety, so she dropped to her knees.

Spence crouched down behind her, wrapping his arms around her, putting his hands over hers, expertly flicking at the controls to adjust the flight. She could feel his breath on the back of her neck and she suddenly found it difficult to think of anything else. She was so incredibly aware of him, and unbidden came a flashback of the last time he'd had his mouth on her neck. And where else that mouth had gone . . .

She wondered if they had time for a repeat.

"Later," he promised, his mouth brushing her ear, sending her already raging hormones into overdrive. "Anything you want."

She nearly dropped the remote but his

big, sure hands were there to hold her steady. His chest was flush with her back, his arms surrounding her, his hands on hers as he guided her through the flight. She tried to concentrate, but her attention span was shot to hell. He smelled amazing —

"Focus," he said.

She *was* focused. She was focused on how the fronts of his thighs were pressed against the backs of hers . . .

"Close out the world," he said in her ear, pulling her to her feet. "Close out everything but this."

She'd like to, but he'd lowered his head so that his whisker-rough jaw brushed against hers, playing havoc with her brain. Her breathing was still accelerated. But not Spence's. Nope, he was breathing calm and even, making her want to change that —

"Colbie."

"What?"

"Honey, you're staring at me and you're going to crash my very favorite drone."

Dammit. She jerked her gaze off of him and felt his chest shake with silent laughter. Forcing her mind to clear, she turned her face to the sky and set her mind to determined concentration.

And the most amazing thing happened. Standing there braced against the light wind and cold air, with Spence at her back making her feel like she could do anything, she flew the drone. Up. Down. Sideways. In a loop . . .

It was the most exhilarating thing she could remember doing, well, other than Spence himself . . .

When they landed the drone together, they sat on what felt like the edge of the planet, looking down over the city, sharing a bottle of water from Spence's backpack.

"Fun?" he asked.

"More than I could have imagined, but . . ." She laughed ruefully and slid him a sideways glance. "You do know this isn't exactly what I had in mind when I asked you to get me out of that coffee shop."

He took her hand and brought it to his mouth, taking a nibble out of her palm that had her sucking in a breath. "Maybe that's coming next."

"Maybe?" she asked breathlessly.

He squeezed her hand. "Do you always need to know the plan?"

"Always."

"Okay, then," he said agreeably, still looking out over their view. "My plan is to unblock you some more."

Anticipation raced through her. "How exactly do you plan to do that?"

He met her gaze, his own so hot it stole her breath. Then he leaned in, his mouth at her ear as he told her his plan in slow, sexy, sensual, erotic detail, leaving her with a shiver that was nearly an orgasm.

"Does that work for you?" he asked.

All she could do was nod.

He flashed her a smile. "Good. Let's go."

She'd never moved so fast in her life, earning her a low, rough laugh from Spence, whom she raced to his truck.

Chapter 23
#HairyMonkeyButts

Spence walked Colbie to her apartment, telling himself that if she gave any sign of hesitation, he'd walk away. He'd go upstairs and bury himself in his office.

And not inside her body.

But as she dipped her head to her purse, rummaging for her key, their bodies brushed together and she stilled, closing her eyes for a beat, like she was trying to remember the feel of him for later.

He'd known the first time he'd ever laid eyes on her, drenched in the fountain, that he was going to have to hold back with her. That he couldn't let her in. That she deserved so much more from him than he could give. Just as he'd known that if he ever managed to step away from her, it'd be nearly impossible, letting go of the only thing that had ever made him happy.

And if that wasn't an epiphany all in itself.

Colbie managed to get ahold of her keys,

letting out a moan as he slipped an arm around her from behind. When she got her door open, she stepped inside and grabbed his hand, dragging him in with her before kicking her door closed. Then she pushed him up against it, making him smile because she was mirroring the move he'd pulled on her the last time they'd been in this very spot.

And God, when she looked at him like that, he was a goner. She'd offered him her friendship. Her body.

And he'd taken both.

He wanted to keep them both. And he also wanted more, so much more. He wanted her damn heart, like she had his.

"About your plan," she whispered against his lips. She was on tiptoe, her hands gliding up his shoulders and into his hair.

"What about it?" His hands were just as busy, burrowing beneath the sexy sweater that had been driving him crazy all morning.

"Were you all talk?" she murmured, "or are you going to back it up with some action?"

Going with show instead of tell, he hoisted her up into his arms and, with her wrapped around him, walked to her bed. "Better move, cat," he said to the black cat sleeping on a pillow.

The cat sniffed in disdain but did indeed hop down. "Good kitty," he said and tossed Colbie down on the mattress.

Before she'd so much as bounced, he had her jeans off and was on her, scooping her in close. It felt good, holding her like this. Folded together so intimately in the quiet haven of her apartment, where no one else existed.

"Meow."

Except the cat. "Go prowling," Spence told her. "We're going to need some privacy."

"True story," Colbie said and then reared up to nibble on Spence's neck.

He inhaled sharply and Colbie stilled. "Did that hurt?"

"Not you, the cat —"

Who'd climbed back onto the bed and was sitting on his ass, kneading it like she was making muffins.

"Claws," he ground out, twisting to pick the cat up and set her back onto the floor.

Colbie laughed, her hands going to his ass to knead — without claws.

"Better?" she asked.

"Much." He kissed her then and they rolled over the bed jockeying for position. He fell to his back, liking the way she looked straddling him, her hair pouring over the both of them like spun silk. He brushed a kiss to her jaw, her chin, fisting his hand in her hair to bring her mouth back to his.

Colbie writhed on his lap trying to get closer and then closer still, flicking her tongue across his lip, galvanizing him into action. Rearing up, he pulled her sweater over her head and nudged her straps off her shoulders, watching as the cups slipped, teasing him with a peekaboo hint of rosy nipple that he had to get his mouth on.

With a moan, she dropped her head back and she rocked the softest, wettest part of her over the hardest, most desperate part of him, and though he'd intended to go slow and love her body until she couldn't take any more, it'd have to wait until round two.

With an arm low around her hips, he yanked her beneath him, tugged the sexy little scrap of silk masquerading as panties off. He freed himself, thankful for the condom he had in his pants from the day before. Colbie reached for him, cradling his body with hers like it was where he was meant to be as he sank into her.

"Spence," she whispered, her gasp of pleasure comingling with his. She arched up into him, sinking five nails into his back and five more into his ass, giving the cat a run for its money when it came to impatience.

He gave her slow, deep thrusts that had her panting his name along with some wordless, frenzied pleas that spurred him on, leaving his best intentions about taking his time in the dust. Incredibly aware of her every movement, the way she coiled herself around him like he was the anchor that kept her from floating away, he heard the exact second her breathing changed, felt her muscles tightening around him. Nudging her lips with his, he kissed her, swallowing her cry as she burst, and just like that, he was done for as well.

They stayed locked together for long moments, trying to catch their breath, Spence fully aware that he'd just let himself fall a little bit harder, certainly harder than he'd intended or wanted. Not that it seemed to matter to his brain what he wanted. His heart had taken over, and for a guy who prided himself on his brains, it was a humbling admittance of defeat.

Colbie was more content than she could remember feeling and hoped she never had to move again.

"Sleepy?" Spence whispered in her ear,

making her smile at the sex-roughened low timbre.

"Exhausted," she admitted. "But it's a fairly regular state for me. I'm writing like the wind here but I'm still a terrible insomniac. You?"

"No. I usually sleep like a baby."

She sighed. "I hate people who can go to sleep as soon as they shut their eyes. It takes me three hours, a minimum of five hundred position changes, and a sacrifice to the gods."

He laughed but it faded when his phone vibrated from the vicinity of his pants, still on the floor.

"Hey," she teased. "At least you know it can't be a sibling asking for money."

"True."

His phone buzzed again. And again he didn't move.

"It might be work," she said.

"Yes, but I'm the boss, so . . ."

She laughed. "You don't need to at least look?"

"I don't want to adult today," he said, nuzzling in closer. "I don't even want to human today. Today I want to dog. I want to lie on the floor in the sun. Just pet me and bring me snacks."

She laughed and he ran a finger across

her breast, giving out a quiet hum of pleasure when her nipple puckered up tighter for him. He leaned over her, pressing her back against the pillows as he licked her like a lollipop.

"Spence," she gasped. Her insatiable need for him no longer shocked her but she was still getting used to it, to days being in this heightened state of awareness and need for him. Sinking her fingers into his hair, she tugged until he looked at her. "I don't want to be that girl," she said.

"Which girl?"

"The one that keeps you from your work or your promises."

"Not your problem." He kissed the tip of her breast and sat up. "And if it helps to know, being with you like this is very . . . motivating." He flashed a smile.

One she was helpless to not return. "So . . . me being here isn't a complete hindrance?"

He pulled her onto his lap and rubbed an impressive erection at her core. "Depends on your definition of *hindrance* . . ."

She smiled, as she knew he'd expected her to.

"I can multitask," he assured her. "I'll get back to things in a minute."

"Well, you *are* the master at the one-minute thing."

"Ouch," he said mildly. "Not exactly what a guy wants to hear — his name and *one minute* spoken in the same sentence."

She smiled. "The only time I think of you and *one minute* together, it's in reference to how fast you can get me off with that thing you do with your tongue."

He smiled a badass smile. "I've got a few other tricks as well," he murmured and pulled her down to him, rolling her beneath him, making himself at home between her legs. "Allow me to demonstrate."

Oh boy . . .

Chapter 24
#OhMylanta

Colbie awoke at the touch of Spence's hand on her hip. It was late afternoon — she wasn't sure what time, but they'd spent the rest of the day in her bed. She was warm and comfortable in his arms, their legs tangled together, her back to him. The fading light slanted through the window, casting a glow through the room.

But that wasn't what made her smile. It was feeling Spence's lips on her shoulder, softly exploring. She could feel the heat of his body against her bare back, the hair on his chest slightly scratchy against her skin as he moved. She lay there for a moment, luxuriating in it all.

How in the world could she lose herself so completely, without a single inhibition, with a man she hardly knew? It boggled her brain.

"I smell something burning," he murmured huskily.

"Just thinking. Why is it I feel like I've known you forever?"

"Because we like each other," he said, "and because we don't need anything from each other either." He rolled her over to face him, his hands sliding down her back to cup her ass, his eyes dark and hungry.

"Not . . . anything?" she asked, wrapping her arms around his neck, making room for him between her legs.

"Well, maybe one thing," he said against her mouth and then went about recharging her batteries again.

And then again, because Spence was nothing if not thorough.

Elle slipped into Spence's office at the ass crack of dawn the next day. But since she was carrying coffee, he forgave her the interruption. Until she spoke.

"So who was the expensive suit with Colbie yesterday?"

He sipped his coffee and went noncommittal.

"Everyone's taking guesses on what's going on, you know. Willa and Pru think maybe Colbie's a corporate spy trying to find out how far you've come with your drone project."

Spence raised a brow.

"Kylie thinks maybe one of her brothers works at some news conglomerate and is pimping her out to try to catch you with your defenses down."

Spence shook his head and drank some more coffee.

"Trudy and Luis think she's after your money."

Spence leaned back in his chair. "And you?" he asked. "What do you think?"

She sat on the corner of his desk, her business suit a siren kickass red today, her heels high and shiny black. "I think that . . . I don't know what to think."

He laughed. "Well, there's a first time for everything."

She laughed a little. "I know, right?" She shook her head. "It could still be a con, you know. It's not like you're being careful."

"And you know this how?"

"Because you were sighted nearly getting in a fight protecting her yesterday."

He wasn't surprised. The building could've doubled for downtown Mayberry with all the gossip and secret spilling that went on, and that included the outlying streets as well. "Maybe there's no conspiracy," he said. "Maybe she just really likes me."

Elle sighed.

"Is it really so hard to believe that a smart, attractive woman with a sense of humor could be into me?" he asked.

Elle straightened, bristling. "Okay, that's not fair. There's a lot about you to like. A lot, Spence. But face it, you've got a horrible track record."

"We all have horrible track records," he said. "It's what leads up to the real thing. It's what allows you to recognize it when it shows up. As you should well know."

She stared at him for a beat and then acknowledged the truth of that with a sigh. "Okay, but I'm going to need you to tell me you're not in love with her after only two-plus weeks."

He paused. He didn't want to lie to her but this wasn't a conversation he was going to have with Elle before he had it with Colbie. "Probably more lust than love."

Elle sighed again, this one pure relief. "Okay," she said. "Lust is fine."

"Thanks for the permission."

She rolled her eyes. "You pay me a lot of money to keep you protected."

"From the press," he said. "From the needs of this building. From the demands on my time for things you can handle. Not my love life, Elle."

"There's that *l*-word again," she said. "So,

you know how Colbie takes notes all the time?"

"Yeah."

"Tina got a peek at her laptop screen the other day at the coffee shop. Colbie had a page up about how deep you have to dig a hole to keep a dead body buried and safe from the elements."

He shook his head, keeping his smile to himself.

"I know," she said. "Kind of insane, right?" Her eyes narrowed, catching on to his amusement. "What the hell is so funny? Mrs. Winslow overheard her on the phone planning some sort of big heist. Even Finn and Sean are worried about you and you're laughing about it."

"Have you talked to Archer or Joe about this?" he asked.

"No. Archer told me to mind my own business, which obviously, I'm never going to do. I've been trying to get to Joe, but he's been avoiding me like the plague, although . . . Shit," she said, looking at her phone. "I did miss a call from him."

"Call him back," Spence suggested.

"Now?"

"Yeah."

Elle pulled out her phone and hit a number. "Hey," she said. "I —" She paused, listening. "Huh. And Archer knows this . . . ?" Another pause. "Okay, thanks." She disconnected, opened her e-mail, and thumbed through something. Two minutes later, she looked up and met Spence's gaze. "You know."

"Yes. But only since the other night, if that helps."

Elle sank to a chair. "And Archer knows."

"He's Joe's boss, so of course he knows. He knows everything. When you sicced Joe on Colbie, what did you think would happen?"

She shook her head. "Not this. But I guess I'm not all that surprised." She didn't look particularly appeased either.

"How about sorry," he said. "Are you sorry?"

"Hey, it could've been any of a million reasons why Colbie was acting shady. I couldn't have guessed this reason. It's a good one though," she admitted grudgingly. "Impressive."

"Hugely so." He had to laugh. "You can't even admit when you're wrong, can you."

"I can admit when *you're* wrong." She sighed. "Dammit. You should've told me who she was. I'd have been . . ."

"Nicer?" Spence asked mildly.

She sighed. "Okay, yes. And I am sorry, but —"

"Sorrys don't usually have a 'but' after them."

"Fine. I was wrong," Elle said. "*And* I'm sorry."

"Wow." Spence smiled. "Did that hurt?"

She ignored that. "*But . . .* something I *wasn't* wrong about?" she asked. "Is that I can see you're falling for her. Like *really* falling, Spence."

"I don't fall."

Her expression softened. "Listen, I actually think she's falling too."

"I'm not as optimistic as you."

That got a laugh out of her. Elle was a lot of things, but optimistic wasn't one of them.

"The problem is, where does this leave you?" she asked. "You're already having a hard time with this project and —"

"It doesn't matter," he said, not wanting to talk about the drone project, which was currently at the top of his shit list. "None of it matters. She's leaving on Christmas Eve and that'll take care of everything."

She stared at him and slowly shook her head. "You can't really believe that. Love isn't that simple, Spence."

He drew a deep breath. "Yeah, well, love sucks."

Elle didn't even try to disagree. "Some-times, absolutely," she agreed. "But the thing is, once you've been hit over the head with it, it actually sucks a lot more to walk away and leave it behind."

"I'm not the one walking away," he said.

"Maybe it'll pass," she said. "Maybe . . . maybe it's just a really powerful crush."

"Deep green," he said.

Elle blinked. "Huh?"

"Colbie's eyes are a clear, piercing green, but sometimes they're more like jade when she's sad or upset."

She was still staring at him. "You've finally gone off the deep end."

"How long have I known you? And the others? And I don't know what color anyone else's eyes are." Not even Clarissa's. "But I know Colbie's. I also know that she bites her lower lip when she's trying not to smile. That her comfort food of choice is mac and cheese. That she loves and cares about her family more than she worries about herself. That she can laugh at herself and life. Hell, she makes *me* laugh at life, and we both know that's a real feat in itself."

Elle was still just staring at him. "Interest-ing," she said. "It's not just any woman who can get *you* to slow down and notice the little things." She shook her head. "I guess I have no choice but to let this go. Or at least try."

"Try real hard," he suggested. "And while I'm asking something of you, I'm going to ask this too — Chasing she's alone out here. No friends, no family. Can't you and the girls invite her to something?"

"Like?"

"Like the chick nights you have where you all get together and . . . I don't know, whatever it is you all do."

Elle looked amused. "Just for curiosity's sake, what is it that you think we do?"

"Look, all I know is that last month you, Pru, Willa, Kylie, and Haley all went to some drag show and ended up onstage. When the club got raided by the police for some shady dealings in the back rooms, everyone got dragged downtown. Archer, Finn, and Joe had to bail you all out."

"You want me to get your girlfriend arrested?"

"No," he said. "I really, *really* don't want you to get her arrested. I want you to include her in your crazy-ass gang and make nice."

"I don't make nice easily."

"No shit." Spence gave her the look that he knew she could never resist. "Just try. For me, okay? If you get the others involved, it won't look like I made you make friends with her."

Elle blew out a sigh and hopped off his desk. "The things I do for you."

When Spence was alone, he stood at the window and tried to gather his thoughts. Yeah, okay, so he was in deeper than he'd thought, or even planned on. But what he hadn't yet admitted to anyone, including himself, was that even if Colbie expressed an interest in making this work, he still wasn't sure they could. Could he change his habits? Let her in, all the way in? He wondered if these worries had anything to do with why his grandpa had picked up and left his family, out of the blue.

And did the old man have regrets?

Shaking his head — there was no use going there — Spence called Colbie. He'd already told her Joe and Archer knew. "Elle too."

Colbie was quiet for a beat. "Okay."

"Don't worry — they'll keep it to themselves."

"They're your people," she said. "If you trust them, then so do I."

His people. He had his people, and she had hers. It already felt as though they were a continent apart.

■ ■ ■ ■

One afternoon Colbie was writing away and getting lots of pages while she was at it, when Elle texted her to come to her second-floor office. Okay . . . When she got up there, she found Pru, Willa, Kylie, Haley, and Elle going through a trunk of costumes.

"Girls' night out," Elle said to Colbie.

Kylie was wearing a headband with a feather in it, a flapper dress, and some seriously high heels. "Hard to snag a good man when you're as short as me," she said.

"But can you walk in those?" Colbie asked doubtfully.

"To be determined."

"There are worse things than being short, you know," Haley said.

"True," Kylie said. "There are actually great things about being short. For instance, when you hug a guy and you feel his heartbeat against your ear, you know exactly where to stab him if he hurts you."

"She's just kidding," Willa told Colbie.

Behind Willa's back, Kylie shook her head. No, she was *not* kidding.

Haley, who didn't like men at all, just grinned. Willa was in only a bra and panties, pawing through the trunk. "The twenties theme is harder than I thought it'd be to pull off. I don't look good in hats."

Pru was in her boat captain's uniform. Or at least the pants and boots. She wore no top and was talking with someone on the phone. "Don't worry," she was saying. "We don't plan to get arrested this time."

Colbie hesitated. "So . . . you got arrested last time?"

"Yes, but that hardly ever happens," Kylie said and tossed Colbie an outfit.

"We for sure can't get arrested again tonight," Pru piped in. "I've gotta work in the morning. Plus I promised Finn."

"Party pooper," Kylie said.

"You in?" Elle asked Colbie.

She had no idea. Back home she didn't have a lot of friends. Janeen and Tracy. Jackson. Andrea Horvath, her editor. Most everyone else had fallen by the wayside when she'd gotten so busy.

"Colbie?" Willa asked.

"I've never actually been on a girls' night," she admitted.

"Why not?" Haley asked. "You and your tribe too busy or something?"

They had all paused what they were doing and were looking at her with varying degrees of curiosity.

"This is a little embarrassing," Colbie said.

"It can't be as embarrassing as when we took Pru to the spa and she screamed the house down during her Brazilian," Elle said.

"Hey," Pru said. "My bits are extremely sensitive."

Colbie sighed. "I don't exactly have a tribe."

They all blinked collectively.

"You don't have any friends?" Willa asked.

"Not ones that I can just call up and go out and get arrested with."

"*One* time," Pru said and sighed.

Willa smiled sweetly at Colbie and squeezed her hand. "Well, you can change that right here and now. Elle put tonight together, including you, so you've got your girlfriends now. Us. Right, guys?"

They all nodded enthusiastically. Well, except for Elle. Her nod wasn't quite enthusiastic, but Colbie got the feeling that she didn't do enthusiastic, so she decided to take it.

CHAPTER 25
#WhatTheFlip

They all finished dressing from the trunk and Colbie looked around, thinking they looked amazing. She glanced down at the clothes Elle had given her. *Clothes* being a loose term for a mini halter fringe dress, headband, belly button–length strand of pearls, and thigh-high stockings with lace trim along the tops.

She didn't recognize herself.

They'd just gotten out of an Uber at some exclusive, fancy nightclub in the Financial District, ready to partake in Murder Mystery Night.

"I just hope I'm the murderer, not the murderee," Elle said. "I don't look good in blood."

The six of them were dressed as — near as Colbie could tell — prostitutes from the Roaring Twenties.

"I wouldn't mind being the bad guy," Haley said and smiled. "Elle plans the best girls' nights out."

"Of course I do," Elle said.

Inside, they headed to the bar. A few minutes later, Pru eyed the line of shots in front of all of them and grimaced. "Tomorrow morning's going to hurt."

They were each given role cards with their story lines and information. Colbie realized she was the victim, but according to the rules, she couldn't tell anyone. She was to mingle until half past nine and then "vanish." But really she'd be allowed into a back room, a greenroom, where she'd be able to drink and eat and watch the next half hour on the monitors as the guests tried to solve her murder.

Elle immediately dragged them all into the bathroom, where she locked the door and then climbed up on the sink — impressive given her five-inch pumps — and blocked the surveillance camera with paper towels. "Okay," she said and pulled out the player card she'd been given. "I'm just a patron. You guys?"

Willa, Pru, Haley, and Kylie all said they were just patrons too. They turned to Colbie.

"We're not supposed to tell," she said.

"I get that," Elle said. "But no way am I letting any of you out of my sight tonight for any reason. So I need to know your roles so I can make sure you stay safe."

"And not arrested," Pru said.

Colbie sighed. "I'm the victim."

"Shit," Elle said. "Okay, we can work with this. Switch roles with me."

"Why?"

"Because no one's killing you on my watch."

Colbie felt herself oddly moved by this. "That's so sweet."

"The hell with sweet," Elle said. "Spence would fire my ass, and I love my job."

Okay, then.

Elle swapped their note cards. "Remember," she said, "we stick together."

They went out to the bar and had a few drinks. By the end of the second one, Willa was wearing a silly smile. "I love you guys," she said, slinging her arms around them all. "Thanks for loving me even though I always smell like wet dog and carry pet treats in my pockets."

"She's a cheap date," Haley whispered to Colbie.

"Hey," Willa said. "But true."

"I usually smell like wood," Kylie said, holding up her glass.

"Sometimes I smell like the bay *and* pelicans," Pru said.

"Well, I smell amazing," Elle said, waving at the bartender, buying them all another round before turning to Willa. "And ride or die, right? To the moon and back."

"Ride or die, to the moon and back," Kylie, Willa, Haley, and Pru repeated, completely out of sync but with such genuine sincerity that Colbie felt a catch in her throat.

"It's so sweet that you guys have each other like this," she said.

"And you too," Willa reminded her.

"Yeah?" Colbie asked, feeling sappy. And maybe a little bit drunk as she finished her second drink. "You'd really include me after only knowing me for two and a half weeks?"

"Depends on if you're going to make a big deal out of it or not."

The catch in Colbie's throat tightened and now her eyes burned too. "I'm sorry," she whispered, waving a hand in front of her face. "I didn't realize how lonely I was until right this very minute, being so far away from home."

"Aw." Kylie slipped an arm around her. "We won't let you be lonely tonight."

"Sure," Willa said. "We're a pretty good tribe to belong to. We always tell each other if there's something stuck in our teeth, and we all carry chocolate in our purses for everyone's various PMS days. Plus we all have our roles. Pru is the voice of reason. I'm the mom. Kylie can fix anything. Haley is our resident healer. And Elle is the protection."

"What am I?" Colbie asked.

"You tell us," Elle said.

Their gazes met and Colbie felt the challenge. "I'm a good storyteller." That's as far as she was willing to go right now, although looking into their friendly gazes — well, everyone's but Elle's; she was avoiding Elle's — she felt a stab of guilt.

"That's it?" Elle asked meaningfully.

"Yep."

"Hmm," Elle said. "I'm not sure Spence needs a . . . storyteller."

Willa opened her purse and handed Elle a piece of chocolate.

Elle sighed and ate it. After a few seconds, she looked at Colbie. "Sorry," she said to Colbie. "Old habits, protecting those I care about."

"Spence wouldn't want you trying to protect him," Pru said.

"No, he wouldn't," Elle said. "And he sure as hell wouldn't want me to say he's having trouble with work, but I'm going to say it anyway because he is."

"Wait." Colbie was trying to process but

felt impeded by the shots. "What do you mean, he's having trouble?"

"He hasn't been able to concentrate or focus."

"Since?"

Elle just looked at her.

Right. Since she'd come into the picture. "It's only been a little over two weeks."

Elle nodded. "Time that he didn't have to spare."

Colbie set her drink down. Was that true? And if so, why hadn't he told her himself? He'd made it seem like everything was fine.

"You know what we need?" Willa said into the awkward silence. "Another drink!"

Ten minutes later, Colbie could admit that Willa had been right. She was feeling no pain. In fact, she couldn't feel her toes. "Huh," she said and looked down. But yep, her toes were definitely still there.

"What's up?" Kylie asked.

"I thought I lost my toes there for a second."

Kylie grinned. "You're a cheap date too." She looked at Willa. "We should call Spence."

"Oh let me!" Pru said, bouncing up and down and clapping her hands. "I owe him a favor. I can hand him Colbie and we'll be even!"

"Hey," Colbie said, pretty sure she should object to anyone handing her over to anyone. Even if a part of her, a big part, quivered in anticipation of being given to Spence for the rest of the night.

"Are you denying you'd want to go home and ride him like a wild bronco?" Kylie asked her.

Everyone stared at Colbie, leaving her in a predicament. "If I say yes," she said with the care of the heavily inebriated, "then you'll all know we're sleeping together. If I say no, then you'll want to know why I'm *not* sleeping with him, and then I'll have to admit that I *am* sleeping with him."

"You do know you're talking out loud, right?" Elle asked.

But the others were all high-fiving themselves and also exchanging money.

"I won," Kylie said, counting her winnings. "But only because Elle didn't bet."

Colbie looked at Elle.

"She didn't want to bet on something that might hurt her BFF," Pru said. "That's why we're here tonight. To make sure you're okay for Spence, that you're not holding him back. And if so . . . well, I don't know what. Maybe off with your head!" she said dramatically.

When no one else laughed, Pru closed her

eyes, smacking her own forehead. "Right. *Don't* tell Colbie that Spence asked us to be her friends or that Elle wanted us to audition her for him . . ."

Colbie blinked and then stared at the others, hating that the alcohol was scrambling her thought process, making her slow as a turtle. "Wait . . . so this wasn't girls' night — it was an . . . audition?"

Pru winced. "Listen, we —"

"No." Colbie stood and grabbed her purse. And a little bit of the edge of the bar so she didn't tip over. "What the flip?"

A warm hand helped steady her. "Whoa, darlin', careful."

It was Tina from the coffee shop, tall as a mountain and dressed in head-to-toe flapper girl, looking fab while she was at it. She took in the now tense group and her smile faded. "Hey. What's wrong?"

"Colbie," Willa said, regret heavy in her voice. "We just wanted to make sure —"

"— That I'm Spence-worthy, I get it," she said. And oddly enough, she did. But it didn't take away from her embarrassment and hurt that she'd been fooled. "You let me think you wanted me here." She shook her head, feeling stupid . . . and drunk — a bad combo. "And I *gushed* about it," she said. "I went on and on, and you let me."

Feeling her throat go tight, she knew she needed out of there, now. "I've got to go."

That's when the fire alarm came on. And then the overhead sprinklers.

And then the lights went out.

Chaos reigned. People screamed and called out, and there was more than a little bit of shoving. Colbie was pushed into a wall and she shrank back against it, not wanting to get trampled. Then suddenly there was a beam of flashlight and a hand grabbed hers and tugged, hard.

She tried to dig in her heels.

"Come on," someone said, and she recognized this voice.

Elle.

Someone else came up at her back.

"Just me," Willa said cheerfully.

"And me," Kylie said, *not* cheerfully, sounding like she'd just run a marathon.

"Pru," Elle called out sharply. "Haley. Tina."

"All right here," Tina chimed in.

They were all soaked to the bone and shivering as Elle led them through the back, past a kitchen, and out a side door into the night.

"Damn," Kylie said and crouched down, wrapping her arms around her bent legs, dropping her head to her knees. "Damn,

damn, damn . . ."

"She's claustrophobic," Willa murmured to Colbie.

Colbie dropped to her knees in front of Kylie. "Chocolate," she said and snapped her fingers before holding out her palm to Willa.

Willa dropped a piece of chocolate — also wet — into her hand and she passed it to Kylie.

Kylie chomped it down and nodded. "Thanks," she said and her breathing slowed. "How in the world did you know that would help?"

"Chocolate fixes everything," Colbie said.

Everyone laughed but Elle, who gave Colbie a long speculative look. Colbie tried to give it back but she was more than a little tipsy, so she ended up cross-eyed, which had her losing her balance and falling to her ass on the sidewalk.

Kylie laughed and hugged her. "Perfect remedy for a panic attack. A friend acting drunk to cheer me up."

"Who's acting?" Colbie said. She managed to get to her feet and wobbled. Dammit. She gripped the wall. "You guys are the only actors here."

Willa winced. "Colbie —"

"No." She pointed at them collectively. Or

at least she hoped she did. Hard to tell since her vision was wonky. "I'm leaving now."

"Sorry, ma'am, but you're not."

This from one of the two police officers who'd shown up out of nowhere. "No one's leaving until we find out who set off the emergency fire system. It might've been a joke, but the building's got a lot of damage, which makes this a felony."

"We didn't do anything wrong," Tina said, putting herself between the girls and the cops. "We're patrons here and were lucky to get out without injury. We're going to walk away."

"Not yet," one of the cops said, a hand on his baton, eyes on Tina.

"Oh hell no," Elle said and stood arm-to-arm with Tina.

"Let it go, Elle," Tina told her. "Just drop it."

Elle jabbed a finger in the cop's chest. "Are you racial-profiling my friend?"

The cop yanked his cuffs out. "Okay, face the wall. All of you."

"Bite me," Elle said.

Which was how they all ended up in the back of a squad car.

Later they sat in lockup long enough for Tina, Willa, and Haley to make friends with everyone else in the cell. Pru and Kylie were more muted but still friendly. Elle didn't make friends.

Shock.

Colbie told herself to relax and take in the entire experience for research but she couldn't. Because tonight hadn't been their idea. They'd invited her only because Spence had asked.

She felt her face flame just thinking of it.

"Stop," Elle said. "You're thinking so hard your hair is smoking."

"You I'm not talking to," Colbie said.

"Fine. I'll talk. Watching you handle yourself tonight, I realized I've misjudged you. You're tough and smart, and you care. That combination is rare and I admire it. I'd apologize for being a bitch, but I can't promise it won't happen again, so I'll just say that I think you're good for Spence."

Colbie shook her head. That was the thing. She *wasn't* good for Spence. She kept him from his work, for one. And two, they had a big geographical problem. "You're wrong there," she said softly. "I'll hold him back."

Elle had the good grace to wince.

"You did *not* say that to her," Tina said.

Elle sighed. "Did you miss the part where I apologized?"

"It doesn't matter," Colbie said. "Look, I

know you're a good friend to Spence. And I want you to take care of him."

"Why?" Elle asked. "Where will you be?"

"New York."

Tina gasped. "You're . . . leaving him? You can't leave him."

"I'm going home."

"But he got dumped last time too —" Tina broke off when Elle elbowed her in the gut.

The guard outside the door pointed at Elle.

Elle gave him an innocent look.

The officer looked at Tina, who in turn smiled and winked at him.

The officer shook his head but relaxed.

Elle started to say something to Colbie, but another officer came down the hall and after consulting a list, he called their names.

They'd been bailed out.

"That was fast," Pru said.

"Not fast enough," Elle grumbled. "I hit my panic button the minute we had trouble at the club."

"Panic button?" Colbie asked.

"Archer is serious as a heart attack when it comes to Elle's safety," Kylie said. "She carries a panic button in case of trouble. She hits it and he shows up, no matter what."

"That sounds either really paranoid or really romantic," Colbie said.

Haley laughed quietly. "A little bit of both."

They walked through the precinct and out into the night. It was cold and raining, but they were still soaked through from the sprinklers, so it didn't matter.

"I'm taking an Uber," Colbie said. "Alone."

"Oh, honey, please don't be like that," Willa said.

"We really didn't mean to hurt your feelings," Pru said. "Please stay with us."

"I'll be fine on my own."

In a rare display of emotion, Elle reached for Colbie's hand. "I can't let you go off without us."

"Your favor is fulfilled," Colbie said. "You're off the hook."

"You're wrong. I told Spence I'd take care of you tonight. All night."

"Well, I absolve you of any responsibility of me," Colbie said and yanked free. Then she turned and bumped into a brick wall.

Which turned out to be Spence's chest. On either side of him were Finn, Joe, and Archer, all looking grimly amused.

Elle made a point of checking her watch.

Archer reached for her and tugged her

into him. "We had a little problem at the site. It's taken care of."

"And so are the charges," Joe said. "You are welcome."

"Hmph," Elle said. "We were actually innocent this time."

Joe grinned. "Whatever you say."

Colbie backed away from Spence because she didn't trust her body not to melt into his, even now when she was really mad.

And also, apparently, still drunk, because she tripped over her own feet. She would've gone down to her ass if he hadn't caught her.

"Got you," he said lightly and looked over her head at Elle. "How much did you give her to drink?"

"Hey," Colbie said, stabbing him in the chest with her finger. "I'm in charge of myself."

"Yeah?" he asked, bending down a little to look into her eyes. "How many fingers am I holding up?"

She blinked at him. There were so many fingers that she couldn't count them all. "That's not fair," she complained. "You're using like five hands. I can't count that fast."

Spence gave Elle a look.

Elle tossed up her hands. "Hey, who knew that she couldn't hold her liquor? She only had three drinks."

"How big were they?"

Colbie tried to roll her eyes and got dizzy. "Dammit," she said and dropped her forehead to Spence's chest.

He pulled her in and kissed her on top of her head. "Come on, I'll get you home."

"Okay, but only because I can't feel my feet. And don't talk to me. I'm very mad at you, you know."

"You can tell me all about it on the ride home."

"I mean it," she said, knowing he was just humoring her. "I'm not that pathetic that I need you to force your friends to pretend to be my friends."

She felt him look down at her, but whether that was in guilt or surprise, she didn't know and told herself she didn't care.

He opened the truck door for her. He buckled her in before going around the hood to get in himself. He aimed the heater vents at her. And the next thing she knew, she was in it, just the two of them. She felt the engine start. It was dark and the motor rumbled, and that was it. She felt safe and cozy, two things that had been in short supply for the past hour — not to mention her entire life — and she closed her eyes.

Just for a minute, she promised herself . . . and that was the last thing she remembered.

CHAPTER 26
#JiminyCricket

Colbie woke up to what felt like a guy in her head jackhammering at her brain. Given how much daylight was stabbing at her eyelids, it was late in the morning. Bracing herself, she managed to squint open one eye and groaned.

A pale, weak sun crept through the window. But it wasn't *her* window. And she wasn't in her bed.

She was in Spence's. With Cinder.

"Meow." The sleepy-looking cat was perched on the next pillow over.

Spence's bedside clock said twelve p.m. "What the ever-loving . . . ?" she started but quickly stopped because even a whisper was too loud for her hurting head. She'd never slept past eight o'clock in her entire life and it was *noon.* She took in that fact and then froze before slowly lifting the edge of the covers to look down at herself.

She wore the thigh-high lace stockings

and . . . absolutely nothing else. "What the ever-loving . . . ?"

"Already said that." This from Spence, who stood in the doorway, propping up the doorjamb with a broad shoulder.

Not naked.

"You," she said and then winced, her hands going to her head to hold it onto her shoulders. The sheet started to slip and she snatched at it, yanking it back up to her chin.

This got a small smile out of Spence. "I've seen it all before," he said in his morning voice, which had a deliciously sexy growly morning edge to it. Not that she was noticing.

"Not when I'm mad at you!" she said. "I don't recall giving anyone an all-access pass to my parts, especially you."

Spence set a couple of aspirin and a glass of water on the nightstand, and she gratefully took them even as she pointed at him. "Stay back." She didn't trust herself with him looking far too sexy for her own mental health.

"Bossy," he said. "I like it."

"You're a sick man."

"True story," he said without an ounce of shame.

"How did Cinder get here?"

"I didn't want to leave her alone all night, so I went and got her."

Okay, so that was sweet. "And why am I naked?"

"You said your clothes were still wet and that you liked to be naked in my bed anyway, and then you executed a pretty great strip show, in which you only fell over twice."

"I *what*?"

"Yeah, you asked for music," he said, "and while I was trying to talk you out of it, you went on without me." He smiled. "Or the music."

"Son of a motherless heifer."

He burst out laughing, sat on the bed with her, and pulled her into him. "I especially liked the dance moves you executed on my coffee table," he said. "You worked around all the drone parts, which was pretty impressive, actually."

She covered her face and groaned.

"I think your bra is still hanging off the TV."

"Stop. Don't tell me any more."

At what was undoubtedly a look of horror on her face, his smile faded, replaced by a whisper of surprise. "You don't remember," he said flatly.

"Reason number 523,002 not to drink

ever again," she muttered.

"What do you remember?"

She pushed away from him to think, letting images flit and play in her head. She remembered being excited about being invited to girls' night out. She remembered the cool club. The drinks. Jiminy Cricket! And then the fire alarm and sprinklers. Staggering outside —

She gasped. "We were arrested!"

"Only hauled in for questioning," Spence said. "Archer pulled some strings."

"You guys came and got us." She narrowed her eyes, remembering the rest. He'd asked Elle and the others to be her friend, like she was some loser. Also, he'd let her think they were each other's muse when in fact he wasn't able to work when she was around. She was so mad at him.

Mad and embarrassed.

And for the first time since arriving in San Francisco, she wanted to go home. She dropped her head to her bent knees.

She felt him shift. Then something dropped over her head. His T-shirt, soft and warm from his body. It fell around her, bringing his scent with it.

It smelled delicious.

"You're having trouble with work?" she asked, her voice muffled against her knees, her eyes squeezed shut as he stroked a hand down her back.

"Someone's got a big mouth," he said evenly.

"If you didn't have the time to spend with me, why would you do it?"

His hand kept up its slow up-and-down on her back, the heat of him warming her. Which she both loved and resented, because it was hard to hold on to a good mad with his hand on her.

"Because I couldn't help myself," he finally said. "I thought I was all work and no play, but with you, it's different. Probably because I knew going in that there was our expiration date."

She lifted her head and met his gaze. "Our Christmas Eve expiration date."

His eyes were full of the same conflicting emotions she knew were all over her face. "Yes."

"I get it," she admitted. After all, she'd thought the same thing. The very same thing. That this was for only a few weeks, the end.

Because who could've guessed that she could lose her heart that fast?

Since all she was wearing was his T-shirt, she did her best to gracefully slide out of his bed with his top sheet also wrapped around her.

Instead she did the opposite of graceful and took a header, hitting the floor.

Spence was at her side in an instant, crouched low. "You okay?"

"Everything but my pride," she said and sat up. She tried to get to her feet, but his foot was on the sheet, which meant she could either start a tug-of-war or lose it.

Luckily, his shirt was long enough to hit her midthigh as she stood and headed toward the bathroom, tugging it down over her bare butt for good measure.

"Where are you going?" he asked.

"To get decent enough to get out of your hair."

"Colbie —"

Ignoring him, she turned on the light and tried to squelch her involuntary scream at the sight of herself.

Thanks to not removing her mascara, she looked like a raccoon. A haggard one. And then there was her hair, which had rioted at some point during the night and now resembled the kind of hair clot one removed from one's vacuum cleaner after not having done so for six months or more.

She nearly screamed again when she realized Spence stood in the doorway.

"So . . . it gets a little worse," he said.

She looked at him, which was a huge mistake because he was shirtless thanks to her, and his jeans were sitting dangerously low on his hips, lovingly cupping some of his very best parts. "How much worse can it possibly get?" she asked, refusing to acknowledge that having him this close was making her mouth water. "You bribed your friends into pretending to be my friends. Then we got almost arrested. And after that, I apparently went all *Fifty Shades* on your ass."

A small smile crossed his mouth. He'd liked it when she accidentally swore, the rat-fink. "Not *my* ass," he said. "But you did say I could spank yours."

Her gaze met his in the mirror. "Over your dead body," she said and made him laugh.

"Tell me the worse part," she said.

"When we showed to pick you guys up, you announced to everyone within earshot that you were going to use this whole experience as writing fodder for the next Storm Fever book."

She stared at him in disbelief because while she remembered thinking that, she absolutely hadn't planned on saying it out loud. "I did not."

He just held her gaze.

"Captain Crunch!"

That had him smiling for real. "The gang will keep your secret," he assured her. "That's what friends do."

"But see, that's my point — they're *not* my friends. And speaking of that, I can't believe you asked them to *pretend* to be my friends —"

"Colbie —"

"No, you know what? I don't want to talk about it." She stalked past him and went looking for her clothes, which were scattered throughout his place. The flapper dress near his front door. A heel here. Another heel there. And sure enough, her bra was hanging from his big-screen TV.

Her panties were near the front door.

Good God. "I'm never drinking again," she moaned, and this time when she went into his bathroom, she closed the door — on his nose — and locked it.

Spence mindlessly searched his fridge while Colbie was in the bathroom. He peered past containers of food without seeing anything except the look of surprised hurt on Colbie's face.

The look he'd put there.

He hated himself for that. There'd been women in the past two years since Clarissa who'd tried to distract him, but no one had been able to pull it off.

Colbie had been different from the start. She understood what it was like to come up against a deadline or to hit a brick wall doing it. He knew without a doubt that she was in his corner, rooting for him, sympathizing with him, perfectly willing to wait patiently on the sidelines.

It was him. He was the problem. He couldn't put her on the sidelines.

Every time he'd lost focus over the past few weeks, he'd assured himself that once Colbie left, life would go back to normal. He'd be back at the top of his game.

He'd been lying to himself.

Nothing had ever been like this with her, and it was going to hurt like hell when she left, because — in spite of himself — he was deeply emotionally attached.

Unfortunately, she was deeply emotionally attached to her life in New York, to her family, her career, and she wouldn't have room in her life for him. He knew this.

Didn't change the wanting . . .

A part of him got that he was simply throwing up his own roadblocks now. Truth was, he was in way over his head and since he didn't know how to do this, when she left, he was going to stick to what he *did* know how to do.

■ ■ ■ ■

In Spence's bathroom, Colbie was trying to
finger-comb her nest of hair when she was
held hostage by a group text.

Kylie:
Colbie — please know that we really do
consider you one of the tribe. And not
just because you're the author of one of
my favorite series EVER!

Haley:
Yeah, you're one of us — with or without
Spence. And not just because I've had
tickets purchased for your movie for the
past three weeks.

Willa:
Fangirling aside — but oh my God, Colbie, or CE, which do we call you? — we
hope you forgive us AND Spence.

Pru:
Yeah, maybe last night was his sugges-
tion, but you should know we all agreed
because we like you.

Kylie:
Even Elle. Right, Elle?

Elle:
Well mostly I like your kickass shoes.

Willa:
ELLE.

Elle:
Fine. I like your shoes and you.

Elle:
And okay, I like you for Spence too.
Don't make me sorry I said that!

It was the nicest thing Elle could've said
and Colbie let herself get a little emotional
over that before blowing her nose and giving herself a stern glance in the mirror.
Toughen up!
When she left the bathroom a few minutes
later, Spence was pulling bagels out of the
oven.
"Seems awfully domestic for you," she
said. "I'm impressed."
"Don't be. It's the only thing I found in
this place to cook you for breakfast."
She felt her heart catch at the gesture.
"You don't have to cook me breakfast,

Spence. I've already taken up enough of your time."

"Colbie —"

She turned away and reached for her phone as it rang. "It's my mom," she said and answered with "What's wrong?"

"Honey, didn't Jackson talk to you? It's getting late in the season and no one's decorated. And I imagine there's shopping to be done, right? It's tradition. Come home. We miss you."

Colbie pinched the bridge of her nose. "Mom, you miss me because I do all the work for the holiday, and I'm not even all that into Christmas to begin with. Maybe until I get back, you and the guys could try making some new traditions."

"Like what?" she asked, sounding worried.

"Like something that includes *you* guys doing the work."

"Well, Kent's baking brownies. That's a good start, right?"

Oh good God. "Mom, whatever you do, don't sell those brownies. Or eat any."

"Why ever not?"

"Trust me, okay? Let me talk to him."

"Do you think he's baking The Marijuana?" she whispered.

Yes, that's exactly what she thought. He

and Eddie would make a dangerous team.

"Those boys," her mom said.

Colbie resisted smacking herself in the forehead with her own phone.

"I just don't know what to do with them," her mom said.

"You could try being the mom," Colbie suggested.

"You do it so much better. Honey, come home already. Oh, here, hold on, here's Kent."

"Yo," Kent said.

"Yo yourself," Colbie said. "Are you cooking pot brownies?"

"I don't know what you're talking about."

Colbie gave up resisting and indeed smacked herself in the forehead with her phone. "Okay, listen to me very carefully," she said. "You're a complete ass."

"Hey."

"The worst part is that it's not even really your fault," she said. "It's Mom's. And mine. I've enabled you. We've enabled you. But I can't do it anymore, okay? You've got to start doing things like laundry and shopping and taking care of the house and yourself."

"Why?" he asked. "You do it better."

She ground her back teeth. "Yes, well, I made a mistake. I shouldn't have done those things for you, because now you're growing up an entitled white boy who thinks he's God's gift and can do anything he wants. And it's not true. You have to earn what you want."

"And . . . I earn it by doing my own laundry?"

"Yes! You need to do your own laundry — including buying your own damn detergent! You also need to cook for yourself."

"Like the brownies?"

"No!" She strove for calm. "Put me on speaker so Kurt can hear this too." She waited until she had both of them. "Listen to me. When I say cook for yourselves, I don't mean drugs, and I don't mean takeout either."

"Aw, man," Kent said. "How about running away from home to find ourselves like you did? Can we do that?"

"No!" She felt steam coming out her ears. "You don't get to do that. You both need to get a job that's more than fifteen hours a week. I don't care if it's bagging groceries — you need it in order to find a purpose in your life, and you need it to learn how to be a contributing human being or you're both going to be jobless, mean to girls, and a drain on society."

Spence was brows up, eating his bagel as

he listened to her going off on her brothers, trying to hide a smile.

"Do you hear me?" she asked the speechless twins.

"Yeah, we hear you," Kent said. "But we gotta go. The pizza was just delivered."

Colbie disconnected and stared at her phone. "I've got to go," she said, more to herself than anything. There wasn't anything keeping her here now anyway.

"So you're leaving early?"

She turned to meet his gaze. "I think it's best."

"Colbie —"

"Look, I need to give you your life back. And clearly I need to go fix mine."

He started to open his mouth, but she knew if he said anything sweet or sexy, she'd cave, so she spoke first. "Look, we both knew this was inevitable, right? I mean, I was going to go back in four days anyway."

"You're running away because of what you think happened last night," he said. "At least be honest about that."

She crossed her arms, feeling defensive because she'd been as honest as she could be with him.

Okay, so maybe not.

But she didn't know how to bare her soul to him without getting hurt. And anyway, now they were out of time. "Last night has nothing to do with it," she said.

"Bullshit. You think I forced my friends to be your friends —"

"You *did.*"

"— And now you're going to use that excuse instead of the real problem to run away. *Again.*"

"Not fair," she said quietly, his shot taking aim right at her heart and hitting it bull's-eye. "I understand that you were just trying to help me when you got me invited to girls' night. I can even accept that maybe I needed that help. But I feel terrible that I've been distracting you, Spence. I wish you could've told me that."

His gaze was intense on hers. "I don't remember ever saying that was a problem for me. In fact, you've turned out to be the exception to my every rule."

She had no idea what that meant. "I practically barged into your life. It was self-ish. Just because I was on vacation didn't mean you were too." She held up a hand when he started to speak. "You've been great about spending time with me. And I'm going to miss you," she added softly. "But I really do think it's time for me to go."

"But you've been writing again," he said.

"Why would you cut that short?"

She didn't want to. Things were going so good that just yesterday she'd sent chapters off to both Jackson and Andrea, her editor.

"Colbie," he said softly, coming closer, setting his hand over hers where she gripped the counter with white knuckles because she didn't want to leave him and she didn't want to leave while everything was going so well with her writing and . . . she didn't want to leave, period.

"Don't go," he said. "Not like this. I don't want to be the reason. Yes, I need to focus on work, but that's my problem, not yours. I needed a mini vacay too. I'll settle back into a routine soon enough."

She shook her head.

"Would it help if I tell you that I'm not expecting more than what we have?"

She gave him a look of disbelief.

"Okay, you're right," he said. "I'd love more with you, and if someone had told me that could happen in three weeks, I'd have told them they had been eating too many of my grandpa's brownies."

"No fair," she whispered.

"I'm not trying to play fair. I'm playing for keeps. Don't panic," he said when she just stared at him in genuine shock. "You've made it clear that you're not in this for the long haul. So I'll take you however I can get you. Long-distance friends with hopefully some seriously good benefits when one of us can travel."

She could scarcely breathe. "I want you to know how much this time meant to me," she said, heart pounding, legs weak. "Getting away from my life for these past few weeks has given me clarity on a lot of things. Such as how much of my own life I've been ignoring. I was starved for simple things, like friends . . ."

He grimaced. "Colbie —"

". . . And affection. And," she went on, giving herself a minute by scooping up Cinder and hugging the cat to her chest, "physical touch as well. You gave me all that and I want to thank you for it. Sincerely."

He shook his head. "Don't do this. What we have here is too special for you to mess it up because you're scared."

"I'm not."

"You are."

Okay, he had her there. And not wanting these to be the last words between them, she forced herself to meet his gaze. "I found myself here," she said softly. "And a big part of that was thanks to you. I fell more than a little bit in love with San Francisco and the people in it." And then because her eyes had gone blurry and her throat too tight to speak, she forced herself to walk out the door.

Chapter 27
#SuckADuck

Colbie was packing her suitcase — with Cinder helpfully sitting in the middle of it, getting cat hair on everything — trying to feel good about her decision to go.

"You understand, right?" she asked the cat.

"Meow."

"You know you're coming with me, don't you? Willa sold me a cat carrier, a comfy, cozy one that you can snooze in all the way across the country right beneath my seat." Or she *hoped* Cinder would snooze all the way across the country. It was going to be an adventure for the both of them, but she couldn't leave the cat behind.

It was bad enough what she *was* leaving behind.

Or rather, who.

She jumped when her phone rang. Jackson's name flashed on the screen as the phone danced across the coffee table while she debated whether or not to answer. In the end, her manners took over and she grabbed the phone.

"Is this supposed to be some kind of a joke?" he asked.

"Um . . ." She pulled the phone away from her ear to stare at it. "What?"

"The pages you sent," he said. "It's a joke, right?"

A ball of anxiety nearly choked her. As did a ball of anger. She'd slaved over those pages! "What are you talking about?"

"Since when do you write romance?"

Colbie tucked her phone into the crook of her neck so she could grab her laptop and open her story file. She scrolled through the pages and took a deep, shaky breath.

Embarrassment tangled with the anxiety and temper, never a good match — especially since he was right.

She was writing a romance. "Oh my God," she whispered to herself.

"I mean, yeah, the writing is good. Excellent even," he said. "But you're a YA author."

She closed her eyes.

"It's that new guy, isn't it," Jackson said.

But Colbie was still stuck on what she'd done. Her writing was different but . . . she'd *loved* writing it. "Okay, yes, it's different. But there's still a story there. I can merge both worlds."

Jackson was silent. A first.

"Look, I'm coming home," Colbie said. "We can discuss it when I get there."

"When?"

"Tomorrow." Her flight was first thing in the morning. She'd be walking away from one of the best times of her entire life. She'd be walking away from new friends. She'd be walking away from Spence.

The thought was crushing, and she knew there was something she had to do before she left. "I'll see you there," she said and disconnected. Then she went to the second floor and knocked on Elle's office door.

Elle opened up and looked at her in surprise. "Hey," she said. "Again, about last night —"

"It doesn't matter."

"It does," Elle said. "I want to make sure you understand that no one meant to hurt your feelings."

"I know."

"And I hope you also know that we . . ." she paused and rolled her eyes ". . . like you. Okay? With or without your kickass shoes."

Colbie had to laugh. "Did that hurt?"

Elle sighed. "Not as much as I thought it

would. Thanks for stopping to see me."

"I didn't come for you. I . . ." She shook her head. "He doesn't have any decorations, Elle. Not a one."

"Spence?"

"No," Colbie said. "Santa Claus."

Elle laughed and put her hand to her heart. "I feel so proud of your sarcasm and cynicism. Spence doesn't have any decorations because he won't let Trudy decorate his place."

"Why not?"

Elle shrugged.

"Probably something stupidly male, like he thinks he doesn't have a right to Christmas because he doesn't have family around other than Eddie. Which is bullshit because we're his family and he never puts anything over us ever."

"Do you have any extra decorations?" Colbie asked. "And how can we get rid of him for a bit?"

Elle picked up her phone and checked something. "He and Caleb are out at Marin Headlands, probably drone-testing." She called someone. "Need holiday decorations," she said. "For Spence's apartment. No, he's not asking. Colbie is." She listened for a few seconds and then laughed wryly. "I do get the irony." She disconnected.

"Willa's bringing you some stuff. She'll meet us at the elevator."

"And the irony part?" Colbie asked.

"Spence has always pushed us to go with our hearts and yet he's managed to hold back on going with his. Until now."

Colbie shook her head. "No, you don't understand. I'm leaving tomorrow morning. But I don't feel right going until I know he'll be okay, that he'll still celebrate Christmas."

Elle just looked at her. "What about Cinder?"

"She's coming with me."

"You're taking a stray cat but leaving behind your man?"

Colbie's heart twisted. Her man . . . "He doesn't fit into the carrier I bought."

Elle shook her head. "You two are both so stubborn you should have your pictures in the dictionary."

Colbie opened her mouth and then shut it. She had no defense.

Willa did indeed meet them at the elevator and the three of them decorated Spence's apartment. At the forty-five-minute mark, Finn called Willa and warned them that Spence and Caleb were back and heading their way.

Willa and Elle vanished, saying something

about not wanting to get caught in the cross fire. Plus Keane had sexted Willa, so she was in a big hurry to get home.

Colbie stayed, quickly changing into the dress she'd worn on her and Spence's first date because she knew how much he'd liked it.

Spence and Caleb walked in the front door less than a minute later, each carrying two drones, looking tense and unhappy.

They set their things down, Spence's gaze never leaving Colbie, who was standing in the center of his now decorated living room, surrounded by twinkling white lights, garland, and mistletoe . . . everywhere.

She might have gone overboard.

There was also a tree in one corner with colorful balls hanging from the branches. She had no idea how Willa had gotten it here so quickly, but she hadn't asked questions in her eternal gratitude.

Spence looked stunned. "When did Christmas throw up in here?"

Caleb, clearly taking in the tension between them, backed to the door. "I've gotta . . ." He jerked a thumb in the direction of the door and then vanished.

Spence met her gaze, his own completely shuttered from her for the first time since she'd met him. "Thought you were gone," he said.

"My flight doesn't leave until the morning." She gave him a small smile. "And I kept thinking about how lonely it seemed in here, the only place in the entire building without holiday decorations."

He held her gaze a moment and blew out a breath. "Look, you're a fixer. I get that. You assume responsibility for everyone and everything around you. But I don't need fixing, Colbie."

"I know."

He gestured around them. "And yet there's stuff twinkling everywhere," he said, still not coming toward her.

Not touching her.

His voice distant.

It broke her heart and she closed her eyes.

"Colbie."

His voice. Low. Sexy. Perfect. Was she really going to be able to walk away? And even if she managed that, how was she going to move on and forget? The lump in her throat became so huge she couldn't swallow. Or speak. Stupid lump.

Then she felt his hands on her shoulders. "Honey, look at me."

She opened her eyes and found his intense and unwavering.

"This isn't easy for me either," he said. "I suck at goodbyes."

She could only nod, but she did step into him and press her face into his throat.

He let out a breath and his warm arms came around her, hard. "We've got a problem."

"What?"

"I want to toss both our phones out the window and then lock ourselves into my bedroom. Tell me absolutely not."

Instead she let her lips brush softly against the hollow of his throat.

"Honey."

"I'm trying." But that was a big fat fib. She wasn't trying to say no at all.

"Last chance," he warned.

She lifted her head and met his intense gaze. "I want this. I want you, Spence, even if it's the last time."

"Colbie," he said quietly, regret heavy in his voice.

She closed her eyes tight.

Apparently getting that she didn't want to talk, he took her hand and used it to pull her slowly back into him, giving her plenty of time to change her mind.

Which wasn't going to happen.

She kissed him and then kept at it, kissing hello and goodbye and just because, because

381

she knew that all this was going to stop soon. When she left. She'd had trouble sleeping because she missed him already, so much.

He seemed to feel the same as her as he put everything he had into the kiss, his hands running reverently over her body. "Did you wear this dress for me?"

"No, I actually forgot how much you like it."

He chuckled. "Liar." He tightened his grip on her. "I'm going to miss you too." He pulled her into his bedroom, and then she was in free fall to the bed.

He stood at the foot of the mattress looking down at her, eyes dark with nefarious intent, and something new swirled through past the sadness she was keeping at bay.

Anticipation.

Lust.

She'd felt the pull of both those things before with him, of course, but this time there was also something else.

Affection.

Deep affection.

New, terrifying, and . . . even more arousing. "Spence." She crooked her finger at him.

He responded by climbing up her body to kiss her hard, both demanding and gaining access to her mouth. Leaning over her, his hands roughly ran the length of her body until she was caught up in a rising tide of hunger and need that didn't give a damn about commitments or declarations of love.

When he pulled her phone from her pocket, she had to laugh.

He removed his phone from his own pocket as well, held up both for her to see, and then vanished.

He was back in twenty seconds.

"Did you throw them out the window?" she asked.

"No. Even I can't bring them back from a five-story fall. I put them in the freezer."

She laughed.

He didn't. She could see the effect she was having on him and it was incredibly empowering. She started to sit up to get her hands on him, but before she could, he slid to her ankles and yanked, making her fall to her back.

She stopped laughing and maybe moaned as he crawled up her body. Holding her gaze, he slowly pulled her hands above her head, pinning her to the mattress beneath him, covering her mouth with his. This was no simple goodbye kiss but rather a "not letting you go before I make sure you never forget me" sort of kiss, and it gave her a full-body shiver of the very best kind.

"Off," he murmured, fisting a hand in the material of her dress, pushing it up enough to reveal her black lacy panties. Then, before she could lend a hand, he'd stripped her himself. Which wasn't to say he did this impatiently. In fact, he spent a lot of time kissing and suckling and fanning the flames over every inch he exposed.

Nope, the only person in a hurry was her as she shoved up his shirt, struggling to get him as naked as she. He came up on his knees to help, shrugging out of his shirt. Her hands traveled the now familiar path of muscles and smooth skin, down the length of his torso and beyond.

He was rock solid and gorgeous, and she had no idea how she was supposed to walk away.

"Colbie."

"Off," she said, mimicking his much lower voice. "Everything off."

A laugh rumbled from him and he complied. Then dipping his head, he licked and sucked a trail down her body, taking his damn sweet time about it too, so that by the time he reached her thighs, every cell in her body was alive, waiting for the moment when he'd press his mouth against her.

She cried out when he finally did, fisting

her fingers in his hair as his tongue worked its magic, leaving her helpless to do anything but quiver and squirm and whimper with each expert stroke as he took her to the edge and held her there for an impossibly long beat before nudging her over.

While she struggled to remember how to work her lungs, he made his way back up her body, planting a series of warm, wet kisses over her stomach and ribcage and then her breasts . . . and then at last his face was level with hers.

His eyes were penetrating, dark with desire. His breathing fragmented as he pushed inside her, hard and thick. "You'll remember me," he said.

Of that she was most certain. "I'll remember you," she promised, already halfway to another orgasm. "Always."

With that, he finally gave her what she wanted and pounded into her, making her writhe against him as she came, crying out his name between shuddered gasps. She knew he came right along with her and reveled in the pounding of his heart against hers as they struggled to come down from the stroke-level intensity.

They fell asleep like that, limbs entwined, sharing air.

When she opened her eyes again, she had

no idea how long they'd been out. All she could remember was cuddling under the covers and hearing the question she hadn't meant to ask escape her lips anyway. "Would you really come visit me?"

"If you ask, yes."

She thought about that long after he'd fallen asleep. Because with their lives so deeply entrenched in their respective cities, three thousand miles apart, she didn't see how this could work. She just didn't. Very carefully, she turned her head and looked at the clock.

Four a.m.

She had to go. Spence was on his back, face turned toward her, entire body relaxed and still, his chest slowly rising and falling.

He was deeply asleep. She could tell he was exhausted. Mentally, physically, and if it was at all possible, emotionally as well.

"I'll remember you," she promised and walked away.

CHAPTER 28
#MUDDERFUDDER

When Spence woke up, Colbie was gone. He knew it before he even opened his eyes; it was in the cold silence of the room. It was in the lack of joy in his heart. It was the pit sitting deep in his gut.

She'd left and it was going to be okay. He was going to be okay. Hell, he'd been okay only three weeks ago, right? Right.

So why did he feel like that time when he was five years old and his grandpa had told him, "There's no Santa Claus, kid. No one's ever going to hand you what you want — you gotta do that for yourself."

Spence blew out a breath and stared at the ceiling. What did he want? That was the easy part.

But he didn't want someone who could walk away from him, or someone he had to chase. He'd had enough of that for a lifetime, thank you very much. He'd go back to work and he'd be fine.

Just like always.

Colbie sat in the kitchen of her family home, the one that she'd bought with her first big royalty check. She'd settled everyone into it so that she could take care of them as she always had.

It was noon.

No, scratch that. That was California time, but she was in New York now. It was three o'clock here and she hadn't slept — although blissfully, Cinder had and was in fact curled up on the rug in front of the kitchen sink because that's where the heat vent was.

She was glad the cat seemed happy. But Colbie needed to find some happy herself. She was exhausted. She hadn't been able to catch any z's, not on the plane and not in the hour since she'd arrived.

There was good and bad news. Bad news — she ached for Spence. She ached for him like she'd ache for air to fill her lungs. Not exactly a newsflash.

Good news — her family had decorated. Yes, she realized this was a very small thing in the scheme of all the things, but hey, she had to celebrate the good stuff, no matter how small. Her brothers had pulled the Christmas boxes from storage and thrown everything up. It wasn't in Colbie's usual orderly fashion. The stockings had been taped to a wall instead of pinned on the staircase railing. The tree had been put up in a corner instead of in front of the window. And the lights . . . good Lord, the lights. They'd used the outside balcony lights to line the crown molding. The tree lights were on the balcony. And the mantel lights were on the tree. It was all wrong and looked a little bit like Christmas on crack but . . . it made her smile.

"What do you think?" Kent asked, standing in the doorway in nothing but boxers and socks.

"I like it," she said. "You guys did it on your own."

He smiled and headed into the laundry room off the pantry, where he grabbed a pair of sweats out of the dryer.

She opened her mouth to get on him about living out of the dryer, but she closed her mouth again.

Because he'd done his own laundry.

He came back into the kitchen and moved to the oven. He turned it off and pulled out what looked like a very loaded casserole dish, and put that on the stovetop.

"What's that?" she asked.

"Linner. Late lunch, early dinner. Put it

together last night cuz it's my turn to cook today and I only had time to make one thing."

She stared at him. "Okay, who are you and what have you done with my brother?"

He grinned. "I know, right? And wait until you taste it."

She tried to pull a piece of the melted cheese out and burned her finger. "Mudderfudder!"

He laughed. "You know that we're legal adults now, right? That we've heard every bad word under the sun and have most definitely used them?"

"You use them?"

"All the time. Just not near you so we don't have to pay." He gestured to the swear jar on the counter, filled with money she'd put in it. "Maybe," he said, "it's time to retire that thing. You could probably go on another vacay with what's in there."

She sighed. "I was just trying to make sure you guys knew right from wrong."

"You were the best role model we could've asked for. Of course we know right from wrong."

She looked at him and he laughed. "Hey, knowing and doing are two different things. We had things to get out of our system." Still smiling, he came close, pulling her out of her chair and into his arms. "You're back," he said quietly.

"I told you I would be."

He tightened his grip and pressed his face into her shoulder and she hugged him back, feeling a ball of emotion in her throat at the way he was holding her. "You didn't expect to see me," she whispered.

Still keeping his face hidden, he shook his head.

She squeezed him, her heart so tight she could scarcely breathe. He, like she, had some abandonment issues, and she'd hurt him by running away. "I'd never just walk away from you guys."

He laughed softly and lifted his head, flashing her that grin that she knew got him whatever he wanted. "We'd absolutely deserve it if you did."

"Maybe," she teased, and then let her smile fade. "But seriously, I was always coming back, Kent. Always."

His eyes grateful, he nodded. "I'm glad. And not just because Kurt cooks like shit. Oh, and you just got a same-day delivery. It was left at the front door." He gestured to the package on the table that she hadn't even noticed. One glance at the return address — Spence's — had her hurriedly opening it up, heart in her throat as she came to a pretty wooden box. Inside, it was jammed with a huge assortment of small note pads and stickies in every color. She stared at it and started laughing.

Had a man ever gotten her more?

"What the hell's all that?" Kent asked.

"It's blank notes for me to use to jot down all my random thoughts," she said.

"Huh." Kent shook his head. "You should marry that dude."

"Can't," she managed around a clogged throat, shaking her head. "I messed it all up."

"As badly as I messed up?" he asked. "I mean, you yelled at me and I got it. I know we've been slow on the uptake but we're trying to change, I can promise you that. I also know it's only been a few days but I can tell you that we mean it. I'm sure we'll screw up more than a few times but we heard you, Colbie. And we're working on it. Sometimes it's that simple."

"Not this time," she said.

"Because you let your responsibilities here hold you back," he said. "You let us hold you back. If San Francisco turns out to be your jam, we're going to try real hard not to hold you back anymore."

Her breath caught. "No?"

"No." He laughed softly. "I mean, we

might all follow you out there, but hey, that's how family works, right?" He pulled free and smiled at her.

"Right," she said and shook her head. "How did you get to be smarter than me?"

He ruffled her hair just as Kurt came into the room.

They looked at each other, his expression hooded. "Hey," she said softly. "Nice to see you. I'm glad you're here."

"I told you I would be," he said.

"I was wrong to tell you what to do," she said. "We're equals in this family. We take care of each other because we want to, not because we have to."

"You really believe that?" Kurt asked.

"I do," she said and looked at the both of them, so identical and yet so different. "I'm sorry I left the way I did, without coming to you and telling you what was wrong. But I'm not sorry I went. I needed it. I . . ." She broke off, her throat constricting at what she'd found for herself in San Francisco, a world away from here. "I loved my time there."

"We know." Kent pulled out his phone, accessed his photos, and brought one up of . . .

. . . Colbie and Spence. It'd been taken outside of the Pacific Pier Building where the paparazzi had caught up with them. She was staring up at Spence with a silly smile on her face. It'd be embarrassing except that Spence was smiling down at her as well, his eyes lit with humor and something else — affection.

The cool, calm, unflappable, stoic man who didn't easily show his feelings was practically glowing with how he felt for her.

And her heart stopped. Just stopped. She didn't realize she'd taken Kent's phone into her own hands and zoomed until he nudged Kurt.

"See? I was right," he said. "She does really like that dude, a lot." He held out his hand.

Kurt sighed and went to the junk drawer, where they kept an envelope of petty cash. Mostly it was used for emergency convenience-store runs or tips for deliveries, and it was funded by Colbie. Or at least it always had been. She realized she'd probably left it low on funds and hadn't given it a second thought.

But the envelope was full now. "Tell me you didn't rob a bank," she said.

"Overtime," they both said in unison, and while she stared at them, Kurt pulled out a twenty and slapped it into Kent's hand.

"You bet on my love life?" she asked with

disbelief.

This was met with a stunned silence as they both gaped at her, mouths open. "Wow," Kurt finally said. "You actually just said 'my love life.' You've never said anything like that before."

"Okay, that can't be true," she said. "Can it?"

They both slowly nodded and she realized they were right.

"All you ever do is work," Kent said. "You don't do life, at least not yours."

"Things change," she said softly. *And how.* "I guess we've all done some changing and growing up, huh?"

Kent smiled. "What exactly happened to you in San Fran?"

"A lot."

The front door opened, and in came Jackson, carrying bags of presents. Probably the presents she'd asked him to have delivered to her family via an e-mail before she left.

He didn't expect to see her. She watched it cross his face, the surprise chased by a flash of something she'd never seen from him.

Uncertainty.

"Hey," he said. "You're here." He sounded genuinely glad to see her. "Can we talk?"

Her brothers vacated the kitchen and she

and Jackson sat and stared at each other across the table.

"I'm not sorry I left," she said. "And I didn't come back for you."

"I know. Colbie —"

"But what happened between us is my fault," she said. "I should never have mixed business with pleasure. And —"

"No," he said quietly. "It's on me. I was wrong to do the same."

She nodded, relieved they were going to be civil about this. "I appreciate that," she said. "But this is my career, and I gave you too much free rein over it because all I wanted to do was write. It was lazy of me, and I shouldn't have done that. I also shouldn't have left you in charge of my personal life. That's on me too. But I'm a writer, Jackson. Not a public speaker. Not a celebrity. I need you to get that."

He started to say something, but she held up a hand. "I know what the books have become and what our world is like, but it's not for me and it's never going to be. I'm always going to want to leave the red carpet for someone else to stumble over. When I asked you not to book any live engagements for me, I was serious."

He grimaced, and in the not too distant past she would've rushed to try to please him by agreeing to stuff she didn't want to do. But no more. She was standing firm.

The problem was, her heart was aching for Spence so much right then that she could already scarcely breathe for all the emotions battering her from the inside out. But something good had to come from walking away from him. "I mean it," she said. "If that's the type of person you want to represent, we're not going to work out."

"Colbie —"

"And something else," she said. "I like my new book. I know it's a departure, but it's flowing for me and I'm happy with it. And I think Andrea will be too because —"

"It's good." He reached for her hand and gently squeezed her fingers. "After I got over myself, I read the chapters again, and there was something there."

She stared at him. "Yeah?"

"Yeah. I called Andrea and she agreed too." He stood and tugged her into him for a hug. "And I'm the one who's sorry," he said against her hair. "I knew how you felt about me and I was enough of an egotistical asshole to be flattered by it. I even egged it on because it seemed to make you write faster. You were right and I'm so sorry."

She closed her eyes and shook her head. "Thanks for saying that. You were an egotistical asshole. But I put a lot on you, asking you to deal with so much more than you should've had to. Let's just move on, okay?"

"Considering that I was certain you'd fire me, I'd like that very much. But . . ." he paused ". . . are we really okay?"

"You mean is my crush over?" she asked dryly. "I can promise you it most definitely is over."

"Good to know," he said on a short laugh. "But I meant can you move on from San Francisco?"

She stared at him, wanting to say yes but unable to do so.

"Because I really thought you'd come back here just to tell all of us that you were moving there," he said.

"I couldn't just move."

"Why not?"

She paused. "I . . ." Huh. She didn't know.

He tugged on a lock of her wild hair. "We all deserve our happy," he said. "And I want that for you. Think about it. Let me know." And then he was gone, leaving Colbie in the middle of her kitchen, feeling more than a little lost.

She should've felt good. Her editor was happy. Her agent was happy. Her staff, her family . . . all happy.

But she wasn't. Because her brothers and

Jackson had been right. She needed to find it for herself. And she had. She'd just left it three thousand miles behind.

God, she missed San Francisco. She missed the people in it. She missed the Pacific Pier Building. She missed the courtyard and the fountain and writing in front of it, listening to the water falling to the copper base. She missed sex. She missed Spence.

She missed sex with Spence.

She really had fallen in love with him. The truth was, she'd never really thought about love before — the heart-pounding, can't-live-without-you kind of love that grows in the pit of the stomach and spreads outward until you're warm all over. The kind of love you know is real because you've got not one single teeny, tiny doubt that he'd be there for you, no matter what.

Maybe she'd never given thought to love for herself because she'd never seen her mom in that kind of relationship. Or maybe it was because she wasn't really sure she *believed* in that kind of relationship.

But something had changed, shifted inside her, because suddenly she did believe in love. And more than that, she wanted it for herself. She wanted what she'd had with Spence. Only she didn't want it just for a vacation from her life.

She wanted it *for* her life.

"I shouldn't have run," she said.

"You can't help it," her mom said, coming into the room. "It's in your blood."

Colbie looked up. "Hey, Mom."

Her mom smiled and hugged Colbie. "I thought I was dreaming when I heard your voice!" She tightened her grip and Colbie patted her on the back, trying to drag air into her lungs. "Can't. Breathe."

"I know." Her mom loosened her grip only very slightly. "But you came! It's a Christmas miracle!" Stepping back from Colbie, her eyes filled with huge tears.

"Oh, Mom. It's okay, don't cry."

Her mom cupped Colbie's face. "Thank you. Really. Thank you for coming when we called. You didn't have to, and we shouldn't have asked, but it's really great to see you — no matter why you're really here."

"What does that mean?"

"I had my cards read and was told that you've fallen deeply in love but that you ran from it."

"Mom." Colbie shook her head. "I told you to stop spending your money on that stuff. You don't need to have your cards read to live your life."

"Maybe not, but how else will I hear about

your life? You don't talk to me. So is it true, then? Did you run away from love? I mean, it would make sense, given that you're here so quickly without any fuss."

Colbie sighed.

"Oh no, Colbie. Really? I didn't want to be right on this one, although I admit, it does make me feel better that you're running away from your man rather than racing home to deal with us, who don't deserve you."

"Mom, I don't want to talk about it."

"Huh. Shock. But maybe you'll listen instead. Follow me." They went to the living room, where her mom pointed to what she'd been doing before Colbie had come home.

Looking at old photo albums, like she did every Christmas. They were from the years before Colbie's birth and right after. The old leather one on top was opened to a page that held an eight-by-ten picture taken on her parents' wedding day.

They were smiling and looked happy.

And young.

"Mom," Colbie said gently. "Why are you doing this to yourself? He left us. He doesn't deserve your regrets and sadness."

"Yeah, about that . . ." Her mom paused. "He didn't leave us, Colbie."

Colbie met her gaze. "I don't understand."

Her mom sighed. "Sit. *Sit,*" she said again, patting the seat of the chair next to her. "We met at a frat party."

"I thought you didn't go to college."

"I didn't," her mom said. "But my friends and I were looking for our MRS degree. Do you know what that means?"

"That you were looking for husbands," Colbie said, not liking where this was going.

"I met your dad at the first frat party I ever went to. He was trouble, of course, I could see it in his eyes, but I didn't care."

"And by *trouble,*" Colbie said, "you mean . . ."

"He had no interest in marriage or a family. Absolutely zero. But when I got pregnant that night, he actually stood by me. Married me to give you a name." Her mom's eyes overfilled and a few tears escaped. "We did our best, but you know how I am. I self-destruct my happiness, always have. I did the same with us. By the time I got pregnant again, we weren't doing well. I knew it was over, that I had to leave. I told myself I was doing all of us a favor. I was leaving him before he could leave us, that's all. Still, it was wrong. I know that now, and if he'd ever tried to see you kids, even once, I'd have swallowed my pride and let him be a part of your lives. But he never did."

Colbie just stared at her in shock. "You left him."

"Yes. And I know. Believe me, I know what a shitty mom I was to ever let you think otherwise. I was a shitty mom in other ways too. I didn't teach you to enjoy life. Instead I had you always looking ahead for problems, letting you fix everything. But that's not life. Life is in the little things, you see?"

"No," Colbie said flatly and stood up.

Her mom caught her hand. "You gotta catch the moments, the precious, good, amazing moments of life. You gotta go after them and hold on for all you're worth. And when someone comes along who loves you for you — and not because of what you do or because you're lonely, but because they love you — you hold on, Colbie. You hold on like you've never held on before. Not because you need it for your life, but because it complements your life." She stood up. She was a good head shorter than Colbie but she put her hands on her hips and managed to glare up at her daughter. "Now, I can see why you'd ignore any advice I might have to offer because your stubbornness is second only to mine, but if you trust me on only one thing, trust this. I've been there, done that, and stole the T-shirt, and it wasn't all that much fun."

"Mom —"

"So don't walk away from what's right for you," her mom said, her voice more serious than Colbie had ever heard. "Although you ran more than walked."

Colbie sighed.

"Baby, if you only listen to me once in your entire life, please, God, let it be this one time." She swallowed hard. "Don't make my mistakes. Okay? Don't let happiness take a backseat. Happiness makes the world go around." She held Colbie's gaze, her own fierce and suspiciously shiny. "Don't be a runner." And then she gave one jerky nod and walked away.

"I'm not a runner," Colbie said to the room.

But she was. And she didn't like what that said about her. Maybe she'd known Spence for only a short amount of time but some things happened in an instant.

Things like . . . standing in a fountain, water dripping off your face as you fell in love with the man standing there with you . . .

Her phone vibrated with a text. Spence.

My life doesn't work without you in it.

She stared at the words until they blurred. "I have to go back to San Francisco," she whispered.

Her mom stuck her head back in, tears in her eyes as she nodded. "Yes! You have to go back."

CHAPTER 29
#FISHANDCHIPS

Spence tried to bury himself in work but there was a heaviness to his daily grind that he knew from experience was grief.

Only on a whole new level.

He'd finally learned how to balance his life and then half of that life had walked away, leaving him out of whack all over again.

The gang tried to cheer him up, inviting him places, bringing him his favorite junk food . . . The guys even took him fishing, and though it'd been fucking freezing and Joe had gone accidentally swimming and nearly lost his nuts, it hadn't distracted Spence.

When they got back, Spence holed up and gave work what he could, and a few days later, he texted Caleb:

Spence:
I've got some shit figured out.

Caleb:

Awesome. So you went to New York after all.

Spence:

What the hell are you talking about? I meant the battery and weight distribution for the drone project. I think I'm close. Meet me at Marin Headlands.

Caleb:

Dude, you're thinking about work on Christmas Eve?

Spence:

Shit. I forgot.

Caleb:

Forgot what? Your brain or that it's Christmas Eve?

Spence:

Marin Headlands. One hour.

An hour later, Spence stood at the top of Marin Headlands, Caleb a few feet away, the two of them braced against the heavy gusts as they watched the drone fight its way through the wind like it wasn't even there.

Another heavy gust sent them both back a step and Caleb's baseball cap off toward Kansas as he looked down at his phone. "That one was seventy-five miles per hour."

They both went back to concentrating on the drone until it was out of sight over the water. They switched their gazes to the tablet on the controls, watching as the drone, several miles out now, kept going without draining the battery. Twenty miles out and it still sent back both clear visuals and clear sound as it executed a hold-your-breath maneuver beneath the bridge, landing on a buoy being battered from all sides by the white-capped, frothy, unforgiving bay.

"Go farther," Caleb said.

Spence did.

"Forty miles," Caleb said some time later. "Battery?"

The drone, still relaying back a picture-perfect visual and sound, came to the bridge again, hovered, dropped down onto a buoy, and . . . stayed there, perfectly balanced.

"Hold it there," Caleb said, the two of them glued to the screen. "Wait for that incoming surge of waves — do you see them?"

Yeah. Spence saw them. They waited. Watched while the buoy was hit by wave after wave. Twice the drone did as it'd been programmed to do when things got too rough. It ascended, hovered in place, and then lowered back down, once again maintaining its position.

"Not even a wobble," Spence said in marvel. They both looked at the tablet. "And the satellite reception held through the wind and water interference."

Meaning if there'd been a doctor on this end trying to see and speak to a patient on the other end, they would've been able to maintain their connection.

"Make the drop," Caleb said.

Spence executed the command and the drone rolled out a weatherproof, impact-protected box that was perfectly set on the tip of the buoy. The landing zone that was *maybe* six inches by six inches.

And the box landed right in the center, precisely weighted so that even with the swells hitting the buoy, making it rise and fall, the box didn't shift.

Spence worked the controls and had the drone reverse the process, setting down and scooping the box back up.

"Still won't stop someone from stealing the meds," Caleb said. "Or snatching the drone."

"We only make the drop after confirming by satellite that there's an authorized receiver on site." Spence shook his head. "That's the best we've got. Patented long-use battery and unfailing connection through our app."

Caleb nodded and turned to Spence, triumph gleaming through his smile. "You did it, man. Amazing."

Yeah, and satisfaction burned through him at the triumph. Satisfaction, but not elation.

The last time he'd felt a surge of a positive emotion had been when he'd been buried deep inside Colbie, feeling like he'd found himself in her fathomless gaze, in her warm arms, buried in her body.

"Storm moving in," Caleb said, tilting his face to the sky. "It's a good night to cozy up to a woman with some good brandy and catch a sappy movie on TV."

Spence arched a brow.

"Hey, women like sappy," Caleb said.

Colbie liked sappy. The thought of cozying up to her in front of a blazing fire, wrapping her up close as a movie made her tear up, comforting her, making those tears vanish . . . "You ever been dumped?" he asked.

Caleb laughed ruefully. "Oh yeah."

"Did you chase after them?"

"The hot ones," Caleb said.

Spence sighed.

"Listen," Caleb said on a laugh. "Honestly? I can make a woman happy. Keeping her that way is another thing entirely and definitely not one of my superpowers. So I'm the wrong one to give advice."

Spence got that. He knew he'd made Colbie happy. Hanging out with her had been effortless. So was making her laugh. And when he got her in bed, she'd absolutely communicated how he'd made her feel there . . . In fact, he could still feel the indentions of her nails in his ass.

"You could talk to Archer," Caleb suggested. "He's managed to snag the most difficult woman who ever walked this earth. I mean, Elle actually smiles now. Get him to tell you the secret to *that* and bottle it."

Spence wasn't any good at asking for help but when they got back to his building, he found himself at Archer's office.

Molly, Archer's receptionist, shook her head. "He's in, but he's . . . busy."

"Client meeting?"

"An Elle 'meeting.' " She put *meeting* in air quotes. "She went in there half an hour ago and no one's seen hide nor hair of them since."

There was a muted sound, a sort of thunk, like something — or a bunch of somethings — falling off a desk.

Joe stuck his head out his office door and

glared at his younger sister Molly. "I thought he ordered corkboard for the walls to add insulation so I don't have to hear what's going on in there."

Molly, who could hold her own with the kind of guys she worked for — which was to say completely badass — narrowed her eyes at his tone. "Hasn't come in yet," she said, her own tone cool, with an added *watch it* implied.

"Shit." Joe vanished back into his office and then they heard him crank up some music to window-rattling levels.

Spence left and hit the elevator. When the doors opened to Willa and Keane locked in an embrace, apparently checking each other's tonsils, he pivoted on a heel and took the stairs.

This sucked. He'd just made an incredible work breakthrough and he had no one to share it with. It felt . . . empty. He'd been alone before, plenty of times. In fact, he'd been alone for most of his life, but he'd never felt this hollow.

He strode through the courtyard, hell-bent on key lime pie, which surely would ease the gnawing pain in his gut.

Except it wasn't hunger and he knew it — it was something he hadn't seen coming. Heartache.

Halfway to the coffee shop he caught sight of his grandpa sitting on a bench staring into the fountain like it held the answers to the mysteries of the universe.

Spence had a short argument with himself, which he lost. Changing directions, he headed to the old man's side.

Eddie didn't look over at him, just kept staring into the water. "Hear you screwed things up pretty good, boy genius."

"Who told you that?"

"I hear all. I know all," Eddie said sagely. The guy's white hair was standing straight up in his best Christopher Lloyd imitation and in spite of the cold, he wore only a Deadhead T-shirt and tie-dyed Bermuda shorts.

Spence shook his head and shrugged out of his jacket, handing it over.

His grandpa pulled it on and smiled. "Warm."

"I've given you a bunch of jackets and other warmer weather gear. Why aren't you wearing any of it?"

His grandpa shrugged, pulling the hood over his wild hair. "Some of my friends don't have a you."

Spence read between the lines on that one. "So you gave it all away to keep them warm."

Eddie didn't answer. Instead he worked his way through the pockets of the jacket, locating a candy bar and grinning with happiness over the find.

Spence gave up with the life lectures and stared at the fountain as his grandpa had been doing. He was exhausted. And . . . dammit. Sad.

"You could try to fix it with her, you know."

Spence let out a low, mirthless laugh. "You've got a helluva lot of nerve lecturing me on my life. Look at yours."

"Exactly," Eddie said, for once his smile and good nature gone. "You're just like I was. My mind was always working ten steps ahead of everyone else. I shut everything and everyone out."

Spence had a feeling he wasn't going to like the rest of this conversation. "I already know this. Dad and Grandma told me a long time ago."

"Told you what?"

"That you chose work over family. How after a bunch of grief from both places, you eventually decided you didn't need either one and just up and left one day."

His grandpa huffed. "There's two sides to every story, you know."

"You have something to say, say it."

Eddie nodded to the bench next to him for Spence to sit. So Spence sat. For a few minutes they were silent.

"You know I was an inventor like you," Eddie finally said. "I had the brains for it. But not for the business side of things. I had a partner. Not as good a man as Caleb, I might add. He stole ten patents out from right under my nose and I didn't even notice. My ability to focus on the work came with thick blinders and everything else fell by the wayside."

Spence stared at him. "So you just left? Your life wasn't all about business. You walked away from your family too."

"I was broke. Broke and humiliated, and had nothing left to offer. I'd lost everything."

"Your family didn't care," Spence said. "All Grandma wanted was you, and she'd have taken whatever part of you she could get. She would've been willing to share you with work. Dad too."

Eddie held his gaze and slowly nodded. "I know that now. Because hindsight is twenty-twenty. What I don't know is how you're sitting there judging me but you're not believing it yourself. Because if you were believing it, you'd be in New York, chasing down the best thing that ever happened to you."

"You can't chase love."

"Wrong," Eddie said. "You can do whatever you want. Life is short, Spence. Don't waste it on stuff that doesn't matter."

"Are you saying family doesn't matter?"

"I'm saying that people make mistakes. So forgive. Love. Laugh."

"Now you sound like a slogan for the Hallmark Channel."

"Hey," Eddie said. "I like the Hallmark Channel. It makes me smile, and you know what? You could use a little bit more of that."

Elle came through the courtyard, holding a box. She looked perfectly put together, the only thing giving away her earlier "meeting" in Archer's office being her overly flushed cheeks. She stopped in front of Spence.

"No," he said.

"I didn't say anything yet," she said.

"You're going to tell me another woman sent me yet another present."

She dropped the box in his lap. "Another woman sent you yet another present."

"Dammit, Elle."

"Open it."

He met her gaze and saw something there that had him sighing and taking the box. In it was a duffle bag much like his old one but not battered and abused — filled with all his favorite candy bars. The jumbo sizes.

His throat tightened but it was nothing compared to the pain in his chest.

"Wow," Elle said. "The perfect gift for you. I've been trying to get you to replace your piece-of-shit duffle bag for a year."

Eddie reached into the box and took a candy bar in each hand. "You're not nearly as smart as you pretend to be if you don't go after that girl."

"That might just be the first thing you and I agree on," Elle told Eddie.

He beamed at her. "See, I've finally worn you down with my charm." He clapped a hand on Spence's shoulder. "Time to use yours, boy, and go get our girl."

Spence rose to his feet. "I need some air."

"We're already outside," Eddie said, but Spence kept walking, heading toward the street and his truck. He pulled out his phone and called Colbie. He missed her. He loved her. And dammit, he wasn't just going to let her go. At least not until he told her.

She didn't answer.

He was still holding his phone when it vibrated with an incoming call. His heart leapt but it was just Finn.

"It's Christmas Eve," his friend opened with.

"Yeah?" Spence said, not feeling the spirit in the least. "So?"

"So . . . you're supposed to be at the pub."

"Why?" Spence asked.

"Because that's what we do on Christmas Eve. We all hang out together. Hurry. I need you for something first."

"What?"

Finn sighed. "Just get your ass over here."

Spence blew out a breath. "Fine."

"Now, right?"

"Jesus, you're out of control, but yeah, whatever."

He was nearly to the pub when his phone rang again and he answered without looking at the screen. "I said I'm coming, I'm fucking coming."

"Spence."

He nearly tripped over his own feet at the sound of Colbie's voice in his ear. Which reminded him that he was a complete dumbass who wasn't supposed to answer his phone without looking at the screen first.

But in this case, he was glad, so very glad he had. Just the sound of her had him in knots, in the very best of ways. "Hey," he said, softening his voice. "Sorry, I thought it was Finn."

"And I'm sorry I missed your call." She paused. "It's good to hear you, Spence."

He stopped at the door of the pub, stilled by a rush of love and heat and hunger. He closed his eyes. "Same."

"Where are you?"

He walked into the pub, his phone still up to his ear as he took in the room.

The place was lit up for the holiday, with soft white twinkling lights strung from the rafters and in and around the hanging lanterns, giving off a warm holiday glow that might have reached Spence if his heart wasn't shrunk to the size of the Grinch's.

Finn and Sean always closed on Christmas Eve. It was their gang only. They always had dinner and drinks together and toasted the holiday in their own way. Usually with a vicious, high-stakes dart tournament and then a round of pool.

"I'm in the pub," he said to Colbie. *And I wish you were here . . .* And it was like the wanting conjured her up. He could *feel* her.

"Me too," she said in surround sound, both in his ear *and* from behind him.

He whipped around and, phone still at his ear, saw her about twenty steps away, at the bar. Their eyes locked and it was all he could do to breathe. She started toward him and he could feel his entire face lighting up. She was in a little black dress and some serious black boots and his heart wasn't the only thing that took notice.

A warm smile curved her lips as her green gaze ate him up much the same way his was doing to her. "I wanted to give you your Christmas present in person."

"You already sent me one," he said inanely, his heart threatening to burst out of his chest.

"That one was a decoy. This one's bigger." She grinned. "And hopefully better."

"What is it?" he asked.

She pulled her phone from her ear, tossed it to the bar, and pointed to herself.

CHAPTER 30
#FUDGENUGGETS

Colbie's heart was thundering in her chest, ricocheting off her ribs. She was going on fumes at this point and grateful that going from east to west had given her three extra hours of Christmas Eve. It'd allowed her to zip her way back here in time for this. For what would hopefully be the best night of her life.

Their life. Spence stood before her looking like the sexiest geek she'd ever seen, all tall, dark, and as rumpled and exhausted as she.

And clearly shocked to see her.

Having no idea what he could possibly be thinking, she stepped closer and put a hand on his chest to ground herself to his calm energy. But beneath her palm, his heart was beating like hers, which boosted her confidence some. "I missed you, Spence."

His hands went on her arms, one gliding up her shoulder to stroke her throat before he tucked a lock of her hair behind an ear.

"Thought you didn't see visiting each other working out that well," he said.

"I was wrong." She turned her face into his palm, planting a kiss in the center of it, over his rough calluses. "I was very wrong, about a lot of things actually." When she met his gaze again, his had grown warm with so many things her throat clogged. It seemed like forever since he'd looked at her like that and she melted as he pulled her to him and kissed her long and hard.

"Missed that," he said, voice rough. "Missed you, Colbie. So much."

She tugged him down for another kiss and then another, after which they were both breathing heavily. She had her hands fisted in his jacket, every cell in her body alive and singing as he nuzzled her temple, then placed a kiss at her jaw. "You going to tell me what else you were wrong about?" he asked.

"You already know."

"Sometimes it's nice to hear." His mouth brushed her earlobe as he spoke and she clutched his arms to get a grip.

"I have a terrible habit of running away," she admitted. "And apparently I come by it naturally." She shook her head. "I thought it was my brothers who needed to grow up. Turns out it was me too. I left you because

422

what I felt for you scared me."

"And . . . you're not scared anymore?"

"No, I'm still scared. Terrified," she conceded. "But I'm *more* terrified of losing the best thing that's ever happened to me."

"You mean writing in San Francisco?"

She choked out a laugh. "You. *You're* the best thing that's ever happened to me, Spence."

He cupped her face and pressed his forehead to hers. "Right back at you," he said with quiet steel.

She gripped his wrists. "Tell me I didn't screw up so badly with you that you're not willing to give me another try."

"Are you kidding?" he asked in disbelief. "I've made plenty of mistakes too, especially when it came to you. So let me show you how willing I really am." He let go of her to fish in his pocket for his phone, bringing up his boarding pass. To New York.

She stared at it. "You were coming to me?"

"Tomorrow morning," he said. "It was the first flight I could get. I'd forgotten to tell you something."

"What?"

His thumb swiped over a few tears she hadn't realized she'd shed. "That I love you," he said with no hesitancy. "I told you, Colbie, I'm playing for keeps. I know that this thing between us scared you and I can give you whatever you need: time, space, patience . . . I can give you all of that and more, but what I can't do is let you walk away."

"I love you too," she said, and at the words she didn't know she had in her, butterflies took flight in her belly.

"For how long?" he asked.

She stared at him, confused by the question. "How long am I going to love you? Seriously?" Unable to find the words for that, she shook her head, marveled, boggled, because somehow, in spite of themselves, they hadn't managed to screw everything up. "So to be clear, we just decided to be together . . . right?"

"Right."

Could it really be that easy? "And about living three thousand miles apart?" she asked.

He shrugged. "I like New York."

She blinked. "But you own this building here in San Francisco."

"I could buy another."

"But you love this building," she said. "You built yourself an entire community and made it home."

"Funny thing about that," he said with quiet intensity. "I thought I needed to create a physical home for myself. I thought that's what home meant. Turns out it's not a physical space at all."

"No?" she asked, hope filling her chest.

"No. See, home is wherever you are."

"Oh," she breathed. "Oh, that's good. I need to write that down —"

He laughed while she fumbled through her big bag for one of the note cards he'd sent. She scribbled down the words and then stilled, looking up into his face, realizing he was waiting out her special brand of crazy. Quickly, she shoved the note back into her purse. "You're pretty amazing, you know that?" she asked softly.

He smiled. "Thanks for saying so in front of our audience."

She looked around. They were alone, just as Finn had told her they would be. "What audience?"

Heads silently popped up from behind the bar. Finn. Pru. Sean. Willa and Keane. Elle. Archer. Joe. Molly. Kylie. Haley. Caleb . . . They all waved.

"Carry on," Sean said. "Don't mind us."

Colbie laughed and turned back to Spence. "So . . . a few months in San Francisco and then a few in New York? Or vice versa?"

"I can go either way," Spence said. "What

I can't go either way on is being without you."

This was met by a thundering applause and accompanying cat whistles. They were all sitting on the bar now, sharing bottles of champagne, starting without them.

Spence bowed and then grabbed Colbie's hand and pulled her in close.

She stared up at him, needing to know. "Are we really doing this?"

"Yes." He kissed her jaw, her cheek. The tip of her nose. There was a smile in his voice, but his eyes were serious. "So let me ask you again," he said. "For how long?"

She closed her eyes for a beat, savoring the feel of him against her. How long? Was he kidding? Forever and ever would *maybe* do it. "I guess until you get tired of me."

He gave her a slow, sexy smile. "I determined on day one that I was never going to get tired of you."

"Never ever?"

"Never ever," he repeated, sliding a hand through her hair to tip her face up. "Think you can handle that?"

"Oh yeah." She kissed him, knowing she was never going to get tired of him either. Never ever.

EPILOGUE

One week later, New Year's

The lights came up in the movie theater but Colbie couldn't tear her eyes off the screen as the credits rolled.

Screenplay adapted from the novel by
CE Crown

When the words scrolled by, the audience went nuts and Colbie beamed.

"So," Spence asked at her left. "What did you think?"

"She loved it!" her mom exclaimed from her right, squeezing Colbie's hand. "Right, baby?"

Colbie couldn't talk. This was her second time seeing her book come to life and it was no less amazing. It'd been an experience of a lifetime and she felt like she was floating.

Behind her, Kylie and Willa were practically bouncing in their seats and thrust their faces close to Colbie.

"It was terrific!" Kylie exclaimed. "Better than terrific! Five stars! Both thumbs up!"

"Yes, all of that," Elle said next to them. "But it wasn't as good as the book."

Colbie's heart felt full to bursting as she shot Elle a smile of thanks. "You all liked it? Really?"

Everyone nodded emphatically, and she did mean everyone. Her brothers and mom had flown into San Francisco the day before to celebrate New Year's Eve and to get a feel for Colbie's new home.

All of Colbie's new friends were there too. The girls and even the guys. Finn, Sean, Keane, Archer, Joe, Caleb . . .

The entire gang.

All of them there for her. She felt her throat get tight.

Spence met her gaze and as usual read her without effort. He pulled her into him, wrapping his arms around her. It was sweet, even if she could feel his chest shaking with his low laugh. "Cute," he said in her ear. "You're cute. And amazing. I love you so much."

She looked into his eyes. He'd flown her family out here, for her. He'd rented the theater out for the movie, for her.

His work world was going a million miles

an hour this week but that hadn't stopped him from being here for her. In fact, he was flying to Europe for several weeks tomorrow to deliver the drone prototypes and he'd convinced her to go with him.

Seemed their lives could indeed be entwined, and the knowledge made her grin ridiculously.

Spence smiled down into her face and kissed her.

She'd thought her heart couldn't get any more full than it was, but she'd been wrong. Her poor organ swelled, straining against her ribs as she cupped Spence's jaw. "I love you back, you know."

"Yeah, yeah, to the moon and all that," Kylie said, thrusting her face in between theirs again. "Blah blah. What I want to know is . . . can we see it again?" She turned to Spence. "You can get them to do that, right?"

Spence never took his gaze off Colbie, brows raised, silently asking if she wanted him to.

She grinned. "Yes, but we'll need more hot dogs and pizza and popcorn."

"And wine," Elle said.

Spence stood up, presumably to make that all happen, but instead of walking away, he went to a knee at Colbie's side.

"Holy shit," Joe said. "Didn't see that coming."

Elle smacked him upside the head. "Shh!"

Colbie's heart had stopped and she stared at Spence. "Did you drop something?" she whispered.

He smiled. "No."

Willa clapped her hands in delight. "Oh my God, is someone getting this on their camera?" She shoved Keane. "Quick, get your phone out!"

"Oh," Colbie's mom breathed on a quiet sob. "I never thought this would happen! She's not good at letting anyone want her."

"Shh, Mom," Kurt murmured and squeezed her hand.

Colbie couldn't concentrate on any of it as Spence pulled something from his pocket.

A small black box.

"Oh my God. Are you sure?" she managed. "It hasn't been all that long and I have a whole bunch of faults that you haven't really gotten to see in full Technicolor yet, so I would advise you give me some more time —"

"I've seen everything I need to," Spence said, voice calm and sure. "You are the light in my world. You make me a better man. You —"

"Yes!" she said emphatically and both

430

laughed and cried when he just blinked.

"I had a whole speech planned," he said slowly. "I was going to tell you —"

"Yes!" she cried again and leapt at him.

He barely caught her, laughing as he rose with her in his arms.

"Honey, you should maybe listen to what he wants to say," Elle suggested. "Cuz he's got some faults of his own and —" She broke off when Spence gave her a long look.

Archer pulled Elle against him, his hand coming up to cover her mouth. "Got her," he told Spence. "But make it quick before she bites me."

Spence's gaze was still on Colbie. "You didn't look at the ring."

"Still yes."

He grinned. "You're that sure of the question? What if I was just going to ask you to —"

"Let me save you some time," she said. "Yes to everything and anything."

"Well that's a little dangerous," Pru murmured. "Giving him free rein to *anything . . .*"

But Colbie wasn't listening. She'd gotten her mouth on Spence and was happily losing herself in the man who understood her, loved her, and wanted forever with her.

Which just might be the right amount of time . . .

ABOUT THE AUTHOR

New York Times bestselling author **Jill Shalvis** lives in a small town in the Sierras full of quirky characters. Any resemblance to the quirky characters in her books is, um, mostly coincidental. Look for Jill's bestselling, award-winning books wherever romances are sold and visit http://www.jill shalvis.com for a complete book list and daily blog detailing her city-girl-living-in-the-mountains adventures.